CRACKER

THE MAD WOMAN
IN THE ATTIC

D1392237

CRACKER

THE MAD WOMAN
IN THE ATTIC

Jim Mortimore

Virgin

First published in Great Britain in 1994 by
Virgin Books
an imprint of Virgin Publishing Ltd
332 Ladbroke Grove
London W10 5AH

ISBN 0 8636 98220

Typeset by Galleon Typesetting, Ipswich
Printed and bound in Great Britain by
Cox & Wyman Ltd, Reading, Berks

For Arthur
(Get well soon!)

And Angela and Andy, Owen and Jackie,
Steve and Belinda and anyone else whose
wedding I missed.

ONE

Monday

It was the off.

His eyes were open, wide open but they looked beyond the university corridor, through the walls, the fresh coat of magnolia paint. The phone was a hard bar of plastic in his hand, turning his knuckles white, but Fitz didn't even notice.

It was the off.

And he could feel the animal thundering towards him, pressing close. He could taste the hot stink of its breath, feel the steam from its nostrils clinging to his eyeballs, hear the roar of the crowd as close as the thunder of hooves; the roar, the buzz; and over it all the pure absolute high of thinking it through, making a choice, a wager, getting it right –

And then the words. The *word*. And the gentle click of the phone going back down on the receiver, capstone to a bad day, a quiet cannonblast of sound; and he stared at the wall and felt like throwing up.

Second. The bloody horse came second.

Second. It was worse than last. At least with last you could see it coming. Knew it from the off. Had some deep down gut feeling it wasn't going to happen. But second. That stank. That was a pisser. With second there was the moment. That ripe, shining, glittering moment when it might have happened. Might have made it. Might even have romped home.

And you might have been right.

But no. Second.

1

And all that adrenalin pumping through your system, through your body, your head buzzed up with the chemical fire of it, your hands and feet shaking with it, your belly heaving with it, all that wasted. Flat. Flushed away.

Nothing. Less than nothing. Bad day.

It had started with the argument with Judith. Nothing new. One of the cards had been cancelled; she hadn't been able to buy something. Forget about the times when she had been able to buy things. When he'd bought her things. *Ground Zero* in the Epsom sweep. *Everything To Gain* in the National. The dresses. The jewellery. The pretty things he knew she loved. The things he bought for her because he loved her. Loved her more than he could ever say. Not that her life revolved around pretty things, of course not. She had a brain on her. That was why he loved her. Not just for the perfect figure; the amazing sex.

And how long is it since there's been any sex, Fitz, let alone any amazing sex?

Ignoring the voice chipping away deep in his mind, Fitz allowed his thoughts to fast forward to the meeting at the bank. That at least had been a success. Then again, what did he expect? Bank managers were just glorified clerks after all. The books must balance. The formulas must be fulfilled. Morrison was the bank manager's name. Fitz felt sure he got the job because he looked a little like Clark Kent, rather than through his ability to manage money. He might have a super body but he certainly didn't have what it took to beat Lex Luthor in a stand up battle of brains. Fitz had told the man what he wanted to hear; the rest was inevitable. Dominoes falling. He wouldn't even have made a bet on the outcome of that conversation. For Christ's sake the man had even complimented him on his choice of colour scheme – a moment's invention for Fitz, the same as the whole idea of the new bathroom itself: pure invention.

He needed fuel. Fuel to feed the fire. He would get it any way he could.

He stared at the magnolia wall and felt like throwing up. It wasn't losing that made him feel like that. Wasn't the waste.

2

The sheer stupidity of it. It was the knowledge. The perfect self-understanding.

From the corridor behind him, a voice lifted angrily: 'Fitz. Come on. You're late.'

You're late. Not *we're* late. No hint of support there. Then again, what else would you expect from a ponce like Geoffreys? Head of Psychology? Head of a bad head, more like. Bad inside. Not even empty. Not even that. Just dead.

Fitz turned. Geoffreys waited at the end of the corridor, his face flushed magnolia from the freshly painted walls, impatience stamped across his features like a head cold.

Bad head. Bad horse. Bad day.

Fitz smiled sweetly as he swept past Geoffreys and into the auditorium. 'Our liver playing us up again today, is it?'

At the podium, Fitz allowed Geoffreys to take his moment with the crowd. 'OK everyone, I'd like to take this opportunity to welcome you all to this, which will hopefully be the first of many guest lectures by the eminent Doctor Fitzgerald.'

Fitz met Geoffreys' dead stare as he took his place at the podium. Dead head. Not even enough stuff in there to be angry.

Dismissing Geoffreys, Fitz gazed out across the auditorium. Faces. Hair. Eyes. And expectancy. Lots of that.

Dolls beneath the auditorium lights, the faces stared back at him, splintered fragments of the same mirror. We're here, they seemed to say. We're waiting. We want you. Bits of you, all of you, we don't care. Give to us. Teach us. Let us know you.

Bollocks.

In front of Fitz was a pile of books, presumably stacked neatly there by Geoffreys before the lecture started. Spinoza. Descartes. Hobbes. Locke. Freud. Bastions of the art. Foundations of the knowledge. Keepers of the flame.

No more.

Fitz sniffed. Placed a pair of wire frame half spectacles on his nose. He picked up the top book, read the title and author aloud. Hesitated. Studied the crowd over the top of his spectacles.

3

Suddenly he moved, with a speed that belied his bulk.

He threw the book as hard and as far as he could, out into the audience.

The mirror shattered. Expectancy was replaced by a dozen different emotions. Interest, affection, amusement, outrage, shock. It didn't matter. They were different now; dolls no more as the feelings spread, ripples on a pond, shockwaves from a bullet, fallout from a bomb.

And he had them.

Fitz picked up the second book. Threw it. A high, wide arc. One of the faces plucked it from the air, waved it in salute, grinning. Fitz ignored the gesture.

Third book. Fourth. Fifth.

'Adler. Jung. Meyer. Sullivan. Horney. Pavlov,' he said as the books described flapping arcs towards the faces. And he thought: Mark. Katie. Judith.

Judith.

And he said: 'End of lecture.'

He walked off the podium to a silence more profound than that of a mortuary. No chairs scraped. There were no coughs. No giggles. No flapping of paper, brushing back of hair. No sighs. No discussion.

At the edge of the stage he hesitated.

They couldn't possibly want more. Could they?

Ah well. They asked for it, the bloody fools.

He turned. Got back on the podium.

'Moral,' he said. He stared at them; expectant faces again, dolls again. The mirror whole.

'Can anyone tell me what's the moral?'

There was no answer from the dolls. Fitz sighed.

He'd pushed them too far.

He'd lost them.

It had been a bad day, the last of a bad weekend, and it showed every sign of getting worse.

The carriage was dirty, the compartment, the whole train. The cushions pumped dust into the stale air as she sat while her shoes scraped grime from the rubber-surfaced floor. She could open the window but the thought of the smoke from

4

the engine, the fumes, the dirt, made her cling helplessly to the seat. Outside the window, above the train, even the sky was dingy. Iron-grey clouds over brick-red terraces. A roof of smoke over the parks and playgrounds, supported by endless ranks of chimneys.

Somewhere in that mess of factories and industry a tiny neon sign glimmered: *Hovis: Home Of The Family Loaf.*

She uttered a short, humourless laugh.

Dad had been a baker until he'd fallen ill. He still looked OK, but the signs were there if you looked, like dirt beneath the sideboard; clinging to the edge of the carpet where you couldn't get rid of it without ripping up a whole chunk of fabric. Dirt. In his lungs. Clinging. Hoover-proof. Electrolux-proof. No Shake-and-Vac was going to shift his problem. The dirt would just keep accumulating, multiplying inside him, unstoppable, relentless. Until there was nothing of him left, just the dirt.

And when he was gone they'd put him in a wooden box and cover it with yet more dirt.

God she hated him. Right at this moment she hated him so much.

Him and Mum. Both of them. They let the boys run their bloody lives. Love? Love didn't enter into it. Not for Charlie, Rich and Dave. Not for the only family she ever had but which, for all the love and support she ever got, might as well have died years ago. They had wanted boys and they got boys.

And then in the heart of summer 1962 there she was, stuck in the middle of it all. A moment alone with Mum fifteen years later had confirmed her worst fear: she had been an accident. An accident! What kind of knowledge was that to impart to a fifteen year old struggling to discover her own identity, to determine her own way in life? Jesus H. Christ how she hated them.

And she was back on shift in less than two hours. Compassionate leave? No thanks, she could do without that. Could do without the time to dwell on it. On them, and on the dirt she could see everywhere she looked, now she knew what to look for.

5

She wished she could leave it all behind. The pain, the sadness. The responsibility. Except she could never leave it all behind. Because they wouldn't let her. At no time in her life had either of her parents shown her the love she hoped they felt for her. At no time had they supported her in her arguments with her brothers. Her choices. Her men. Her career. Her life.

Now they wanted her. They all wanted her there. It was as if they'd already put him in a coffin; as if only she could see he was still alive, still vital. She wanted to grab him, shake him, scream at him: *it's still out there, Dad, your life. All the things you ever wanted to do, they're still out there waiting for you. Go and grab them, grab them and hang on hard before you can't grab onto anything any more. Take hold of your life. Make it mean something, anything. Don't let the bastards take it from you!*

She pulled out a tissue, blew her nose, shoved the tissue back into her bag.

Christ, it was so hot.

Sheffield came and went. Manchester was an hour away.

Somewhere a door banged loudly.

She pulled a book from her bag and tried to read. The carriage door opened and a man came in. Short but wiry. Balding. Glasses. Halfway attractive in an older-guy kind of way. Nondescript clothes; a rumpled suit. A case which he placed on the luggage rack above her head. The case was small, like a sample case. Was he a salesman? Collapsing with a sigh into the seat opposite he smiled the way you do: strangers on a train. *Sorry: I'm in your space, I know. It won't be long. Only an hour to Manchester.*

She gave him a perfunctory smile and, head nodding slowly in time with the train, returned her attention to the pages of the book.

'Do you mind if I open the window?'

'What?' The book folded into her lap, fell between her knees, hit the floor with the dull slap of paper.

'The window. It's awfully stuffy in here.'

She shook her head, picked the book up, opened it again. Stared at the pages.

6

The man stood, legs brushing hers as he moved past her to the window. 'Let the grime out eh? Let a bit of sunshine in.'

She didn't look up. 'Sure.'

He sat beside the window, nearer now. Rocking to the movement of the train.

A rush of cold air spilled across her and she shivered. He probably thought it was clean.

Glossop came and went. Manchester was twenty minutes away.

The man stayed. She could hear him breathing in the cold air to the rhythm of the train. In. Out. In. Out. Inandthenout. Inandthen –

'Good book, is it?'

'Pardon?'

'I only ask, you see, because you haven't turned a page yet.'

'What?'

'Since I got on, you haven't turned a page. That's forty minutes. Either it's really boring or it's so riveting you can't help but read it over and over again.' He smiled. Ingenuous. Nondescript.

'Going to give me three guesses?'

'Look, I'm sorry. I'm just not good company right now, OK?'

The smile faded. 'Of course. I understand. I'm sorry.'

'That's OK.'

'Um . . . do you mind if I smoke?'

'The whole carriage is non-smoking.'

'Uh . . . of course. Stupid of me. Sorry.' A hesitation. 'Look . . . do you want me to leave?'

'No. No, don't be silly.'

'Shall I stay then?'

'Do what you like.'

'I do believe I will.'

Suddenly. The man stood suddenly. Face blank, eyes burning with embarrassment that hadn't yet touched his cheeks.

Though he was short he towered over her as she sat, rocking to the rhythm of the carriage. He swayed before her. Close enough to touch, close enough to smell.

7

And abruptly he moved closer –

And reached out for her –

And –

'Get away from me!'

– she stood, surged upwards, book forgotten, hands shoving at his chest; and he was falling, eyes widening in shock, almost fear, one hand clutching the case he'd placed on the luggage rack above her head when he'd entered the compartment.

She stood gazing down at him. He cowered back against the dirty seat, wisps of hair blowing in the draught from the window, his case clutched protectively to his chest. There was that look in his eyes. That dead look she'd seen so often.

Born victim.

'Oh my God,' she whispered. 'I'm so sorry. I thought – I thought . . .'

She held out a hand to help him rise.

After a moment he took it.

When a man's scream of terror came from further down the carriage, her eyes widened for a split second. Then book, bag, dying father and fellow passenger forgotten, Jane Penhaligon, Detective Sergeant in the Manchester Metropolitan Police Force, shoved back the door so hard the glass window cracked as she left the compartment at a dead run.

Fitz screamed inside. They were hooked. Faces, the lot of them. Just hungry faces.

He'd definitely lost them.

Still, he had to try. They'd shown the spark; well, some of them had. If he pushed. If he really pushed they might see it. Might get it. Might take it home with them. Some might even think about it; in between the football, or the soaps, the pets, the kids, the parents, the partners. One or two might even use it.

'The bride in white sees herself as the widow in black.' There. A statement. Not quite a fact but stated with the authority of one. Ambiguous. Thought provoking. The faces ate it up. An hors d'oeuvre. A prelude to the feast. Fitz gave them the starter: 'She's only just married him but already

8

she's planning for the day she'll bury him, and she'll be centre stage again.'

One or two satiated faces there. Women mainly. Couldn't handle the extended metaphor. Weren't going to make it to the sweet. Perhaps they just hated him.

Judith.

The main course? 'I rehearsed the death of my father for years. I even got a little bored: I knew all my lines but he was still alive. I didn't get my opening night for years.'

Dead silence.

Well. The crowd went wild for that one, Fitz.

Judith, please.

They deserved what was coming.

'So go and lock yourself away in a room for a couple of days, or months, or years, whatever it takes, and if any of you have the patience or the humility or the sheer guts to do it, study what's in here, in your heart. What you really feel, not that crap you're supposed to feel. It'll scare you. No: it'll bloody well terrify you. But that's tough. Listen to yourself. To your own, scared, inadequate, worthless selves. The things you'll find out will teach you more than anything, more than anyone else ever could.'

And just to prove to himself that he could do it, he threw them a little grin, a sacrificial lamb, just a hint of levity; sugar with the spoonful of medicine.

'Even me.'

He studied them. Was there a hint of diversity there again? Was the mirror trembling, might it crack again? Could he get them back from the edges of their bland, undifferentiated lives?

'And when you've studied, when you've listened, when you've shed a little light on the dark recesses of your soul, *that's* the time to pick up one of these.'

The last book, Skinner, sailed flapping into the audience.

He turned. 'And that, ladies and gentlemen, really is the end of the lecture. Doctor Geoffreys will presently be coming round with the contributions bucket. Thank you and good-night.'

● ● ●

There was no answer when George Wilde knocked on the door of compartment four, carriage ten of the 11:44 Glasgow–Manchester intercity. The window blind was down and there was no answer. Just the blatting noise of a couple of plastic tea cups on the floor outside the compartment jigging to the beat of the rolling stock, and the soft slurp of what looked like some very dodgy British Rail tea sliding out from the darkness under the door itself.

Tea in which someone had stepped, by the look of it.

George had been a guard for twelve years, and he dug the rolling stock beat pretty good himself. Twice round the Earth, that's how far all the miles he'd clocked up on British Rail would take him. Twice round the Earth or halfway to the Moon and back. Same as the distance that would be covered by all the veins and arteries in the human body if removed and placed end to end.

He'd told them that in the canteen on the morning break. They'd laughed, of course. What did he expect? There was no respect from the youngsters on the job. The androgynous boys and girls. They moved to a different rhythm from George's; a different tempo. All square and lifeless, impatient. Thought they knew it all, they did, but not a one of 'em understood the rolling stock beat. No feel for the job. No instinct. Faces in a crowd; all the same face. None of 'em would stand out. None of 'em had the bottle to take a chance. Do the job right.

No respect for it, see? No respect for the job.

He'd told them *that* in the canteen on the morning break. They'd laughed. Called him an old hippy, over the hill, a joke, a walking cliché.

Well. Maybe he was a walking cliché. At least he cared.

Cared enough to notice the darkness in the crack beneath the door beside the jigging coffee cups. Sharp enough to realise there should be light under that door, at least half an inch. From the outside or, at least, if the blind was down, from the compartment lights.

Unless the door was blocked, and that was a safety hazard. There were rules governing that sort of thing. It was probably someone having a crafty smoke. Come to think of it there did

10

seem to be a touch of the old Benson and Hedges wafting under the door. Bloody fools. Ought to know better. Did they think safety regs were made for someone's entertainment?

Well he'd soon put a stop to it, whatever it was about.

George knocked on the door. Again there was no reply. He shrugged. Slid the door open.

'Now, look here,' he began, 'I'm afraid we can't have no . . .'

He stopped.

Saw who was in the compartment.

What was left of her.

Everything kind of blurred out then for a while.

The voice at his shoulder shocked him into awareness. He turned. There was a girl. Small. Pretty. Well, sort of. Thin-nish. Red hair. Well sort of. Waving something at him. A wallet. A card.

'I'm Detective Sergeant Jane Penhaligon, Manchester Met,' said the girl. 'I'd like you to stop screaming now, sir. You'll alarm the other passengers.'

George shut his mouth. Pointed soundlessly into the compartment.

The girl looked in the direction of his pointing finger and her lips narrowed to a thin line.

That was all.

15:45–17:30

They took it away from her. Of course. What else should she have expected?

Bloody Bilborough. Bloody Beck. Worse than all three of her brothers put together, both of them.

She stood to one side as the cavalry swept through the train. Bilborough nodding to the commuters, suit crisp and clean, a contrast to her own off-duty jacket and jeans. Beck shadowing him, glowering, black eyes narrow, roll-up stuck behind one ear, suspicion of everyone and everything evident in every look, every movement.

'– about the delay ladies and –'

'– be moving again as soon as –'

'– nothing at all to worry –'

'– second pal, honestly, alright?'

She trudged after them. In the wake. Just for the hell of it she tried to imagine them in a Sergio Leone movie. *Once upon a time in Manchester Victoria.* Somehow she wasn't surprised how easily the mental picture of Bilborough and Beck in long coats, boots, spurs and six guns standing on the platform of an entirely different train station formed in her mind.

She suppressed a giggle. That at least was easy.

Bilborough turned then, beckoned her forward to join them in the empty corridor of carriage ten.

'Sweeney?' His voice was soft. Educated. If he hadn't been such a dim sod she might even have found it attractive. DCI Bilborough was the Met's new golden boy. A rising star. Well. Everyone knew what they said about things that went up.

She nodded. 'Looks like it.'

Beck scowled. Sometimes she wondered if he ever did anything else with his face.

'You've done well, Sergeant.'

Gee. Thanks a whole bunch, pardner.

'Thank you, sir.'

'Scene of crime not here?' That was Beck, struggling hard to squeeze the words out past his scowl.

'On the way. Pathology too.'

There was the sound of a flushing toilet. Someone wandered out of the loo at the end of the carriage. She introduced him. 'George Wilde. The guard. He found her.'

Bilborough offered a perfunctory handshake. 'DCI Bilborough, sir. We'll need your shoes.'

'Do what?'

But Bilborough was already past, Beck in tow, coasting along the corridor to compartment four, and his expression said it all. She imagined them in waders, checking through the train's septic tank for flushed evidence, and grinned to herself.

She offered a shrugged apology to the guard as she followed.

'Did you touch anything in here?' Beck again. Arrowing in on the important stuff in as aggressive a manner as he could get away with.

George shook his head.

'Sorry, sir? What was that?' Neither Beck nor Bilborough was looking at him; both were staring at the inside of the compartment.

'I said no. I didn't touch anything. I'm not as stupid as some young people think, you know.'

Bilborough turned, unsmiling. 'Quite.'

She joined them at the door to the compartment. Everything was just as she remembered it. Particularly the girl. No more than eighteen or nineteen. Hard to tell with all that blood. The carriage was red with it; black with it. A crumpled shape in the corner showed where her clothes had been flung; a shape marginally less crumpled than the girl herself.

She forced herself to look at the girl's face. Her eyes were open, fringed with blood. There was no expression there. In her experience there never was. No horror, no surprise, no pain, no regret. The reality was that when you died there was simply nothing of you left at all.

Her own eyes moved on.

The girl was naked. She was shaven. There were cuts in her breasts and chest, her neck, her hands. Deep straight cuts. Razor cuts. One finger hung by a thread of skin, the bone white and jagged, the flesh ripped. Not a cut then. Torn in the struggle.

She had been young, beautiful. Under once perfect skin the muscle tone was good. She had been fit. Healthy body; healthy mind. The book she'd been reading, flung into another corner and trampled underfoot in the struggle, confirmed the supposition: Jung. She'd been a psychology student; looks, health, intelligence. She'd had it all. Now she was just a lump of meat.

She let her eyes wander around the carriage, noting details in a holistic kind of way, storing it all for later retrieval and analysis. Eventually her gaze fastened on the window, where a droplet of blood had slipped free from the top part of the

13

frame. Dusty yellow sunlight glinted on the liquid as it moved sluggishly down the glass. Other stripes hung beside it, unmoving.

Her eyes moved on, eventually settling back on the girl. Alchemists of the fourteenth century had once thought that everything in the world was made up of five elements. Earth, air, fire, water and something called phlogiston. This was the name they attributed to that substance which left an object when that object was burned; the element that accounted for the difference in weight between the intact original and the ash that remained after combustion. That premise was all rubbish, of course, but it had a parallel here today. One she noticed now: something had left the girl in death, some spark . . . Something. She imagined it, soul, psyche, whatever it had been, swept out of her in the blood jetting from the mouth. The second, straight, red-lipped mouth newly opened in her throat. And she felt sick. Sick to her stomach, as if she were the one who'd been violated.

Whatever the path report said, it would be irrelevant. In her own mind Penhaligon already knew the conclusion.

Sweeney.

Bilborough was talking: 'Statements from everyone on board. Reason for journey. Names and addresses. Proof of identity.'

Beck was nodding, taking in the instructions, Brylcreemed hair bobbing slightly, unlit roll-up wobbling precariously behind an ear.

Bilborough went on, 'A seating plan of every compartment. Who sat where. Who got on, who got off; where they got on, where they got off.'

'Right.' Beck pushed past Penhaligon with a muttered apology. Bilborough himself stayed at the scene, staring at the girl. Penhaligon studied his face. A little sensitivity there. Perhaps he wasn't such a dim sod after all.

Behind her, George Wilde said, 'About me shoes. Do you want them now, or what?'

Without turning, Bilborough said, 'Yes please, sir. Give them to DS Penhaligon here, if you would.'

● ● ●

Three quarters of a mile away in the student bar of Manchester University Fitz drew back his foot and levelled a mighty kick at the fruit machine he was playing.

It bleeped.

A titter of laughter trickled around the students who were lounging and chatting in the room. Dolls, all of them. Plastic, all of them. All the same. All the bloody same. Even when they smiled, they were dolls. And they were all part of the mirror.

Anyway, only one smile held him nowadays. One rare smile.

Judith.

Some muttered comment followed the laughter. Something about his size, probably; his weight. He thought about responding. Then he thought about kicking the machine again. Thought of the satisfaction it would give him, how small it would be compared to, say, just making Judith smile. A natural smile, not forced or sarcastic. A natural smile. God she was beautiful. Why did he do it to her? Why did he do it to all of them? Mark. Katie. But especially Judith. Twenty years. Oh, God. What he wouldn't give to see her smile just once. Tell him it was OK. Tell him she understood. Understood the highs, and lows that made the highs even better.

Giving in to self-indulgence, Fitz kicked the fruit machine. It bleeped again. He thought he detected a smug note in the bleep. Well, why shouldn't the damn thing be smug? It had his money, didn't it? And what did he have? Not even a smile from his wife. Not even that.

Geoffreys entered the room ten minutes and two pounds fifty later. Fitz knew it without turning; heard it in the subtle change of ambiance; the delicate redirection of attention away from him. The man's timing was immaculate. Bloody immaculate.

Foot poised to kick the machine again, Fitz said, 'A hundred and twenty.' He said it without taking his eyes from the flickering lights, the tumbling neon fruit.

'It'll have to go through accounts.'

Nudge. He thumped the button. Two cherries, a lemon.

'Oh, come on. I could do with it now. In readies.'

15

'Can't be done.'

'I'm out tonight. With Judith. I was counting on the money for that.'

'Fitz, I'm really sorry. My hands are tied. Anyway. The lecture wasn't quite what I expected.'

The machine bleeped. *Collect or gamble?* No question there.

'Yeah well, you know, a little controversy, a little phoney passion. They lap it up.'

Why did he say that? He didn't believe that.

A cherry, a blueberry, a bloody orange.

Did he?

'Take it on the chin, Fitz. It's inevitable. Can't fight city hall, you know that.'

Bollocks.

Fitz grunted a monosyllabic answer.

Nudge.

He thumped the button.

Nudge. Nudge. Nudge.

Jackpot. Jackpot. Raspberry.

'Bloody machine's taking the piss!'

'Fitz, do you want to borrow a few pounds? I can manage a tenner if you –'

Fitz clamped his teeth around his high tar, sucked, said nothing as the words washed over him.

Instead of leaving, Geoffreys leaned closer. He didn't say anything though. Maybe he was getting the point.

With a flamboyant gesture, Fitz smacked the play button one more time, then turned without waiting to see the mismatched line of fruit he knew would align across the machine's casing. Dismissing Geoffreys' sympathetic expression he thundered across to the bar, and reached for his drink.

His fingers closed around the monkey-nut bowl.

'Where's my drink?'

The kiddie behind the bar looked blank. How often had he seen Mark display that same expression; most notably when in Fitz's presence?

'My drink,' he explained with exaggerated calmness. 'I left it here, in a pint glass, while masochistically allowing

16

myself to be whipped silly by R2D2 over there,' he hooked a thumb to where Geoffreys was pumping money into the fruit machine.

The kiddie blinked. 'A pint? Of bitter, you mean?'

Fitz sighed. Nodded. 'This is the student bar, is it not? What else would you serve? Unless I am to believe you now have the power to transmute the kind of radioactive sludge into which I would not immerse my worst enemy into liquid gold?'

The kiddie blanked again, sniffed to cover his pause, wiped a glass thoughtfully. 'Yeah, well. Thought you'd finished, didn't I?'

'Finished? Finished! There was at least a quarter of an inch of fluid left in the bottom of that –' Fitz stopped. What was the use? Without another word he turned to leave the bar. As he passed the fruit machine, Geoffreys was collecting the tenner jackpot.

Bastard. *Bastard.*

Fitz hit the street in a black rage. The cold, dusty wind did nothing to cool him off. His mood was not improved when the half hourly bus whipped past while he was just ten feet from the stop.

Another few minutes bad tempered stomping brought him to the taxi rank outside the Arndale Centre, where he cruised in front of a young mum with a kiddie in a pram and an elderly couple with two Woolies shopping bags apiece.

The cab, with Fitz inside, shot away from the Arndale in a cloud of grime.

The cab driver was from Liverpool, his voice a nasal whine. 'I'd prefer you not to smoke.'

Tough.

Fitz drew on his high tar, said nothing. Inside his head the road drills were starting up.

'It's been scientifically proven that I inhale twenty per cent of everything you smoke.'

The road drills were hammering louder now. He could feel his eyebrows quiver.

'Gerrit for free, though, don'cha?' Fitz couldn't tell if it was the jibe or the piss-take Liverpool accent that earned him a bad tempered scowl from the cabbie as he opened the driver's window. A blast of cold air sailed back and smacked Fitz around the face. 'Do you mind?'

'No mate, I don't. And I'm not getting cancer off you, right?'

Bastard.

He told the cabbie to wait outside the house while he got some money. That got him another black look. The world was full of them.

In the sitting room Mark was sprawled across the sofa; ponytail clasped by a rubber band, torn jeans, *mammal* T-shirt, frown of concentration. Fitz checked the sofa for burns. At least he wasn't smoking in here yet.

The telly was on. Loud. *Home and Away*. Jesus. Eighteen years old and already hooked.

'I'm booking you into a detox clinic. Is next Wednesday good for you?'

'Eh?' Mark's eyes never left the screen. Sine wave junkie; suicide with an electron gun at his head.

'Never mind. Where's your mum?'

'What?'

'I said: where's your mum?'

Irritation. Concentration broken. 'Dunno.'

Fitz planted himself between his son and the television. 'Where?'

'Shift up, Dad, I'll miss it.' Mark wriggled further along the sofa, peered around Fitz, added, 'What did you say?'

'Have you any money?'

Absorbed. 'Sorry, what?'

'I'll put my bloody foot through that bloody thing!'

Mark's eyes shifted the tiniest amount.

'And don't you dare say "What?" again or I'll brain you. Have you any money?'

'No.'

Fitz sighed. A face. A doll. His own bloody son, just one more facet of the mirror.

Leaving his son to his addiction, Fitz called up the stairs. 'Katie?'

18

'In here, Dad.' Her voice led him to the kitchen. Ten years old. Head a good deal older. Real potential there. Homework spread across the kitchen table. Conscientious. Must have done something right there. 'Have you any money, love? I have to pay the cabbie.'

Katie shook her head, eyes solemn. 'No, Dad. Sorry.' Then she dug into her pocket. 'I've got fifty pence left over from dinner time,' she said.

Fitz melted. 'You keep it, sweetheart.'

Judith was in the bathroom. So was her bag. His second suit had been cleaned, there was nothing under the bed but his slippers, the Japanese urn they kept the monthly milk money in was empty; the money spent last week on a new Glenfiddich.

In the end he paid the cabbie by cheque. The payment for waiting time was half again as much as the fare.

'I suppose you're expecting a tip.'

'It'd be nice.'

Fitz flung the cheque at him. 'Lift your bloody dahlias in winter.'

Fitz was sure the cloud of filthy smoke that hit him in the face as the cab roared away was deliberate.

Bastard.

Back in the house Fitz headed for the drinks cabinet, his bottle of Glenfiddich. Should be able to smooth out the rest of the day with a good drop o' the – He stared at the bottle.

It was empty.

He walked deliberately slowly across the sitting room to the sofa, held the bottle upside down in front of Mark's face. Saw a distorted reflection of the television picture in it, mapped onto his own features. 'Have you been at this?'

'No.' Arrogant. Irritable.

'You're lying.'

'I'm not.' Indignant.

'You're lying.'

The explosion. 'I haven't bloody well touched it!'

Judith swept into the sitting room, face composed, pointedly ignoring both her son and her husband. Mark shuffled upright on the couch, swung his feet to the carpet. Chewed his lower lip while saying nothing.

Fitz was momentarily taken aback by the vision of his wife. Every time he saw her it was like the first time. She was always fresh. Always. She'd had her hair cut. And done something to her face. More make-up. Less. Something. She was beautiful.

'Two hours, Fitz,' she said. 'We're going out.'

She looked at the whisky bottle.

'Preferably sober,' she added.

Fitz swallowed. 'No choice, have I?' He grinned. The disarming grin. The grin she'd fallen for twenty years ago. She didn't react. He took her hands in his. *There. Still friends. I love you. I love you.*

He kissed her.

She let him. This time.

Penhaligon watched the pathologist, Albert Copeley, standing over the girl. No. Hovered would be a better word. Gazing intently at the motionless body.

As if it might get up and do a jig, she supposed.

Clutching a plastic bag filled with George Wilde's British Rail issue size twelves, Penhaligon herself hovered, just beyond the door to the compartment. Bilborough was beside her, eyes alert, also watching. Inside the room was the path photographer. Murphy, Penhaligon thought her name was. And Nease, the scene of crime man. The weirdo.

All three had arrived while she'd been interviewing George Wilde. His story held water; the only curiosity was his remark about someone smoking. There had been no cigarettes or matches in either the girl's clothing or her purse. There was no ash on the seats or floor of the compartment, at least none they could see beneath the blood. Perhaps the killer was a smoker. If so where was the evidence?

'Was it Sweeney?' Bilborough's voice, mild but insistent, brought her back to the present.

Copeley bent – no, swooped – low across the dead girl's mutilated body. Tweezers glittered in the camera flash like claws hunting for prey. 'Blonde pubic hair. She wasn't a natural brunette.' He frowned. 'It's odd; you don't often see that. A blonde dying her hair. Obviously wasn't image conscious. Couldn't have been susceptible to peer group pressure either. Perhaps she was getting too much attention from the boys, felt it would take the heat off.'

Bilborough turned to Penhaligon. 'Sound plausible to you?'

She shrugged. 'Wouldn't know, sir.'

Bilborough studied her for a moment before returning his attention to Copeley. 'Fine. Very good. Very observant. But was it Sweeney?'

Penhaligon didn't know why Bilborough pushed so hard. That much had been obvious from the off.

Copeley pushed back his spectacles; added, at his own pace, 'Throat cut, pubic hair shaven. A cursory glance shows no traces of semen. I'll have to wait til we're back in the lab to be sure, but there's no bruising or distension of the pudendum. And the tiny bit of pubic hair we've found is all one colour. There's no other evidence of penetration.' He pursed his lips, shook his head; a short, bird-like movement. 'All Sweeney's trademarks.'

Penhaligon frowned, rubbed one finger idly along the plastic sheathed shoes that she still held, tapped thoughtfully on the heel. Jazz time.

Sweeney killed them but didn't rape them. Didn't hate them. Loved them. Loved them and killed them.

Murphy snapped a picture of one wall, an arc of blood high off the floor. As if this was a signal, Nease spoke. His voice was that of a man ten years younger, almost childish, full of the enthusiasm of the obsessive personality. 'This is a classic.' His eyes were bright. He reminded Penhaligon of a kid she had been at school with. Tony . . . ? Yeah. Tony Chapel. Tony who had collected dead things that came out of weed choked ponds. Anything wet and slimy. Nease turned to Murphy. 'Can you get one in relation to the window? Thanks.' As the flash bloomed again he turned to study his reflection in the blood-spattered wall mirror. Adjusted his tie. Then, 'D'you see the blood pattern? High up then sloping down?'

21

Hard to bloody well miss it, actually.

'He had her facing this wall.' Nease hooked a thumb at the mirror. 'Right. She's up against the wall. The blood pressure's sky high; she's fighting for her life. The blade pierces the carotid artery; for a split second it's a tiny hole in a high pressure pipe so the force is amazing.' Nease stretched up onto tiptoe, pointed to the space above the luggage rack on the same side of the compartment as the mirror. 'Here. Take a look at this – see, there's the blood at its highest point.' Nease shrank back onto his heels, his arm sweeping around to end up pointing at the dead girl's face. 'Then the cut gets bigger, the pressure drops, *she* drops, and what's left in her, six pints of blood, say, bubbles out onto the floor until the heart stops pumping.'

He straightened. 'It's an absolute bloody classic.' Glanced at Murphy. 'Can you get one of me pointing to it? I'll just do this.'

Posing before the arc of blood Nease shot an apologetic look towards Penhaligon. 'Something for the album.'

She couldn't tell if he was a black humorist or a sad bastard. Then again, did it really matter?

Bilborough said as the flash went off, 'It's safe to presume he's covered in blood, then.'

'Oh, lathered in it, I should think.' Nease hesitated. 'Unless . . .'

'What?'

'Well, it's the Joanna Delling case. You remember it. Seven years ago. Never seen anything like it. Identical *modus operandi* and the killer never had a spot of blood on him. Stood behind her all the time, held her until she was dead. Must have been strong as an ox. Unique. Absolutely unique.' He sniffed.

'And the chances of the same thing being the case here?'

Nease shrugged. 'Not likely. Not likely at all. But . . . possible.'

Bilborough was satisfied. 'OK,' he said to Copeley. 'Zip her up.'

Clutching the bag containing George Wilde's shoes, Penhaligon moved away. She knew what would come next:

22

Prints. ID. Family. They'd give it back to her then, for sure.

'Sir,' she said quietly, as they walked back down the corridor towards the compartments where Giggs, Jonesy and the rest were still interviewing.

'Yes, Sergeant, what is it?'

'Nease, Copely, yourself. You've all assumed the killer is a man.'

Bilborough jerked a thumb back at the compartment, unconscious imitation of Nease. 'Are you trying to tell me a woman could have done that?'

According to Edgar Allen Poe a monkey could have done it.

'You heard Copeley. There was no rape. No penetration. We know that no trace of sexual fluid was found on the other murder victim, Patricia Garth. All I'm saying is maybe we should consider the option.'

'Patricia Garth was found in a caustic lime pit by a railway siding. She'd been there a month. I couldn't even tell what sex she was, let alone if she'd had any.'

'Look, sir –'

'No, Penhaligon. The killer's a man. I know. I . . .' Bilborough hesitated. 'I just know.' He sighed. 'Give the shoes to Jimmy Beck. And get on the blower to ID, OK? Chase them up a bit. I want to find out who she is – was.'

Penhaligon nodded. From behind came the crisp rustle of a body bag closing. From ahead came voices. Giggs, Jonesy, interviewing: '– a salesman? What do you sell? Portable vacuum cleaners? That sounds –'

Bilborough's voice held her attention. 'We can't just keep calling her Number Two.'

'Of course not, sir. That'd be bad for morale wouldn't it?'

19:30–21:15

Sure enough Bilborough gave it back to her. Half past seven that same evening, half a mile from the Appleby's house in the burbs he gave it back to her with the words, 'You take the mother, OK?' Casual. Studied. Predictable.

23

'Yes.'

'You're good at that kind of thing.' Defensive.

I've had plenty of practice.

'One condition. I'll do it on one condition.'

Bilborough changed down for a crossroads, flicked the lights on. Night was coming down, a blustery rain with it. 'What's that then?'

Penhaligon stared out of the windscreen, tracked the dying sun with expressionless eyes. 'Consider it. Just consider my theory about the killer. Do that and I'll deal with as many mothers as you like.'

Bilborough drove the last half mile in thoughtful silence. Penhaligon didn't press the point.

Two hours ago, ninety seven minutes after the girl had first been discovered by George Wilde, the passengers had finally been let out of the train. They trickled onto the platform in twos and threes, dribbled away into the gathering evening; an observer might have thought them strangely reluctant to leave the scene of the crime.

Penhaligon knew all about this. While most people had a healthy aversion to any kind of violence, if you shut a group of strangers up for long enough with a room full of death, something changed. It was inevitable. Once the initial surprise was gone, the fear, the anger; something else took over. Resignation set in and with it a kind of group dependency. There you were taking statements, reassuring people, calming them, being a bloody mother to them. They warmed to you after a while. Even those that didn't, the over-eager beavers, the irritating, self-important prats, engendered a kind of false family-feeling in the others which merely strengthened their bond with you. So when the time came to cut the old psychological apron strings and tip them all back into the big empty, was it any surprise that most of them were reluctant to leave?

Even Beck had had his own admirer, a twenty-two year old mountaineering enthusiast called Francis with a very obvious predeliction for the sleazy-copper look. Penhaligon grinned to herself when she recalled Beck's expression as the bloke had eagerly scribbled down an address and phone number for him to use on follow-up.

And then they'd gone, trickled away into the gathering night with their baggage and their hopes and their heads full of stories to tell. And she'd been left with a zippered girl, a bag full of shoes and slightly more than two thirds of the Magnificent Seven.

Leaving Giggs and Jonesy to dismantle the intercity in the Victoria stockyard, she had taken the lift Bilborough and Beck had offered her back to the station at Anson Road. There she'd carried the bag of shoes down to forensics – the nuthatch – for Copeley to analyse before spending the next two hours with Beck in incident typing up interview reports.

Around seven fifteen that evening ID had pulled off a minor miracle. The girl had previous. As it turned out the 'previous' was failing to buy a British Rail ticket the month before. Unwilling to face a three month prison sentence or tap her parents for the cash, she'd cut into her student grant to pay the fine.

Penhaligon wondered, as Bilborough braked the two-litre gently to a halt, if Jacqui Louise Appleby had bought a ticket for today's journey. If she had any clue just how far this particular trip was going to take her.

'So you'll take the mother then?'
'Will you think about what I said?'
'I'll think about it.'
'I'll take the mother.'

Ann Appleby opened the front door with a pensive look, a tea towel clasped in her hands. Two minutes from now the tea towel was to become the most important thing in her life. For now all she saw was the redhead in jacket and jeans, the man beside her tall, bland faced, almost friendly.

'Mrs Appleby?' The redhead's voice was soft, in no way intrusive, yet it jarred. Oh God, how it jarred. That was the moment when Ann Appleby felt something inside her head cut loose, felt herself floating away inside. She didn't register the girl's name, didn't need to see the wallets, the ID cards.

Jacqui.

'Simon . . .' Her voice was firm. How could that be? She

knew why they were here. How could her voice not show it?
'Simon!'

Then her husband was there, and they were a wall against the night, the fear.

But that didn't change the fact.

And all this before the redhead, the man; all this before they'd even stepped across the threshold.

'Yes? What can we do to help?' Simon smiled a welcome. He didn't know. Hadn't got it yet.

'Police officers? Well. I suppose you'd better come in then. Is there something we can do to help?'

No. Don't let them in. Keep them out. Keep her out. She's the one. The one who'll say it. The one who'll take me apart.

Simon led them into the sitting room. 'Sorry about the mess,' she heard the words as if down a long white tunnel. 'Our daughter's away. Long weekend. We're taking the opportunity to do a bit of late spring cleaning. Can I get you anything? Cup of tea?'

He grinned brightly. The grin wrapped around the end of the tunnel, a grotesque distortion in white of the man she knew too well to love.

'Mrs Appleby, shall we sit down?'

No! I won't sit still for this. Won't sit still for this fact!

Then the redhead told them and even Simon understood.

Later, in the back seat of the car, Ann Appleby clutched the tea towel to her breast and stared at the back of the redhead's neck. She did not feel Simon beside her. She did not see the umber clouds, the rain splattering against the windows. Only the girl. The girl and the man driving the car.

You poor love, oh you poor love. He made you do it, didn't he? Made you tell me?

Jacqui.

The Ambassador had been fully booked for the whole evening but Fitz hadn't batted an eyelid. He'd pushed and as usual he had got his own way.

As the Maitre D' crumbled before him, Fitz knew he was pushing, but it was too late by then. Anyway, he did it all the time, did it unconsciously, automatically; without thinking.

26

Without thinking. Which was funny really, because as a psychologist he did nothing *but* think about most things. Most people. Most situations. There was always something to grab you. Some motive. Some clue to indicate who a person was, what they were about. And once having seen this clue he could never let it go. Had to dig. Had to delve. Find out what was behind the mirror. It had been going on for so long in his life it was almost a game now. Fitz's game. And he was the world champion.

Take the waiter for example. Long hair, long face. Girl-friend problems? Maybe. Boyfriend problems? That could be even more interesting. He seemed too old to be here. At least in his late twenties. Built like a boxer. But clumsy. And the eyes. A little wider than normal. A little more fixed. Was he on something? Steroids? Desperate to make it and prepared to pay the price, any price, for success?

Instead of asking for an ashtray, Fitz had deliberately allowed the waiter to see him flick ash from his cigarette into the table centrepiece. It was a newly acquired habit; he liked to practise. The man had barely reacted. He'd taken away the vase of flowers and replaced it with a cut glass ashtray. No mention had been made of the fact that the Ambassador was an entirely non-smoking establishment.

What could he deduce from that, Fitz wondered. Did he need the job so badly that he was scared of making a fuss for fear that he, Fitz, would make a bigger one in return, cause an affray, maybe complain so much the waiter lost his job?

Fitz sighed. This was a load of crap. He was on edge. Right on the edge. Teetering. Judith did this to him. Every time. Somehow. Twenty years together and now this: five weeks of hell. Sheer hell.

The worse thing was he couldn't even remember when their life together had begun to come apart. The slide from happiness to bitterness had been an insidious one. It was also a bloody logarithmic scale; the further you went down it, the steeper the slope, the harder it was to crawl back up again.

He blamed Judith for it of course. No, not her, himself. But he took his anger out on her. Displacement. He saw it all the time in his punters. Sorry: clients. The anger he felt was towards himself – but somehow it always ended up hitting the fan over Judith. Was it any wonder she was mad at him in return?

He looked at her, across the table, framed by two empty seats. There was symbolism for you: the table was their relationship; the seats their destination. It was a wide table. And the seats were only big enough for one.

Bollocks.

Study what's in here. *That's the time to pick up one of these –*

Fitz picked up the cloth-covered menu. Looked at it for a few minutes without seeing it, re-folded it and fanned himself casually.

God, how were they going to get through this?

He looked up. Judith was staring at the ashtray.

He glanced at his watch, the wide strap a narrow thread compared to his wrist, the metal casing almost swallowed by flesh. Eight thirty. Jo and Mike would be here any minute.

Look at me, Judith. Look inside me. I know you can do it.

Judith looked up then, caught his eye. Must have seen something in it, for she drew breath, started to speak, 'Fitz, I –'

But Jo and Mike arrived at that moment and Judith's response, whatever it might have been, was lost in the round of greetings as they were shown to the table and took their seats.

Fitz studied the couple as they sat.

Stop staring. It was just bad timing that's all. You can ask Judith what she was going to say later.

Jo and Mike were Judith's friends. Jo was Judith's age, a single mother with a four year old daughter, Natalie. She was a lecturer; women's studies at Sheffield U. She was bright, far too intense, a bit over made up. Tonight she wore her hair piled into ringlets and a dress exactly the right size for her. That was unusual; the other times Fitz had been in company with Jo she'd always worn jeans and jacket; the perfect, not-quite-stereotypical liberal. And now the glamour. Understated, handled fairly well, but there nonetheless. Mike was obviously having some small effect on her.

Her current boyfriend, Mike, looked like he could be a businessman of some kind; fairly important; definitely not self employed; no signs of stress, no fretting about being away from the books, the job. Middle management then. A fairly safe job. Woolies. Something you didn't take home with you. A job there were enough hours in the day to perform adequately and still have some left over for a life of your own as well.

Mike looked on the right side of forty. He was fit, with a thinker's face, but strangely quiet. And deferential to Jo. Nothing obvious. Didn't pull out her chair or anything. But he paid attention to her. All the time. And he didn't ask any questions. Not one. Fitz sucked on his high tar and wondered briefly if Jo wearing a dress tonight was a reward of some kind for Mike. It wouldn't be unheard of. Should make for a few interesting conversational gambits later in the evening; later when the drinks had started to fly.

The waiter appeared at his elbow. 'Would you care to order, sir?'

'Yes please.' Ignoring Judith's warning stare, aware that he had been staring himself. 'Give me a scotch and dry.' Without thinking. 'Make it a double.' No, not without thinking. Thinking too much. 'And a couple of bottles of house white,' he added. 'If that's alright with everyone?'

The waiter jotted all this down on a little pad stamped with the restaurant's logo. 'So. A double scotch and dry, two bottles of house white. Now would you like anything to start?'

Fitz grinned; crumpled his face in that way Judith had once found irresistible. 'Do you have any more of those cute little ashtrays? The ones with the water in the bottom and the flowers growing out of them?'

Judith laughed then; the wrong sort of laugh. The *I don't find that funny* laugh. The *shut up Fitz you're embarrassing me* laugh.

God, how were they going to get through this?

She'd been frightened; scared to get out of the car. Not here. Not at this place. But the mortuary had been like a school, red brick outside, cream walls inside, wooden bannisters and fixtures. A noticeboard in the corridor. The smell of scrupulously clean walls and floors.

Just like a school.

She wondered how many children came here. Came here instead of the playground, the park; how many came from the park.

Jacqui. What were you doing on that train? You shouldn't have been back until tomorrow. What were you doing on that train?

The man, Bilborough, led them from the car park through a set of corridors and into a small ground floor office. The redhead followed. Silently.

Simon was beside her, his arm in hers, his movements stiff, almost eager, and she felt herself slipping again, that thing in her mind ripping loose, flying away somewhere on a path of its own.

If I get there quickly enough it won't be her. If I get there quickly enough it simply won't, so I'll walk a little faster, just a little faster now, and it won't be her, won't be her things they'll show me. Won't be her ring, her watch, her book, her purse.

But they were.

And *dear Lord there's blood on her purse. There's blood on everything. Oh Jacqui, Jacqui, love, what were you doing? What were you thinking of to come back so early? What were you doing on that train?*

The lemon sole had been lousy. Judith had hated it, Fitz could tell. He saw the slight twitch at the corner of her jaw as she took the first mouthful, saw her eyes narrow minutely. He hadn't been so keen on it himself for that matter. He'd thought about complaining. Thought about how Judith might react to that, how embarrassed she might be, thought about it until the moment passed.

The conversation returned to normal, skipping gaily from one superficial subject to the next.

With the sole gone the way of all fish, a couple more doubles inside just to take away the taste, and his Barclaycard safely ensconced on the waiter's silver tray, Fitz thought the sensible thing to do next would be to make the coffee conversation as interesting as possible.

Jo was an intelligent woman. Definitely not a face. Not part of the mirror. But when Fitz asked how much she paid her childminder, the shutters slammed down fast behind her eyes.

Oho. Guilty as charged m'lud!

'Go on then.' Fitz ignored a warning glance from Judith, and pressed the point. 'How much do you pay her? Tell me, I dare you.'

'It's none of our business.'

'It's just a conversation, Judith.' To Jo he added, 'Two? Two fifty?'

'Fitz.' Quiet. Controlled. 'It's none of our business.'

'Three pounds an hour? How much?'

Jo leaned forward. 'How much do you pay?'

'We don't have a childminder.'

'No but when you did use them. How much did you pay?'

Fitz settled back in his chair. 'It was completely different.'

Judith sighed. 'A pound an hour.'

Jo pounced. 'A pound an hour! Talk about the pot calling the kettle black.'

It was the off. 'Yeah well, I mean, I don't spout on about exploitation. I don't spout about equal opportunities.'

'I don't spout!'

Aggression as defence. He saw it every day. 'You do. You spout about your life. You spout about your kid. You spout about everything. Social reform, politics, everything. And feminism, you spout about that too, all that bullshit.'

'It's not bullshit!'

Judith glanced at Mike for help. 'Let's talk about the weather shall we?' *Or Australian soaps, or the state of British Rail tea or the rate of bloody income tax for Christ's sake, anything, anything but this!*

But he was away and he was right, he knew it; leaning forward, pushing, pushing the words out fast, faster, and there was a power in him, something mean and angry, something impossible to ignore, the truth. 'It's bullshit. It's complete unadulterated bullshit. You're paying some poor downtrodden cow two pounds an hour to look after your child. Your child. The thing that means most to you in all the world. Two pounds an hour. And –'

'– Fitz we'll talk –'

'– you've got a –'

'– again when you're –'

'– cleaner. You've got that –'

'– not so drunk so –'

'– black woman that comes to –'

'– pissed, Judith for Christ's sake, how do you –'

'– clean the house! She comes to clean the house doesn't she?'

Fitz blinked in the momentary silence. 'Of course, ideally she should be a Filippino, but she's black so that's OK –'

'Fitz. Drop it.'

'I will not drop it, Judith.'

I can't. Don't you see? It's important. It's dangerous. It's bloody exploitation!

'Jo!' Almost a shout. 'Look at me!' It had started as a bit of fun, an intellectual discussion. Where had it changed? 'Am I right?' Was that desperation in his voice. In his own voice?

'What?'

'Jo.' Soft. 'Tell me: am I right?'

Softer. 'Yeah.'

Later, he would think back to this moment and know without a shadow of a doubt what he should have done. He could have, should have let it go. Just let it go. The evening would have taken a beating, true, but not a fatal one. Nothing a day in the dog house couldn't cure. But he had to follow it up. Had to get in there, had to push. Had to dig for the truth. Had to see what was behind the mirror.

'So. How much do you pay her? No don't tell me, the going rate, am I right? I am aren't I? What is it this time? Two? Two fifty? Less? More?'

'A little more.' Resigned. 'Three.'

Mike leaned forward. 'We all know the point you're trying to make.'

Fitz slammed him back in his seat with a glance. 'Oh you

do do you? Understand the point I'm *trying* to make?' Whipped his gaze back to Jo. 'Three pounds an hour. Three lousy pounds an hour. Some kids get more pocket money than that. Three pounds an hour? She could make more than that in sodding South Africa!'

'No she couldn't!' Hesitation. Weariness. Surely not shame?

The prosecution rests m'lud.

But of course he didn't rest. Couldn't. Had to push it; push it right off the edge. Had to find out where it would land. 'So you pay this woman three pounds an hour to clean your house so you can go out and teach women's studies for twenty pounds an hour. Do you not think that's a teeny weeny bit hypocritical?'

'Everyone has to earn a living, Fitz –'

'Yeah, right, sure, so there's you up on the podium talking about equality and freedom and feminism and all that bullshit, all that bullshit Jo, and she's at home, your home, with your kids instead of her own, with your lousy three quid an hour in her purse and her bloody arm shoved halfway down your lavatory –'

Coffee.

He could taste coffee.

It was all over his face, trickling down his neck, under his collar.

He blinked; tiny droplets of liquid flipped away from his eyelids.

He picked up his napkin.

Jo wasn't looking at him. She was looking down at the table, just placing her empty coffee cup back on the saucer. Then she did look at him and something in her eyes told Fitz he ought to count himself lucky not to be blinking away pieces of bone china instead of just lukewarm coffee.

He looked at Judith; she refused to meet his gaze, used her teaspoon to chase the last of her baked Alaska around the dish.

Mike was looking at Jo, expression mild. What shall we do next? Go for the cheese course?

And then the waiter was back. With his little silver tray.

And Fitz's Barclaycard. And the unpaid bill.

Fitz finished wiping his hands and face, crumpled the paper napkin and dropped it onto the waiter's tray.

'I think what we have here,' he said, 'is a failure to communicate.'

They let Ann go into the chapel first, alone.

Inside the room the lights were low, concealed, an up-lighter casting a gentle glow over the tiny altar at the far end of the room. The walls were concealed by drapes. Unobtrusive, velvety smooth in the gentle light. A stained glass window depicting the crucifixion stood above the altar, focal point for those unwilling or unable to confront the truth.

Jacqui lay on a steel table, a cream coloured shroud pulled up to her neck. Her eyes were closed. Her skin was pale, just as she remembered. She looked beautiful but tired. So tired.

Oh Jacqui. Oh Jacqui. There. We'll get you home soon and you can go to sleep. Jacqui. There, there, we're here now love, Mum and Dad are here. We'll take you home soon and you can go to sleep.

She moved closer, footsteps absorbed by the drapes. She reached out with trembling fingers to touch her daughter's cheek. It wasn't cold. Wasn't hard. Had they done something to it? Something with chemicals to keep it soft?

She bit her lip, felt tears on her own cheeks.

And then Simon was beside her. Without looking she knew he would be studying the walls, the stained glass window, the lights, anything but Jacqui. Interesting room. Nice drapes. He'd have to look at her soon. Have to.

She reached out behind, felt him take her hand in his own, the skin rough and warm. With her hand in his she leaned over Jacqui's face and kissed her gently on the cheek. For a moment they were a family again. It was the nearest they'd come for a long time. And even though she hated him for being able to cope, she said, 'Oh Simon. Simon. It's OK. I'm here. You have to look. You have to look at her now. It won't get any better until you look at her.'

And then he did, and she felt her fingers crushed in his,

and in that moment she felt something of her daughter pass
into her and, touching them both, felt as if she were one link
in a chain forged by love and shattered by death.

Oh Jacqui. I'll leave him soon. I promise.

I promise.

When the waiter told him they could take cheques only to the
limit of fifty pounds, Fitz didn't blink. He simply got up from
the table and cruised towards the bar by the cash register. The
waiter, big as he was, had to hurry to keep up.

And as he cruised, he pushed.

'Look I'm not used to being treated like this. You've got a
problem with your technology, fair enough, happens all the
time, but they're not my problems, right?'

The waiter almost caught Fitz by a table for eight, but Fitz
performed a neat end run around a female toilet posse and the
waiter was ensnared by a conversation concerning the relative
merits of Sheffield Wednesday versus Manchester United.

Fitz grinned to himself, leaned nonchalantly against the
bar by the cash register, allowed the man to catch up.

'Did you get all that?' he enquired brightly.

'Yes, sir, I did.'

'And?'

'I'm sorry, sir, I'm afraid it's not simply a matter of
technology.'

'What are you trying to say?' *I know you, I know all about
you, you irritatingly desperate, pumped up little –*

'Your card has come up trapped, sir. That means there may
not be sufficient funds in your account to settle the bill. And,
er, we're therefore unable to take a cheque from you either.'

The words bounced off Fitz.

'Tell you what,' he held up a hand as the waiter began to
protest, 'No. Tell you what, I'll pay by cheque, and what I'll
do is, I'll sign the back, that'll guarantee the cheque for the
bank –'

'I'm sorry, sir.'

'– and I'll even write my name and address -'

'I'm sorry, sir.'

'– on it so you can . . .'

35

Fitz wound down. It wasn't going to happen. A sudden weariness flooded through him. He felt tired, drained, washed out.

Felt, in fact, like one of his own clients.

'Perhaps I'd better fetch the manager, sir.'

Yes, sure, you do that. String me up by the balls for all to see, an example; here rots Fitz, a man unable to keep his accounts in order and too proud to pay his bill by washing dishes –

And there was Mike, an ingratiating smile plastered across his face, a sliver of plastic in one hand.

'Here, use this.'

'Thank you, sir.' Obsequious. Faintly damning of Fitz.

'Must have some kind of problem with the computer . . .' Unable to meet Mike's concerned gaze, Fitz looked away. The evening was taking a real beating; he wondered what else could possibly go wrong. Then across the crowded restaurant his eyes met Judith's, and in the moment before she looked coldly away, he knew.

22:00–Midnight

Penhaligon had a police driver take the Applebys home. She stood with Bilborough in the car park of the mortuary as the tail lights of the Rover vanished into the night. She said nothing, wondering. What was going through Ann Appleby's mind? How would she feel if she'd had a child brutally murdered?

The truth was, childless, she couldn't know.

'Don't try to get inside their heads,' Bilborough's voice was quiet, inflectionless. 'You know better than that.'

'Yes, sir. I know better than that.'

'Good.' Bilborough hesitated. 'There's a pub I know round the corner. It's a good pub. Quiet.'

She looked at him then.

'No thank you, sir. It's been a bloody long day.'

'Sure.' Another hesitation. 'By the way, how were your parents?'

'Fine. How about your wife?'

That got her a look. 'We're hoping it'll be a girl.'

'That'll be nice.'

'Actually anything will do.' A pause. 'Well then.' Bright. Last edge on a tired voice. 'Lift home?'

'I'll get a cab. Thanks.'

'Sure. Autopsy's scheduled for tomorrow.'

'Be there or be square, eh, sir?'

Did he smile in the darkness? She couldn't see. She left him to the Volvo and went back into the mortuary to call a cab.

When she got home the phone was ringing. She thought about ignoring it. Picked it up instead.

'Oh. Hi, Mum. Yeah. Yeah. I'm fine. Yeah. That's right: went straight to work in the end. Do I? I'm just tired that's all. How's Dad? The same. Right. OK. Yeah. 'Course I will. 'Bye.'

Too tired to shower, too tired even to sleep she shrugged off her jacket, switched on the telly and collapsed on the couch.

Film 94. Barry Norman, bless him, the only normal man in her life, reviewing the new De Niro movie.

Soothed by his voice, she slept.

Later she awoke screaming, head full of the night, face twisted with memories –

– *and a balding man cowered before her while her father suffocated, lungs choked with dirt, and a girl was brutally killed and shaven and her family pushed and pushed and pushed and* pushed *while somewhere an open door banged shut time and again to the rhythm of a train hurtling through an endless tunnel –*

Why me? and *Why not me?*

Why me? and *Why not me?*

Why not me!

She told him in the car. Not in words. Not even in looks.

The silence that filled the air between them was a live thing, bitter, furious; an animal. The truth was an animal, Fitz knew that; if you didn't muzzle it, it came for you, straight for you, for your throat.

She stared straight ahead, eyes on the road, the white dazzle of shopfronts and streetlights, the red blur of brake lights from other vehicles. The colours smeared together in front of Fitz, and it wasn't just the alcohol doing it either; it was the fear. The terror. Because he knew. He knew what she was going to say. He'd known it from the off, he just hadn't been prepared to admit it. Just push it under the carpet with all the other dirt, hoover it up later, or maybe it won't happen. Maybe it'll go away on its own. Make jokes, tell her you love her, make it better, make it right.

Except he hadn't, had he? Hadn't told her he loved her. Not for ages. And she noticed things like that.

'I love you Judith,' he said suddenly. There. Finally, it was out. But too late, he knew it. Saw it in her tears gleaming green in the dashboard lights. He'd kept the words in too long, starved them of the air they needed to live. They were tough words, those, but not indestructible. They suffocated, just like anything else. It just took a little more time that was all.

She said, 'How bad this time?'

He gazed desperately at her, mouth working silently.

Bad Judith. Really bad, maybe terminal. I'm dying, Judith, we're dying. Help me!

She never took her eyes from the road.

'Over the limit on both cards. Two grand overdrawn at the bank.'

Judith sucked in a sharp breath. Braked to allow a Morris Minor, one of the new custom jobs, to pull out in front of them from a sidestreet. Headlights dipped in thanks. Judith's expression never changed. She accelerated smoothly away, following the red glow of the Morris's taillights.

'Judith?' Hesitant. Apologetic.

'Nothing else?'

'No.'

She glanced at him then, just a second, just long enough to let him know the answer had come too quickly.

'I raised five grand on the mortgage.' *Oh God what have I done? What have I done?*

'Told them it was for a new bathroom.'

Judith uttered a short, humourless laugh. More of a snort, really. 'How did you . . . ?'

'Forged your signature.'

'I see.'

'I –'

But she was speaking, and the words came out of her like breath, inevitable, unstoppable, and she was right, and he knew it; the truth was at his throat. 'Why not a normal addiction, Fitz? Heroin, cocaine – do too much and you're dead? Why pick something so bloody limitless!'

Fitz crumpled. 'I love you, Judith.' *I can make it right. We can make it right. Just believe in me, Judith. Just trust me this once and it'll never happen again, I promise!*

Silence.

'Judith?'

Silence.

'Judith?'

'You've got a damn funny way of showing it, Fitz!'

And later, as she thrust whatever she could grab of her clothes into an overnight bag, as she led a sobbing Katie by the hand from the house, and the car roared as she slammed it out onto the road, something cut loose inside Fitz's head, something ripped itself out of his heart, went spinning away into the night.

And he knew. Really knew.

This was the low, the flip side of the winning coin.

This was losing.

Everything else was just make believe.

– compartment door and saw her, arms wide to receive him, and he was on her, and her face was jerking inches from his own and her mouths were gaping in horror, both of them, but her screams were lost in the roar of the train and the banging of the compartment door –

TWO

Tuesday

06:30–10:15

Margie owned the dog. The Grey. That's what Dad called it. The Grey, like it was a colour or something, not her friend. She raced him sometimes. Well, Dad did, in between bouts of screaming. Sometimes she thought that was all he did. Scream at her, at Mum. And race the Grey. All he did since the job at the fitters went down the river.

She hated it. Hated the screaming. But the funny thing was, after a while you got used to it, and that's when she got most scared of all. Because something inside told her that letting it happen was as wrong as doing it. And she wasn't big enough, or old enough, or fast enough to stop it.

Not yet.

That was why she was out so early this morning. Not because Dad was screaming; he was still fast asleep. Not because there was a danger to Mum; she was off to work at Woolies before his eyes opened.

She was out here with the Grey because she was like the Grey.

She was in training.

For the day when it happened. Whatever it was.

She didn't know what form it would take, or when it would take place; at fifteen she didn't even know the words to describe what she was doing, not even to her mates. Dan, Sally, Kosi; they were all out here on the mess; larking, jumping around and about the tracks. She wasn't on the mess, wasn't larking, wasn't tagging. All she knew was that

41

something was going to happen, it was going to involve her Dad, and she was going to be ready.

She was in training.

And training could only happen here. Here, where the tracks shone silver in the flat morning sun, where the grass and the bushes whispered advice above a light breeze, where school not only wasn't open yet but didn't even exist.

Here where she was a grown-up.

Where she could think and decide, plan and prepare.

Here. This was where it happened.

Here with the Grey.

Here where the trains played.

And so she ran. And did squats and push-ups among the bushes. And grabbed cinderblocks and bench pressed them on the concrete slab where an old water tank squatted, rusting quietly in the sun.

And she thought about things. Over and over again. Not school things, history, geography, they were important but she would think about them later; Dad. Mum. Where the money had come from for the Grey now Dad had lost his job. Things. Mental exercise. Push-ups for the mind.

Whatever was going to happen, whatever it was, she was going to be ready.

But she wasn't ready for what the Grey found among the bushes that morning.

Who he found.

Wasn't nearly ready.

When the call reached Bilborough he was halfway through a press conference PR had set up at Manchester Victoria.

PR in this instance was represented by an officious know-all called Parsons. (Ms, no first name or initial.) The same Parsons, Ms, had collared Bilborough the moment he'd walked through the incident room doors.

'The Chief Super wants this on the early news,' she'd said.

'Hello,' he'd said. 'DCI Bilborough. I'm in charge here. And you are?'

'Parsons. Ms. They want it to have impact, high profile.

We've decided it will look best if you present it at the scene of the crime. I've set it up with BR. We've got clearance to use platform three.' She'd checked her watch (slim, gold band, executive, high profile; like her clothes, her hair, her face, her manner), added, 'We'll have to hurry. I've set up the meet for six thirty.'

'You're new to this job, aren't you?' he'd said.

And the shutters had come down behind her eyes.

They had remained that way through the drive to the station, the lecture ('This is your first homicide apart from a domestic, my twelfth,' she'd told him. 'You do not use words like identical,') the hint of disapproval in her face at his choice of tie ('Plain, far too plain, no-one relates to plain these days, especially the media, and you have to make them relate to you or we none of us look our best,'), had only lifted before the cameras.

And facing that same wall of cameras and flashes and interested commuters he'd said, 'Sorry to keep you waiting ladies and gentlemen. In a moment Ms Parsons here will take you over to the scene of the crime and you can take some pictures. For now I can tell you there are certain similarities between the murder of Jacqui Appleby and the recent murder of Patricia Garth at Oxenholme Railway Station. My officers are working on the assumption that these two crimes are linked. Our first priority is to trace everyone who got on or off the train between –'

And that was when his bleeper had gone off.

Now he was walking alongside the track in the burbs, three miles from the outskirts of Sheffield, with Parsons, Ms, thankfully left far behind with the madding crowd.

Jimmy Beck slouched along the hardcore beside him, roll-up stuffed in the corner of his mouth, dodging the sleepers, filling him in.

'Jumped from the train. Smashed himself up, you can tell where he landed. Dragged himself as far as he could, blacked out. Must have been there all night, the bastard. Shame it didn't rain.'

'Don't tell that to forensic. Bad weather could've soured it for us. If it is him.'

Beck snorted. 'It's him as sure as rain on Sunday. Bastard. I'd like to –' Beck sucked on his roll-up. Sniffed. Flipped back his hair over a receding crown. 'Yeah, well, you know what I mean.'

Bilborough grinned as he crunched on over the hardcore. Jimmy Beck was a hard man to misunderstand.

Some way off four kids were sitting on the edge of a rusty water tank. One of them, a girl, held a dog by the collar. A WPC was crouching beside them, notebook in hand, pencil flashing in the sun. More uniforms were scattered here and there, together with a couple of track men, orange jackets vibrant against the greenery. Ambulance attendants were parting the bushes, at work with their white padding, glinting chrome, glass, whole blood.

'Who're the crowd?'

'Just kids out messing. Walking the dog like. One of 'em found him.'

'Statements?'

'Enough to fill a bucket. The girl with the dog keeps going on about her dad. Sounds like he might be violent. Might want to pass that on to Sheffield Met.'

'Good idea.' Bilborough looked up as something thumped in the air. Rotors. A medical chopper swung low across the tracks and set down a hundred yards away. The paramedics hit the ground running, Doctor close behind clutching a zippered medical bag. Manchester casualty, on the ball, taking over from the locals.

Bilborough watched the Doctor run and thought she seemed awfully young.

'Would you jump from a moving train?' He yelled the words above the thump of rotors, but they came out introspective anyway.

Beck missed the difference. 'If I'd killed someone I would.'

Reaching the verge, Bilborough pushed his way through the bushes behind the paras, stared down at the man lying before them on the ground. He was tall. Lean. Lathered in blood. His clothes were slashed and full of gravel, similar cuts in his face and hands were black with smoke and grime, crusted with blood and sap from crushed vegetation.

Beside him the Doctor was kneeling with the paras, tucking away her stethoscope as they adjusted a neck collar and inserted the needle of a venflon into his hand, a prelude to connecting the drip feed. 'The cuts to his face and hands are superficial. Left radius and ulna are both fractured below the elbow, maybe some ribs too. Concussion. Easy as you get him on the stretcher, we've no real idea what's going on inside yet.'

Beck muttered something under his breath, earned himself a sharp look from the Doctor. Only then did Bilborough notice her face. Old eyes in a young head. Old and tired.

Bilborough threw Beck a look; he had the grace to shut up.

To the Doctor, Bilborough said, 'I'm coming with you.'

She shrugged, bulky in the flight suit. 'No argument from me.'

Beck said, 'Let me go.'

'Jimmy, I want a suspect to interview later. And I want a murder weapon. So you keep the lads at it, OK?'

Beck frowned, nodded.

Bilborough tried to ignore the disappointment in Beck's face. Jimmy was a good detective but his track record was all that kept him on the force sometimes.

In the chopper the man blinked, struggled to move, slumped back into the stretcher. Bilborough stared down at his face, the ground dropping away beyond the midships port, flattening as the sound of rotors fired up to deafening levels.

'We're taking you to hospital.

'Are you . . . ?' The man's voice cracked. His face crumpled. His eyes were swollen, bloodshot, but beyond this they were like the Doctor's; old, tired, glazed with . . . he couldn't tell, with something. Obsession? Loneliness? An over familiarity with death?

Frowning, Bilborough moved aside to allow the Doctor to get closer to her patient.

Her patient, the killer.

Was Beck right? Was this Sweeney?

By God he hoped so.

'I'm not a Doctor. I'm a policeman.'

And you, pal, are very definitely nicked.

Penhaligon looked at the phone, one of twenty or so in the incident room, and scowled. It was the only expression of discontent she would allow herself. After all she was a professional. Even if Bilborough had taken it away from her again. At least she had the satisfaction of knowing that she was keeping an open mind, never an easy task, particularly at this time.

Racked with dreams about her father she'd been unable to sleep all night. Two doors along the street Fred Lannock had come home from his oil rig at three in the morning. Party time. She'd welcomed the noise because it meant she could hide from the dreams in wakefulness. She'd fallen asleep in front of Sky Gold at four, planning to set off for work an hour or so early, grab a coffee and bagel, maybe a sneaky kip, at the Mountstevens down the high street.

What happened was she overslept.

And slipped in the shower.

And spilt her double strength Red Mountain over the week-old Zildjian cymbals she'd bought for the drum kit.

She limped into incident room three quarters of an hour late and that's when she found out about the man. Bilborough and Beck had shot away like a good pair of racing Greys, leaving Giggs and Jonesy to cover the phones.

And her, as it turned out.

She picked up the phone, placed her finger on the dial pad, hit two numbers, stopped, slowly replaced the phone. She looked up and caught Giggs' eye. 'Got a problem with that?'

He grinned. 'No, indeed.'

At his look she softened, realised she'd been both aggressive and defensive, smiled to take the edge of irritability off her words.

Giggs and Jonesy were OK. Both were in their late thirties. Giggs was a bit on the quiet side, thoughtful, sensitive. Rumour control had it he was going through a bad patch with Emma. Not odd considering that, despite their similarities, their closeness, Giggs had always had an eye for a pretty girl. Jones on the other hand was always bright. Always interested. Nose into everything. Too bloody cheerful, if she were honest. She'd take either of them ten times over rather than Bilborough or Beck.

She grinned back at Giggs, said, 'If I hear the words *"Good morning, sorry to bother you sir, I'm DS Jones of Anson Road police station and I understand you travel regularly on the Manchester–Glasgow intercity service,"* one more time I think I'll break his neck.' She jerked a thumb at Jones, poised with his hand over yet another telephone.

Jones feigned a look of hurt innocence. 'If I hear those words one more time I'll ruddy well let you,' he said. 'How many people does a 105 hold, anyway?'

'It wasn't a 105. They have open plan compartments. This train had separate compartments with a connecting corridor. It was an 82, maybe 83. Good rolling stock those years, before privatisation.'

Jones slowly replaced the receiver. 'You boring fart, no wonder Emma's leaving you,' he said with a grin.

Giggs scowled. 'She's not leaving.' He grinned. 'She never found out.'

Jones shrugged. 'Lucky bastard. Anyway, whatever the number is, it's too many. Especially since they think nothing of selling you a ticket for a seat and then allowing you to stand when the train is full, even if First Class is empty all the way.' He glanced sideways at Giggs. 'If I were you mate, I'd think about booking my seat to the STD clinic before it's standing room only.'

Giggs threw a coffee cup at Jones, who batted it away for six with the telephone handpiece.

Penhaligon felt herself begin to loosen up. Perhaps it wasn't going to be so bad after all. An easy day on the phone after yesterday. A couple of gallons of coffee while she wiped off all the names on her list. Then Bilbo and Gandalf would discover this bloke they'd found on the lines was nothing but a hobo, or an accident, or a jumper from some other train, nothing to do with Sweeney at all, and they'd be back to square one. Her square. Her theory.

47

She picked up the phone. Hesitated once more. Replaced the receiver again. Why should she have to wait as long as that? Bilborough had said he'd consider her theory. Hadn't actually told her to drop it in so many words. She was a bloody DS wasn't she? Alright it was only six months since her promotion but what did that matter? She had a brain; they had a case to solve. Check out all options. That was the *modus operandi* of the Met these days. Well, it was hers anyway.

That was sorted then. 'So long, boys,' she said, rising suddenly, smiling at their curious looks, grinning particularly at Giggs. 'I'm going out; I may be gone some time.'

Judith . . . mm . . . Judith . . . Jooodiiith . . .

Fitz sighed, rolled over.

Fell off the couch.

'Hell and bloody damnation, what –'

Fitz struggled back to a sitting position, back against the couch, and knuckled his eyes. His vision smeared. Something smelled awful – scotch, coffee, stale sweat – God, it was him.

He pushed himself back onto the couch, swearing at the cushions which folded irritatingly beneath him, then snapped back down with the viciousness of the wire on a kingsize mousetrap.

He tried to blink away the tears crusting his eyes but that only glued them together a little more firmly.

Then he heard footsteps.

'Judith?'

A click.

'Judith?'

Thank God, it had all been, cliché of clichés, a bloody nightmare. OK, he'd had a bit of a bender, losing the cash, the race; making the wrong choice, that was it, but at least she was still –

A dim light glowed in front of him. A shape moved back and forth in front of it. There was a sharp *snap*; curtains being pulled back. A shaft of brilliant light transfixed him. He cried out and screwed his eyes tightly shut. Knuckled them again, harder this time, and eventually felt able to open them.

'Judith?'

It was Mark. Eyes wide, taking it in; the sight and smell, taking him in; the picture of a perfect father; asleep in his second best suit on the couch, reeking of alcohol and coffee and God knows what else, minus half his family and most of his sanity –

'What are you doing up at this time?' Even though his head felt like it was stuffed full of cloth the words came out sharp. Too sharp. But they had a mind of their own, those words, acted independently of his brain. 'Wet the bed again or something have we?'

'Gotta sign on, ain't I?' Cold. Hint of contempt.

Mark left the room; left him alone in the room. Alone with the silent telly and his memories of the night before.

The restaurant. Oh God the bloody restaurant. That's where it had happened. Where it had got out of control.

The truth.

Somehow it just didn't seem to matter that he'd felt what he'd said. Believed in it with all his heart. Somehow the truth had turned on him, got past the chair and the whip. Taken him down, screaming and kicking; no not even that, no protest at all, because hand in hand with the truth came shock, the freeze, the thing that makes you lie down and die when the wolf comes knocking. Shock and then after that surprise, because the one thing he would have said, would have bet would never get the better of him, was the truth. It was his profession after all, his life, his passion; digging for it, luring it out from that dark corner where it liked to hide and from which it sometimes pounced, taming it, putting it on display. A game. His rules.

And now here he was, deep in that same corner and the truth was wielding the chair and the whip. And he was cowering from it. Like an animal. Collared, like a bloody animal.

Well, no more!

This was it; as bad as it got. But there was hope yet. Judith had Katie, had his heart; Mark wasn't fighting in anyone's corner; but Fitz still had his mind. There would be a way out of this. Had to be. Twenty years was too big an investment to flush. Bigger than raising five grand on the mortgage, bigger than anything. There was no way he was going to give it up, any of them up, no way on God's green Earth.

The sound of the downstairs toilet flushing jerked Fitz into full wakefulness; he shuffled his hands around on the couch for his high tars. Found them eventually, squashed into the space between one end cushion and the arm of the couch. Extracting the ruin of a cigarette from the packet, Fitz shoved it into his mouth and began to fumble through his pockets for his lighter.

As he lit up the blurry glow in front of him resolved itself into the familiar shape of the television; the face of the Breakfast TV news announcer. He blinked. His neck was killing him. At least the sound was off. He didn't know if he could cope with that this early in his newly single life.

The picture changed on the television as he rose to switch it off.

'What?' Fitz's head whipped round fast, his neck cricked and he grunted with pain.

There was a girl on the screen. A girl he knew.

Jacqui. Jacqui . . . oh bugger it, what was her last – Appleby! Jacqui Appleby!

Cut back to the newswoman, mouth working frantically, silently, no hint of emotion in her eyes.

And back to Jacqui, posed, a dazzling smile, greenery in the background.

And the newswoman, face serious.

He blinked, tried to lip read, got nowhere. Dug under the cushions for the TV remote.

'– *inally on a lighter note the custodians of the cottage where poet William Wordsworth once lived with his sister say they're having to –*'

But Fitz wasn't listening. He was into the kitchen at a dead run, feet pounding, floor shaking, and there was the radio on the fridge, and he was grabbing it, as the road drills began to hammer inside his head, thump and hammer, and clatter and he was twisting the dial –

– bloody thing, come on, come on come –

– and Queen banged out of the speaker, thumped into his head, a chorus with the drills.

'". . . *here we stand*," '

'". . . *and here we fall* . . *"* '

And he was in the hall, head full of memories, eyes down searching for the morning paper, memories of that day, but there was nothing, just the Racing Post, and then the clatter of Mark on the stairs and Queen and the drills –

'Has the paper come yet?'

'You're holding it.'

'The other bloody paper!'

'In the bog.'

'". . . *history don't care at all* . . ." '

And he was on the move again, as Mark came down the stairs, cold expression turning to concern, down the hall to the bathroom, wrenching open the frosted glass door, grabbing the paper looped over the side of the bath; didn't have to open it to see the massive headline splashed across the cover page, didn't need to read the words to know what they said.

And he sat on the closed toilet seat; just sort of collapsed, shrank in on himself, hands working without thinking, folding the paper neatly into smaller and smaller squares while Mark peered in through the frosted glass, eyes wide.

'Dad? You OK? Dad?'

He kicked the door shut in the face of his son's concern.

Oh God. Jesus. Jesus. Not her. Not Jacqui. Not this. Jesus. Not this!

'". . . *we're just waitin' for the hammer to* . . ." '

'". . . *hammer to fall* . . ." '

10:30–12:15

After a while Fitz got off the toilet seat. Not because his arse was on fire, or he realised there was no point in sitting there drowning in self pity, or because he was alone in the house with nothing but memories and the ghost of Jacqui Appleby for company; but because he really wanted to go.

The realisation made him giggle. The giggle turned into a guffaw as he pulled the chain, imagining that was his troubles he was flushing. The guffaw exploded into laughter as he ran a bath, cooked breakfast, turned off the taps, wolfed down his breakfast while the bathroom filled with steam, wolfed it down because he was hungry, famished, and that was a surprise; forty four years old and still capable of being surprised; the surprise itself was a surprise, and that realisation came when he was in the bath so he didn't even notice the laughter turn to tears, into belly shaking sobs, didn't notice anything as he fell asleep, cried himself to sleep, there in the bath; waking some time later when the water was tepid, the bubbles flat like old beer, to stare at his wrinkled knees and discover that despite everything he felt, somehow, slightly better.

He rose, dried, dressed, threw open the French windows to purge his own smell from the sitting room, perched on the edge of the couch, toying with the TV remote. Would there be anything more about Jacqui on there? The mid morning news? What about Judith? Where was she? Her father was on holiday for two weeks, or he'd have assumed she was there. A friend's then. Jo's? Maybe. How would he find her? Get her back? Make her see she was wrong, that they couldn't live apart, that the love between them was too strong to allow that to ever happen.

He stood, paced; agitated, unable to decide what to do next. Did she want him to chase her? Did she want him to hold back? And what did he want? Did he want to chase her? Did he want that?

God, Fitz, call yourself a psychologist? You don't even know what your wife wants from you, not even that. Forget about the fact that you've been married for twenty years and have two kids and should bloody well know each other by now!

And he pulled on his shoes, and laced them, grabbed his raincoat, headed for the door, for the street, checking his wallet for the cash to buy flowers for Judith, flowers and maybe a trinket for Katie, closed his eyes when he saw how little money remained in there and then, when he opened his eyes, saw he was still in the sitting room, still there and staring at the drinks cabinet, and he was opening it, without thinking, reaching for the Glenfiddich –

And then he stopped.

Stopped because he thought he saw the truth crouching there in the corner of the cabinet, the dark corner behind the Raven House glasses, right by the corner of the mirror where the light from the room got all twisted and fractured, hiding there, at the edge of the mirror, waiting to pounce, waiting for him.

· The Glenfiddich was dead, of course. He picked up a tumbler, stared for a long time at the vodka beside the mirror, decided in the end it was too close to the dark corner where the truth glared at him with flat eyes, those flat, feral eyes.

Shutting the cabinet, he returned to the couch, forced himself back into the cushions, surprised at how soft they were, no hint of this morning's mousetrap there now. He forced himself to relax.

To relax and acknowledge that the truth was out now, out of the cabinet, prowling around inside his head.

And the truth was he couldn't think about Judith for a while. Couldn't think about her or Katie or Mark because there was something more important in his life.

Steel. Enamel. Blood. Bone.

Penhaligon stared around the mortuary through misty clumps of her own breath. Nothing changed. All human life came to this eventually. A few pounds of chemicals. A funny smell. And then nothing.

A smocked figure, Copeley was hard at work on the naked body of a man. The man appeared to be in his forties, but it was hard to tell because about three quarters of his face had been pushed back into his skull. Copeley's angular body was stark in the antiseptic light, pneumatic bone saw clutched in one hand, suction device in the other. He was meticulously removing small sections of bone.

'Penhaligon, isn't it?' He spoke without looking up from his work, breath mask pumping in and out with the words. 'Met on the train if I recall.'

53

'That's right.'

'Can I do anything for you?'

'What about . . .' She gestured towards the cadaver.

'Fell from Otley Tower, some time around three this morning. His name was Mallinson. He was a company rep. Sold advertising space, apparently.' The saw whined. Bone splintered. 'I'm told it's a cut throat business.'

Penhaligon licked her lips. 'He jumped?'

'That's what we're trying to find out. One witness says he was in a fight; the witness himself was – and is – very illegal. Drugs, alcohol, you name it. Apparently there was a heck of a party going on there.' Again the saw whined. Then Copeley racked the saw and began to probe gently into the skull with a scalpel. 'Obvious cosmetic considerations aside, my work here is primarily reconstruction; there was extensive damage to the facial tissues, apparently he landed on a parking meter.' Copeley lifted free a section of bone, placed it carefully in a metal tray at his side. 'Thing is, we don't know if he was punched before he fell. With the witness so totally unreliable, this is the only way to decide whether the death can be classified as manslaughter or simple death by misadventure.'

'I see.'

'Anyway,' Copeley put the scalpel down gently on the stainless steel instrument tray. Scalpel and tray were smothered in blood, as were Copeley's overalls and gloves. 'I expect you've come about Jacqui.'

'That's right.'

'Well, we've had to delay the post mortem I'm afraid. I don't have anything for you as yet.'

'That's OK, I only came here to run an idea past you anyway.'

Copeley shrugged. 'I'm all ears.'

'When you do perform the post mortem on Jacqui Appleby I'd like you to keep a special look out for certain chemicals present in the skin around the genital area.'

'Oh?' Copeley took a step closer. 'What chemicals?'

Pnehaligon handed Copeley a list she'd made.

The pathologist cocked his hand on one side as he studied

the list. She could see his mind zeroing the names like a bird after prey. 'It's true there were no razor marks around the pubic area. But why do you think Sweeney shaved her with depilatory cream?'

Penhaligon pursed her lips. 'Can this information come to me before it goes to Bilborough?'

Copeley shrugged. 'You're all in the same department. I should think so. Now why the cream?'

Penhaligon studied the pathologist. 'Well think about it. A cut throat razor on a train doing seventy miles per hour? How's he going to shave her without leaving marks?'

'You think Sweeney's a woman, don't you?'

Penhaligon pursed her lips. 'Interesting theory. I'll get back to you on it.'

'Sure.'

Penhaligon nodded her thanks and left the mortuary. As the door swung to behind her she heard the whine of the bone drill notch upwards as Copely swung it into use again.

It sounded as impatient and irritable as she was.

Fitz walked to the high street, took a bus into town. This late in the morning he earned himself a few funny looks from the OAPs.

Look at him. Just on the wrong side of middle age. Why isn't he at work? Where's his job? His car? Why's he on the bus, our bus?

Fitz knew exactly what they were thinking, leered right back, only stopped when an elderly gent dressed in black clutching a cheap bouquet shuffled along the bus away from him, nervous eyes wide, edgy.

Fitz shook his head, turned his attention to the outside. It was actually sunny; just a hint, not much for May, but there you go. It was showing willing, and in Fitz's book that was good enough.

He leaned close to the nervous gent as the bus approached his stop in the high street. 'I'm my own boss. A psychologist. I keep my own hours and I don't have to justify them to anyone,' he grinned, straightened up as the bus drew to a halt, added, 'If she's gone, she can't bully you any more. Can she?'

He didn't even look at the man as he stepped off the bus. But there was a new spring in his step, something that hadn't been there for some while, now he thought about it. As if Judith's leaving him had actually burst the dam, let all that crap that he now realised must have been weighing him down for months out into the light of day. Out into the sun to dry up and drift away, like . . . Fitz shook his head, endeavoured to keep the bounce in his stride. He was doing altogether too much thinking lately. It was time to take some time out from his personal life. Get back to the business of running a business.

Fitz's office was on the second floor of a building whose rent he shared with a number of other private medical practices in the heart of Manchester. His punters – sorry, clients – weren't among the richest or the poorest; Fitz didn't believe in exploitation. He believed in helping people. He charged what he felt was appropriate, allowed his accountant to handle any problems arising from his fairness. In truth he sometimes liked to allow a wealthy hypochondriac onto his books just for the pleasure of intimidating them. The cure was invariably nothing more complex than a simple demonstration that he, Fitz, understood them better than they did themselves. And in truth, he did, most of the time. At other times he was winging it of course, playing the game, but still his success rate was high; the game was his, the rules also. To date no-one had complained about his work, and if a fair few had changed to a different practice, still he had enough clients to see him through the year without worrying about where the next mortgage payment was coming from.

And if he was completely honest with himself he relished the challenge that some patients brought.

This morning he had scheduled a couple of hours for a middle aged husband and father of three named Peter Hanrahan. Peter was the classic jealous obsessive. Normally Fitz wouldn't have allowed the man to take up more than an hour of his time, but Fitz had a feeling about this one. It wasn't the money. Hanrahan really needed help. Fitz felt he could give it.

Although he'd planned to cancel his appointments for the

day, Fitz didn't do that. OK he needed the money. But as much as he needed it, Peter Hanrahan needed him.

Penny, the building receptionist, buzzed Hanrahan through ten minutes early. Fitz nodded thoughtfully. Hanrahan was always ten minutes early. Exactly.

He knocked tremulously on the door, waited before poking his head around the jamb. 'It's only me.' Small man, small voice. Tired. Weary voice. A drone. Elevator music.

Well, Fitz would do his best to shove a bit of sparkle into the man's vocal orchestration.

'Hello, Peter. Come in.'

'Shall I sit down?'

'Don't you always?'

Hanrahan nodded.

Ten minutes later and they were into it. '. . . and when I get on the phone, it's just as bad. They say "Who is it?" I say, "It's only me. It's only Peter." '

Fitz jammed his last high tar into the corner of his mouth, lit up thoughtfully. Hanrahan, an extreme worrier, had been unfolding slowly for a couple of weeks now; in all that time Fitz had noted little improvement. Except once. Once when Hanrahan's wife, Jilly, had been away for a long weekend with the parents. Some family disaster or other. Hanrahan had been scared shitless he might have forgotten to do any one of the endless chores she'd left him; failed to keep the house clean, provide for the pets, anything. But he'd also been a little more lively, assertive. Just a shade more of a spark to him. That said a lot to Fitz. Sang a chorus to him with the elevator music.

'They get on to me and "It's Charlie. George. Fred." Not "Only Charlie. Only George. Only Fred." '

Fitz nodded, staring absently from the office window. Grey on grey. The sun had done a turnabout. Bloody cowardly solar body. Afraid of a bit of cloud.

'It's a big fanfare of trumpets with them. With me it's "Only me." It's always "Only me." You understand the point I'm making?'

'More to the point, do you?'

'Of course. Of course I understand. Only me. Massive

57

inferiority. Low self esteem. It's not low self esteem, it's sub-bloody-terranean self esteem. A woman fancies me; I say, my God what kind of woman is this that fancies me? Where's her wooden leg?'

'Uh huh.'

Was that a cloud? Did it look like rain? Was provoking Hanrahan by ignoring him doing any good at all?

'A woman marries me? Jilly. Well. She must be from outer space. She must be a Martian or something –'

Abruptly Fitz swung his chair around so he could look directly at Hanrahan. He stubbed out his cigarette, holding the little man's gaze all the while.

'OK,' he said. 'That's it. Session over.'

'What? I don't understand . . .'

Fitz stood. 'Peter, I'd like you to make an appointment with Penny for next week. I'm sorry. I have to . . I have to cut this session short.'

'Of course.' Dazed. Unbelieving. 'If you think that's best.'

'I do. I'll see you next week, Peter. Goodbye.'

'Uh . . . Goodbye then. Goodbye.'

When Hanrahan had left the office, Fitz closed the office door, leaned his head on the window, and stared out at the blustery rain just beginning to fall.

And he thought: displacement. That's what I'm doing: displacement. Judith's left me and naturally I feel like shit about that. No-one likes to feel like shit, least of all me. So what do I do? Care for the clients. Worry about a dead girl. And what should I be doing?

And he knew the answer to that one too:

Getting her back.

For Bilborough the morning was proving to be one of almost endless frustrations. The mysterious man had lapsed back into unconsciousness as the helicopter circled above the train lines; the Doctor had wanted to take him to Sheffield because it was nearer. That was no good for Bilborough because it would place the man outside his jurisdiction. The red tape involved in getting him back again would be monumental. Davis, the Chief Super at Sheffield Central was not exactly famous for his powers of cooperation. So he'd had to argue himself blue in the face with the Doctor, who'd been anything but cooperative.

'Look mate, I couldn't give a toss whether your man's a killer or a sugar pig,' she'd screamed eventually above the roar of the engines. 'In my book he's a patient. He needs treatment and he needs it quickly.'

'Fine, he can have whatever treatment he needs, but he'll have it at bloody Manchester not Sheffield. OK?'

'No, it's not OK. The man needs x-rays. He may have concussion, he may have blood clots, tiny clots you'd need a microscope to see, being carried even now through his arteries to his brain. If they get there he could have a stroke, maybe even die. Is that what you want?'

'Believe me, Doctor, if you'd seen what this bastard did to a nineteen year old girl on that train you might not be so sure yourself about what you'd want for him.'

And all through this the pilot had the chopper at station keeping. 'This whole argument is going to be ruddy academic when we run out of fuel,' he yelled eventually. 'Got enough cash for a cab have you mate?'

Bilborough had stared at the man. 'Can you land at Manchester?'

The pilot had looked away. 'Yeah.'

'Then bloody well do it, before I arrest you for obstructing the course of justice.'

Neither the Doctor, the paras or the pilot had said another word to him during the rest of the journey – all of ten minutes – but he did notice the pilot seemed to find every air pocket between there and Manchester. When eventually they set down on the roof of the hospital it was as much as he could do to prevent himself from hugging the concrete apron or lurching over to the guard rail and puking on the high street shoppers six floors below.

But if Bilborough thought his problems were over, he was mistaken.

They were met by a gaggle of casualty staff and a shortish, middle aged man whose face was lined with an infinite weariness.

Bilborough joined him as the Doctor finished her verbal briefing on the patient.

'Doctor . . . ?'

'Charge Nurse. Ben Medley.'

'Nurse Medley, I need this man processed through casualty as quickly as possible. He's the prime suspect in a murder case and I need him awake and in a condition to talk within the hour.'

Doctor and Charge Nurse exchanged looks as, behind them, the paras transferred the patient to a hospital trolley, then handed him over to a couple of casualty nurses who in turn wheeled him carefully towards the open lift doors. Then the Doctor simply shook her head and climbed wearily back into the chopper. As she slid the door shut she yelled to Bilborough, 'Processed? Processed? He's not a bloody lump of Dairylea you know!' The door slid shut, the rotors banged even louder and the ship took off.

Medley looked at Bilborough and said in a perfectly even voice, 'What was that you were saying about miracles?'

Christ, didn't they understand? Didn't they care what the bastard had done?

'Just get on with it, will you?'

He rode down with them in the lift, watched as the nurses efficiently removed the man's torn and bloodstained clothing and replaced them with a hospital gown, stood by while Medley performed half a dozen reflex tests, checked the pupillary dilation reaction, stroked the sole of the man's feet with a bic.

Eventually Medley shrugged. 'It all seems normal. He's unconscious, but that's to be expected.'

'Great. When can we have him talking?'

One of the nurses shot Bilborough a nasty glance. Medley calmed her with a look of his own. 'Fetch Mitch. She'll want to see this, I expect.' To Bilborough he added, 'Mitch Turner is the casualty consultant. She'll want to check him over, probably authorise x-rays, standard stuff.' As Bilborough sighed impatiently, Medley drew him a little away from where another nurse was adjusting the man's drip. 'A word to the wise: watch what you say. Mitch isn't half as patient as I am.'

At that moment the nurse returned, trailing a tall woman in her late forties, dressed in Doctor's whites.

Bilborough found himself tense with no apparent reason. The consultant didn't say a word, merely rechecked all the tests Medley and his staff had made. She completely ignored Bilborough. He might just as well not have been there.

Finding himself a little intimidated by this behaviour, Bilborough adjusted his tie and concentrated on how good it would feel to eventually have this bastard in the dock facing life for murder.

Then Turner spoke. 'Pupillary dilation is as you said. And the standard reflex tests are positive. Good. What's he on? That's fine. Who put that drip in? The venflon's a mess, sort it out will you? And we'll need x-rays of the skull and that arm too by the look of it. Good! Oh, and get rid of the garden gnome will you?' She hooked a dismissive thumb at Bilborough to illustrate her words, bent over the man and began to feel tenderly and slowly around his skull. 'You say there's no obvious fractures or depressions . . . ? Has anyone checked for clotting . . . ?'

Bilborough found himself ushered effortlessly from the cubicle by the nurse who'd glared at him earlier. 'You can wait in reception if you like.'

Bilborough blinked. 'With the patients?'

She nodded. 'The AA guide to Manchester accommodation gave us three stars last year.' She added deadpan, 'I don't recommend the food though.'

The next hour took forever to pass. Bilborough found himself scrunched in a plastic chair between a man in his early twenties dressed in football strip favouring a swollen knee, 'It's smashed, me bleedin' leg's smashed to buggery and they still made me wait, can yer believe it?' and a woman in her fifties with her arm in a makeshift sling, the fingers of one hand bruised and beginning to blacken. The woman leaned across Bilborough to reassure the footballer, 'They're good here,' she said. 'They are, really. I know sometimes you have to wait, but that's not their fault; that's the government, that is, cutting the funding. Privatising the industry.'

With immense relief Bilborough saw Jimmy Beck stride

61

through the double doors. He stood. 'Jimmy, thank Christ for a sensible face. I'm just about to go bugshite.'

'So what's the SP on our man then?'

'Search me. They tell you bugger all around here.' Bilborough sighed, tried to maintain a more professional approach. 'He regained consciousness in the chopper, briefly, but lapsed again before we got here. The Doctor on the chopper said there was no threat of a heart attack, though he's obviously banged up a bit. Bust his arm apparently.'

'I'd like to bust more than his arm.'

Bilborough became aware the footballer was staring at them curiously. Even the reassuring woman had fallen silent. He led Beck to one side of the waiting room, halted between a rubber plant and a drinks dispenser. 'OK, tell me what the wierdos found.'

'Copeley's a complete nutter, you know that? He and Nease swanned around that bit of track like bloody ballerinas – yeah, well, anyway. Jacqui's was blood group B and that's what they found on the clothes, and on the ground all round where we found him. We checked the train door, his fingerprints are all over it. Giggs and Jonesy have got four descriptions of a man going in and out of the carriage – he fits them all.'

'Murder weapon?'

Beck sniffed. 'Not yet, no.'

'Jesus.'

Visions of the man walking free surged up in Bilborough's mind. 'We can't afford to lose the cutter, Jimmy.'

'Look, there's twenty five miles of track – it's gonna take some time.'

'Well don't let it take too much time. You want the bastard to walk?'

'No boss, you know I don't.'

'Well then, get on it, OK?'

At that point Mitch Turner walked into the waiting room, spied the two policemen and came over.

'The gnome's got a little friend has he? How nice.'

Beck scowled, caught Bilborough's eye. *Who's in charge here?*

Bilborough frowned. 'How is he?'

'He has a broken arm, some ribs. There's no damage to the skull. Lucky, really. For you.'

Bilborough picked up on that one. 'He's awake?'

She nodded.

'We've moved him up onto C ward, one of the private rooms. Thought that would be best – there'll be no interruptions when you interrogate him.'

He seemed lost; lost in the pale blue-striped hospital issue pyjamas that were two sizes too big for him, but also lost somewhere within himself.

Somewhere deep inside.

Lost and searching.

Bilborough stared down at the man, propped up into a half-sitting position in the bed, felt his lips narrow to a thin line at the sight of him, his lost eyes, his blank face.

'I'm DCI Bilborough. This is DS Beck.'

'Hello.' Mild. Gentle. 'You were in the helicopter.'

But Bilborough was already way past the pleasantries, into the business of the day. 'Could you tell us your name please?'

'Yes of course, I'm . . .' The man in the bed blinked rapidly. 'I'm . . .' He seemed to withdraw even more into himself, if that was possible. He opened his mouth, but no words came.

A tear slid out of one eye.

'I can't remember.'

You must be fucking joking!

Beck rolled his eyes. 'You can shove that right now, you –'

Bilborough stopped him with a glance. 'Are you trying to tell me you can't remember your name?'

The head shook, eyes downcast. Then they lifted, full of pleading. 'I don't remember anything. I remember . . .' He sighed. 'I don't know where I am either.'

'Manchester Central Hospital.'

'That doesn't mean anything to me. What's Manchester? Is it a big town?'

Beck was off. 'Look you stupid bastard, we know you did

63

it; faking amnesia is going to get you nowhere. You hear me? Nowhere! I'm on to you you sick bastard, and I'll –'

Bilborough shook his head. 'Jimmy. It doesn't matter. Leave it.'

Beck spread his hands. 'For Christ's sake, boss if we give this bastard an inch he'll take us for everything we've got! Now what are you going to do about it?'

Bilborough lifted his eyes to meet Beck's. The rage the Detective felt was obvious. His face was flushed, eyes black and glittering.

'Out.'

'But –!'

'Jimmy. Out. Now.'

Beck threw a contemptuous glance at Bilborough.

'Or shut up.'

Beck began to say something. Thought better of it. 'I can handle it,' he said softly.

The man on the bed glanced at Beck, let his eyes come back to Bilborough. They were wide with fear, but there was trust in there. A plea for help that made the policeman uneasy.

'There was a girl killed,' he said. 'On the train.'

Beck pounced. 'You remember that?'

Bilborough let it go this time, interested in the man's reaction.

'No.' Shake of the head. 'I've heard them all talking. The hospital staff. They think I did it.'

Bilborough leaned closer. Here was the opening. 'Did you?'

The man wiped his face with his mobile hand. 'I don't know.'

'You can't remember.'

'No.' Mute, eyes wide, filled with the need for absolution. *No bloody chance, pal.*

'You were in her compartment.'

'Your clothes were covered in her blood.' That was Beck, chipping in with his two pennorth. 'Just because you threw away your wallet doesn't mean you're gonna get away with it. We'll find it. We'll find the razor. The razor you killed

64

Jacqui with, the one you opened her throat with, and we'll have you, mate, we'll have you, you murdering son of a –'

The man looked from Bilborough to Beck and back again. He was cowering in the bed, tunnelling back into the pillows, his face twisted into a terrified mask.

Bilborough put out one arm to restrain Beck, who was pushing towards the bed, leaning closer and closer to the man. Beck shot him a glance. Shook off his hand. He backed away though. Bilborough didn't take his eyes off the man. His good hand was up in front of his face, palm outwards, defensive. As Beck retreated Bilborough realised the man was staring at his hand. As he watched the man turned it over and over in front of his face. Then slowly, he held it out to Bilborough.

Bilborough found himself faintly repelled by the gesture. 'What . . . ?'

'Please.' The man was shaking. He leaned forward suddenly. By the time Bilborough reacted, the man had taken him by the hand.

Beck made a disgusted sound.

A moment passed in silence.

The man's hand was warm, smelled faintly of antiseptic. There were puckered ridges where a nurse had stitched a few of the deeper wounds. The hand was damp with recently wiped tears.

'What's your point?'

The hand squeezed; Bilborough felt a certain strength there, beyond the weakness. A strength backed up by the calluses on his palms and fingers.

'I'm a manual worker. Aren't I? Some kind of manual worker. How else could I have calluses like that on my hands?' Desperation. Clinging on to any straw of information. *Who am I?*

'Yeah.' Bilborough became aware that Beck was staring. Placed the man's hand back on the bed. All the strength in it had gone for the time being.

'We're also investigating the murder of Patricia Garth at Oxenholme Railway Station, about five weeks ago. Do you remember it?'

Again the blink, the trembling voice. The fear; the fear of

self-understanding. 'Twice? I've done it twice?'

'Possibly.' Keep it hard. Don't give him an edge.

'Oh dear Lord forgive me . . .'

Bilborough leaned close again, searched intently for a reaction, any hint, a germ of the truth, but the man was gone, lost somewhere inside himself again. Somewhere no-one could reach him. Yet.

'Now listen to me . . .'

He stopped. It was no use. The man folded back on his pillows, back into sleep. His eyes flickered, rolled upwards, closed.

The door opened and Doctor Turner came in. One look at the patient was enough for her. She took his pulse, smoothed the ruffled bed covers.

'That's it gentlemen. He needs to rest. We wouldn't want him to die of a heart attack before you had a chance to hang him now would we?'

Beck scowled at Turner, spun on his heel and left the room. Bilborough followed thoughtfully but no less angrily.

12:30–14:15

Fitz stood outside the florist in the high street, studied the prices in the window, compared them to the amount of money in his wallet, tried to decide whom he should present with the single bouquet that was all he could afford. The Chinese believed in the I Ching, the ability to determine a future based on random events, as in, say, the flip of a coin. Idly flipping a fifty pence over and over between his thick fingers, Fitz tried to decide if the flowers he was about to buy should go to Judith, or to Jacqui Appleby's mother.

Ten minutes deliberation brought no answer. It didn't help that the Salford Project where Judith worked had its offices less than ten minutes walk from here. It would be so easy just to slip in, catch her on a break, talk to her, make her see that he needed her back.

Fitz was on the point of going in when there was a cheerful voice beside him, 'Hello Fitz!'

He turned; Lise Kistasami, receptionist from the Salford Project was standing beside him. 'Long time no see. Alright are we?'

He stared at Lise, took in her suit, her neat hairstyle, her friendly smile.

Judith wasn't staying with her then. She didn't know.

He mumbled something, threw a look back into the florist window. Lise grinned suddenly. 'Oh yeah; seeing another woman are we? Got a bit on the side, Fitz?'

If only it were that simple.

'Uh . . . listen, Lise, could you . . . oh, never mind. Could you just say "hi" to Judith for me?'

' "Hi" to Judith, reckon I can remember that one no problem. Catch you later, big guy.' Lise tipped her fingers in a friendly wave and angled off down the high street.

Fitz looked at the fifty pence piece he had been about to flip to determine the eventual destination of a bunch of flowers, stuffed it back into his pocket, pushed open the door to the florist and walked in.

Penhaligon replaced the telephone with a sour look. Bilborough seemed to think the duty squad was his own personal army, to be deployed as and when he saw fit. He liked to think of people as specialists. And by God once he had an idea in his head about your speciality that was it.

'Penhaligon? Bilborough. We've got Sweeney bang to rights but he's not talking. Claims the fall from the train gave him amnesia. We can't sit on this any longer. The parents have a right to know what's going on. Can you handle it?'

She realised she was scowling when Giggs threw her a sympathetic look. 'You got the mother again?'

'Apparently you guys are the most methodical. So you carry on with the checks on the train, try to hunt down the murder weapon. I take the mother. Apparently I empathise well.'

'Sorry, Pen.'

'And we're now also looking for a wallet, chequebook, library card, in fact any ID that might have belonged to the killer.'

'There was nothing on him when they found him then?'

'Apparently not. Anyway – catch you later.'

'Hey Pen – you driving?'

She nodded. 'Uh huh.'

'Don't kill too many pedestrians will you?' That from Jonesy. Big grin.

Penhaligon played up to it. 'Jonesy, there's nothing wrong with my driving.'

'Sure killer. The grannie with the pram was a complete accident.' Jones pretended to hide behind his telephone. Penhaligon looked at Giggs for support but he was laughing silently, helplessly.

'Silly buggers,' Penhaligon swung out of incident, headed for the car park. She didn't allow herself to grin until she was well away down the corridor.

Bilborough wouldn't let Beck anywhere near the meeting with hospital administration. He was too volatile. Beck had his uses, like all of them, but Bilborough was determined to handle this one on his own. This required the gentle touch; the subtlest of pushes. He must allow no hint of his own impatience to show through. The slightest hint of persecution and it would all go to the dogs.

The man – the killer – had remained asleep only a short while before regaining consciousness. A brief test had shown that he remembered every detail of their previous conversation. Bilborough had immediately arrowed in on what he assumed to be a legitimate loophole in the man's cover story – only to be disappointed and frustrated in turn when Doctor Turner had told him the fact that the killer could now remember recent events was no indication he should be able to remember things from further back.

'The difference between short and long term memory is a subject still under investigation by the world's leading psychologists,' she said, which didn't make things any better at all.

At his insistence Doctor Turner had run a time consuming battery of tests. None of the tests were particularly easy to perform, or to assess. He had split the couple of hours' waiting time between keeping Beck's temper on a short leash and phoning into the station with an update and instructions for the duty officers.

Two hours had gone by. Now he stood before a group of senior hospital administrators while Beck kept a close watch on the closed door of the room in which the killer was again snoring quietly, if not peacefully. And despite his best intentions, his own patience was starting to crack.

'How long are you planning to keep him here? He could go on feigning amnesia 'til the cows come home.'

The hospital administrator, Doctor Chong glanced at Turner. She said patiently, 'We don't know that he's feigning it.'

'Of course he's feigning it.' Calm. Don't antagonise them. Don't make them defensive. They're the power here. Not you. Not yet. 'You've done test after test and there's no physical reason whatsoever.'

'None that we've found.'

Chong added, 'There are emotional and psychological factors to take into consideration.'

'He's murdered two young women. They're emotional and psychological factors. I understand them perfectly.' Stay calm. 'Can I ask a question? Suppose he was simply refusing to speak; you know, if he was perfectly alright in every other respect, just wouldn't talk. Would you keep him in then?'

Turner pursed her lips. 'No.' The answer came with great reluctance.

'Well that's exactly what he's doing.'

'DCI Bilborough that is an altogether unsympathetic view of the circumstances.'

Don't lose it now. 'Doctor Chong, I'm simply stating the facts as I see them. That's what I'm trained to do, what I'm good at. And the fact in this case is: that man should be in a police station, not a hospital bed.'

He watched them waver, exchange glances. Waited. Smiled inwardly as they fell.

'The patient is strong enough to take a measured dosage of pentothal. We'll try that.'

Ann Appleby watched the florist van through the French windows. She kept herself masked by the net curtain. Needed the space. The flowers were a lovely gesture, but they brought the outside world with them, pushing into her home, her life, her grief. She needed some time to herself. Time to grieve.

Simon was out there now, blank faced, automatically thankful, accepting another armful of flowers from the van driver, bringing them into the house, stacking them carefully in the sitting room to join the others spread across the carpet, the furniture, the top of the piano.

Ann stood quite still, clutching the lace curtain, staring out of the window. And Simon made another journey, this one the last thank goodness. And now the driver was getting into the van and then it was moving, pulling out onto the road, receding into the distance, a cloud of fumes; and she wished letting go of Jacqui could be that easy.

And then she caught sight of her reflection in the window: the face of a woman who wants to let her only daughter go. Who's impatient to let her go. Chaffing at the bit to let her go.

Oh Jacqui, I'm sorry, it's not that I don't love you, honestly, it's just –

But of course she didn't know what it was that made her feel like this; so cold. Distanced. Irritable. Even the way her husband thanked the florist seemed unnecessarily obsequious. And now here he was again, closing the front door carefully, expression calm, a tower of strength, there for her, always there for her; and didn't he realise she needed her own space, didn't want him hovering around? God, Jacqui was hers, wasn't she? He hadn't given birth to her had he? Hadn't suffered as she had suffered. The agony. The ecstasy, but dear Lord the agony, the fear and then, *Mrs Appleby, I have to tell you that your baby hasn't turned; there are other complications that mean we're going to have to deliver her by caesarean section*, and then the rubber mask, the sweet smell that ever since had reminded her of the failure of her own body, the knives, the blood, the cutting – and he hadn't even been there. Through the hours of physical labour, the mental agony, the fear that Jacqui would come out some-how . . . wrong; hadn't even been there. And yet she'd been

70

such a beautiful baby, had beaten all the odds, had grown through childhood into such a beautiful woman. And now all that effort, the pain, the heartache, the indescribable effort of it all, everything had been for nothing.

When Simon took her in his arms to comfort her, she didn't even have the strength to be angry with him for not understanding why she was crying.

Then from outside there came the sound of another vehicle pulling up. She didn't need to look to know who it was. The firm, single knock on the front door only confirmed her fear.

'You get it,' she told Simon. 'You let her in.'

He left her in the sitting room, with the flowers. Returned a moment later with the policewoman. The redhead. The girl who'd told them about Jacqui first of all.

'I'm sorry, I don't remember your name.'

'That's perfectly alright, Mrs Appleby, I understand.'

Simon added, 'It's DS Penhaligon, dear.'

The redhead – Penhaligon – nodded her thanks. 'Actually, Jane is fine.'

Ann watched the girl bite her lower lip. 'Are you alright?'

She took a deep breath. 'Mrs Appleby. I have some news for you.'

There was a moment's silence. And she knew. 'They've found him, haven't they? The man who did it?'

The girl nodded. 'Yes. But . . . There's something else you have to know.'

'Please,' Ann moved aside a stack of wreaths, gestured to the sofa thus revealed. 'Won't you sit down?'

'Thanks.' A beat. 'Lovely flowers.'

'Aren't they?' Ann felt her mind whirling. They'd found the killer. They'd found him. So what was the problem?

'Mrs Appleby, I have to tell you, the man we have discovered is –'

There was a loud knock on the front door.

Penhaligon fell silent.

'I'll get it,' Simon left the room.

There was an awkward silence, filled by the sound of voices from the hallway.

71

'Can I get you a cup of something?'

Penhaligon half smiled, nodded. 'Thanks. That would be nice.'

Ann headed for the kitchen by the door at the back of the room, avoiding the hallway. She had no desire to see who was out there. To meet them, to let them into her life. When she returned with a pot of tea and several cups on a tray the sitting room held one extra person.

He looked vaguely familiar from somewhere, a huge man, a sympathetic expression, perched uneasily on a chair Simon had cleared for him, dwarfing it effortlessly.

'I'm sorry, do I . . . ?'

Simon introduced him. 'This is Doctor Fitzgerald. He taught Jacqui's psychology class.'

'Ah,' Ann nodded, aware that Penhaligon was shuffling uncomfortably on the sofa. 'Well, thank you for dropping by Mister –'

'Fitz, Mrs Appleby. Just Fitz. I heard the news this morning, I'm so very sorry to trouble you. I knew Jacqui you see. She was a lovely girl. I'm really sorry.'

There was a warmth in his voice. Ann tried to look away but found herself drawn in by that voice. So calm, so warm, so . . . comforting. And Penhaligon was staring now, eyes wide with interest, as Simon thanked Fitz for his kindness.

'Doctor Fitzgerald brought these for us,' said Simon, gesturing to a new bouquet.

Fitz glanced around at the room full of flowers, smiled sheepishly. 'A redundant gesture under the circumstances . . .' Abruptly he stood. 'Well, I suppose I'd better be going, I . . .' He half turned, then turned back, and Ann saw his face harden, eyes sparkling with determination. 'Look. I'm a psychologist. That's how I knew Jacqui, you know that. She was a student of mine. I want to help. I'm good and I'll catch him for you.'

Ann rocked backwards with the force of his words. Licked her lips. She began to answer but Simon was already speaking.

'The police are coping, thanks all the same.'

Ann watched Fitz follow Simon's glance towards Penhaligon. He turned to study the diminutive woman sitting cross legged on the sofa.

Penhaligon stood to meet his gaze, introduced herself.

Fitz offered his hand. Penhaligon took it.

'I'm afraid unless you're here by invitation from the Applebys I'll have to ask you to call back later –'

'You've found him haven't you?' The words were stated as fact. How did he know? 'Found the killer?' Ann felt herself come under Fitz's exacting scrutiny, watched as his gaze passed across her to Simon, then back to Penhaligon.

The policewoman said nothing.

Fitz pursed his lips. 'There's something else isn't there?' Turned again to Ann. 'Something you haven't been told.' Back to Penhaligon. 'You've got him but there's something wrong.' A pause as Fitz chewed his lower lip thoughtfully. Lifted his head, examined the ceiling, abruptly lowered his gaze to the policewoman.

'He's dead ... no that's not it.' A pause. 'He's claiming amnesia. That's it isn't it? I'm right aren't I? He's told you he's lost his memory.'

His words were shocking in the silence.

Ann realised Fitz hadn't let go of Penhaligon's hand yet. She was aware of something passing between them. Some spark. She could almost feel it, like static, splashing out from them, juddering through the furniture, her own nervous system.

Penhaligon released her hand from Fitz's. 'Mrs Appleby, I'd like to apologise for Doctor Fitzgerald's utter lack of sensitivity in this matter. But ... it is true. The man we believe is your daughter's killer is claiming total amnesia. Obviously you'll be kept informed as the investigation proceeds. I ... I wish I could have brought you better news.'

'Thank you.' That was Simon. He was like a scratched record today. 'Thank you anyway.'

Penhaligon was heading for the door. With her hand on the handle, she turned. 'Mr and Mrs Appleby. If there's anything you need, please call me at Anson Road.'

Ignoring Fitz completely, Penhaligon left the room. 'I'll see myself out, thanks.'

As Simon followed Penhaligon to the front door Fitz

turned to Ann and she saw there was a look of apology in his eyes. 'I'm sorry. That was very tactless of me.'

'It doesn't matter.'

'Yes it does. You don't want anyone smashing into your life now, I can see that. You need to grieve. I'm sorry.'

He turned to leave, but Ann stopped him with a word. 'Wait.'

He turned back, expectantly.

'It's true, I . . . well I didn't want anyone else to interfere. I didn't want to have to deal with that, with people who care in the wrong way. Do you understand?'

'Of course.'

'But with you . . . it's different. I know. Somehow I know that you care . . . in the right way. Do you understand?'

He nodded.

'What will you do first?'

'Well . . .' Fitz chewed his lip momentarily. 'That would depend on what tests they've run at the hospital.'

Ann shrugged helplessly.

Simon re-entered the room.

Ann went to him and took his arm. 'I've asked Fitz to help us.'

Simon nodded slowly. 'DS Penhaligon said he had amnesia. Can you prove he hasn't?'

'There are tests.'

'How would you go about it?'

Fitz looked up for a moment, considering. 'Well, since he's claiming amnesia, he's obviously not that badly hurt. I assume there's no skull damage?'

Ann winced, held on to Simon's arm a little tighter. There was something almost brutal about the way Fitz handled the truth. But she put up with it because she sensed instinctively that it was the only way to go forward.

'No.'

'Well. I'd have to establish that it wasn't due to organic causes. I'd run a liver function test – the chief cause of amnesia in a murder case is alcohol – then I'd run a blood sugar test for hypoglycaemia. Then there's schizophrenia and epilepsy so I'd need an electroencephalogram.' He pursed his lips. 'I don't know. I'd have to see him.'

'But if it was none of these?' Simon. Pedantic as always.

'Well. If there's no brain damage and no organic reasons I would say he was having us on.'

Having us on? Having us on? It was Jacqui! Jacqui he was talking about. Having us on!

'Will you help us?'

Fitz took Ann's hand; she felt a strength radiating from it.

I want to grieve for my daughter. I can't because now he's standing between us. He's in the way and I want him out of the way – forgotten. I want to be able to grieve . . .

And Fitz knew what she was thinking, knew what was in her mind.

'I know. And you'll be able to grieve soon. I promise.'

He felt the questions rather than heard them, an intrusion, like the needle in his hand, an intrusion into him, the outside world pushing in, opening him up, exposing what was inside. And he knew he should be resentful, angry even, but all he felt was relief.

They'd explained it to him when he'd awoken again that afternoon. He assumed it was that afternoon. The policeman, Bilborough, was still here, still pushing. He had a nice face though, Bilborough, a warm face. And his ears stuck out in a friendly way. And that was pleasant too. But not as nice as the questions, because they would show him the way into himself, right down into himself, but maybe that wasn't so good, because then he might not like what he found there, but then maybe even that would be alright, because self understanding was very important, everything he had ever been taught had aimed towards that, aimed him towards that goal. That shining goal. Understand the self.

'– remember being on the –'

'– what you were –'

'– the girl –'

'– Jacqui –'

'– who you –'

'– what your name is?'

Focus. Focus on the answers. Answer the questions. The

75

questions are your friends. They want to help you. And the Doctors, they want to help you. Everyone wants to help you. They're your friends too.

'I remember the noise . . . the lift . . . the helicopter . . . I remember someone spoke to . . . me . . .'

A nice voice. A warm voice. Or had it been that it was a voice capable of being nice but was harsh just at that moment? No. It wouldn't have been harsh. Not when everyone was being so friendly. So –

'That was me. I am a police officer.'

' . . . DCI . . . Bilborough . . .'

'Yes. Now do you remember being on the train?'

' . . . Bilborough . . . that's a nice name. Friendly. Do you know your ears stick out?'

'You don't –'

No.

'– remember being on –'

Of course not, didn't I just say so?

'– the train?'

'No. I just said . . . Hang on. No. I didn't did I?'

Did I say that?

'– obviously isn't going to remember anything of any –'

'– you give him another –'

'– reached the limit of his –'

'– wouldn't make any –'

'– sense? He stopped making sense half an –'

'– do you want to –'

'– else for it. We'll have to let him –'

'– have to let him –'

'– let him –'

Bilborough stared down at the man. The killer. The stitches in his forehead reflected the concealed light in the hospital room, glinted with a silvery sheen, like metal.

The man's eyes slowly folded shut.

Bilborough sighed. The whole afternoon had been a washout. A waste. He reached for the off switch on the tape recorder whirring quietly beside the bed, and that was when the man spoke.

76

'I know my being like this is annoying you. I know. But it's destroying me.'

Bilborough was transfixed by the note of anguish in the man's voice. 'Is that him or the pentothal?'

Turner frowned. 'It's him. You often get a last minute thing like this, just before they go under.'

And then he was speaking again, and Bilborough was pumping up the recording volume to compensate, leaning closer to catch the words the man breathed out, straightening triumphantly as he slipped finally into a tortured sleep.

'Prove to me I did this and I'll confess . . . I promise . . . I'll sign anything you want . . . I'll confess.'

And then the words dissolved into a gentle snore.

Bilborough flicked off the tape recorder. He felt like leaping up and slapping the ceiling; he allowed himself the thinnest of smiles instead.

Got you pal. Bang to rights.

17:00–23:00

Bilborough's good mood had evaporated by the time he got back to Anson Road. There were too many other things that hadn't yet been tied up. A suspect without a weapon – even if the suspect was prepared to confess – was of little use. Motive had to be shown in order to ensure a full sentence. The murder weapon had to be found.

Incident was up as he and Beck barrelled in through the double doors. The usual chat was just a touch lighter. The sound of phones ringing was almost merry. There were even one or two smiles. Tom Jennings and Chandra Jandhu were manning the phones. Penhaligon was updating a wall chart, chomping aggressively on half a Twix. Giggs had the other half stuffed in the corner of his mouth like a cigar. He and Jonesy were poring over an ordnance survey map of the Sheffield–Manchester main line route. They were exchanging what they obviously thought were private grins.

'I suppose the news has got round then?'

There was the usual barrel load of flip answers. Morale was

definitely up and that was good, but sometimes Bilborough wished they could all be just a shade more professional about it.

'I suppose you want me to declare a public holiday.' That got them. 'Well. In case any of you are new to police work there are still one or two minor points to clear up. Firstly: I want a continuous log of all phone calls kept; Tom, Chandra, grab your bics. Penhaligon, how did it go with the mother?'

'Actually there's two of them, sir. Their names are Ann and Simon. And it went pretty much as you might have expected.' She looked like she was going to add something, but Bilborough nodded, cutting her off. For now just the facts were enough. He wanted no more half baked theories.

'Good. Giggs, Jonesy, tell me you have a murder weapon.'

That got the biggest silence of all.

'Er . . . well . . .' Giggs grinned. 'We've got a bloody great Chinese puzzle that used to be a train, boss.'

Ten years younger and Bilborough could easily have imagined the high fives Giggs and Jonesy would be exchanging now. It wasn't good enough. 'That's no good. I don't need a Chinese puzzle. A Chinese puzzle isn't going to send Sweeney down. Do you understand?'

'Yes boss.' Dead silence. 'Sorry.'

'That's OK. Now look everyone. I know it looks like a wrap but the reality is it's a long way from that. We've got to find the murder weapon. Without it we might as well all give up now and get jobs as milkmen. Clear?'

There was a much subdued chorus of affirmatives.

'Alright then. Giggs. When you've finished that Twix there's a waste bin over there. No origami dinosaurs or paper planes, OK?'

Without waiting for a reply he turned to enter his own office. With the door shut behind him he breathed a sigh of relief. Coffee. That's what he needed now. A gallon of double strength before the call home to check on Catriona.

He blinked. There was a man perched on the edge of his desk. A big man. Crumpled suit. Crumpled face.

'Who are you?'

Behind him the door opened. Penhaligon poked her head into the room. 'Sir, this is Edward Fitzgerald. Doctor Edward Fitzgerald. He knew Jacqui. I did try to tell you he was here. Doctor Fitzgerald – DCI Bilborough. In charge of the investigation.'

Fitz nodded to Penhaligon. 'And it's Fitz, OK? Just Fitz.'

Penhaligon withdrew without acknowledging Fitz's words. Bilborough thought he heard subdued mutterings from incident. Mutterings and – perhaps – a giggle.

He shut the door rather harder than he intended.

When Bilborough turned back into the room Fitz was on his feet, hand extended, holding a card. Bilborough took the card. 'So you knew Jacqui.'

'I'm a psychologist. She was a student of mine. Her parents want me involved, right?'

Bilborough sighed. 'Look Doctor Fitzgerald –'

'It's Fitz.' Patiently.

'Look Fitz. You see that lot in there?' He jerked a thumb to the glass wall dividing his office from the incident room. 'They've got half a century of experience between them. If I need a psychologist I'll be sure to let you know. OK?'

Fitz frowned. 'You've got him up at Manchester Central, right?'

'Yes. So?'

'They're a bunch of wankers up there.' Bilborough felt himself come under scrutiny. 'You know that don't you? A bunch of wankers.'

'They speak very highly of you.' Keep it dry. Maybe he'll go away.

'Doctor Chong speaks very highly of everybody. How else do you suppose she became administrator?'

'That's a very cynical attitude, Doctor Fitzgerald.'

'Fitz.' Was that exasperation in his voice?

'Look. Homicide and amnesia are heavy. You need to know what you're doing and I do know what I'm doing.'

Bilborough licked his lips, felt the pressure of the visitor's words as he held open the office door. 'Doctor Fitzgerald. I have a bloody great investigation to coordinate, it's been a hell of a day, no-one wants us to do overtime and my wife's having a baby. I'm sure you'll forgive me if I ask you to leave now.'

Fitz pursed his lips, walked slowly to the door. 'I understand. It's your first child isn't it?'

Bilborough said nothing but his eyes narrowed.

'You see, only someone that's never been there could say "My wife is having a baby." My wife. Having a baby is something you do together. Believe it or not.'

'I believe you.'

'Then believe this: I've forgotten more about amnesia than Chong or anyone else at Manchester Central will ever know.'

Bilborough nodded tiredly. Holding the door open was beginning to hurt his arm.

Fitz took the hint, cruised out into incident. Bilborough followed him out, token politeness. As the main door closed behind the psychologist a phone began to ring.

Bilborough looked around. Penhaligon was staring at the phone on her desk. 'If I have to answer that phone I am going to rip off someone's arm.'

Christ, what was the matter with everyone here? Bilborough felt like screaming at Penhaligon. Instead he wearily reached over, picked up the phone, held it to his ear. A man's voice said, 'The killer is a woman.'

Bilborough sighed. Another nutter. 'And your name is, sir?'

'Aren't you listening to me? I said the killer's a woman. I saw her leave the compartment. She's got mauve highlights in her hair. You know, like a punk.'

'You saw her leave the compartment?'

'Just after the guard screamed.'

Giggs was making circular movements in the air with a finger. *You want a trace?*

Bilborough nodded. To the phone he said, 'You know her?'

'She's got mauve streaky hair. Blue eyes. Freckles.'

'And where were you when you saw her?'

'Uh . . . by the toilet at the end of the carriage. I . . . er . . . I have to go now.' The phone went dead. Bilborough looked at Giggs, who shook his head slowly, indicating there hadn't been enough time to trace the call.

Bilborough made a disgusted noise, put the phone down, aware that he had everyone's attention, not the least of which belonged to Penhaligon. 'One for you Penhaligon. Reckoned Sweeney's a woman. Reckoned he saw the colour of her eyes and that she had mauve streaks in her hair. He saw all that in a juddering train corridor at a distance of thirty feet. Jesus. Sad bastard probably wasn't within a hundred miles of the train.'

Bilborough shook his head, began to return to his office, stopped, turned back. 'Oh yeah – and the good news is there's no word on overtime yet.'

Bilborough re-entered his office to a chorus of groans. He reached for the coffee jug, bubbling quietly on the percolator.

There was a knock at the door. He groaned. What now?

The all-too-familiar face of Parsons, Ms, appeared around the door. 'DCI Bilborough. Good afternoon. As you can imagine the Chief would like a good cross section of today's events to make it onto the early evening news. I've come to discuss the various methods of information dispersal we at PR have deemed to be appropriate and run a few of them past you for your input. Of course an immediate selection would be a good idea to ensure maximum press coverage, as I'm sure you'll understand. Oh, and you'll be pleased to know I've managed to borrow a tie for you to wear. Hm, is that coffee? How thoughtful. Thank you.'

How did she manage to say all that without taking a breath, he wondered.

When he got home Fitz saw with mixed feelings that Judith's car was parked in the drive. Inside, the house was strangely empty. Mark was still out; and there was no cheerful chatter from Katie, no music from the radio. The only sound was the light tread of feet and the clunk of suitcases opening and closing coming from the upstairs bedroom.

Fitz closed the front door quietly at the bottom of the stairs, listening. He closed his eyes for a moment. Inhaled. He could smell her. Her perfume.

Clunk. Slap. The sound of a closing zipper.

Fitz put one foot on the bottom stair. It was going to be easy now. She was here. She'd have calmed down by now. He would talk to her, they'd get it sorted out. This couldn't go on forever.

With his foot on the bottom stair, Fitz hesitated. Could he handle this without a drink, just a finger to give him that edge, that fighting heat –

Bollocks.

He'd won her heart without alcohol, hadn't he?

He cruised up the stairs, along the landing, knocked on the bedroom door, sailed in.

She turned, one hand on a suitcase. Two more were piled on the bed, including Katie's overnight bag. She looked at him, said nothing.

'Judith.'

'Fitz.'

'Ah . . .' *Christ it's so good to see you. So good to see you. Stay a while, will you? Let's talk? The kids aren't here so we can make a good job of it this time, a proper job.* '. . . Do you want a cup of tea?'

'No thank you, Fitz, I do not want a cup of tea. I want my clothes, and Katie's. I want to leave my address for Mark and I want to go.'

'But . . . I want you stay.' *I need you to stay. I love you.*

'It's always been about what you want hasn't it Fitz? That's what this whole thing's about: what you want.' A hesitation. *Come on. Give me that smile. Give it to me. We can make it right.* 'And let's face it, who'd be saddled with a wife and kids when you can have have all the dogs or horses or . . . or bloody tiddlywinks our mortage can afford? Eh Fitz? Would you?'

No! I want you! I love you!

'There. Didn't think you'd have an answer for that one.' She zipped the case closed and pulled it past Fitz out onto the landing.

'You're hardly being fair.'

Judith pushed past him, grabbed Katie's overnight case. He followed her into his daughter's bedroom.

'Fair? Look at this, Fitz.' She waved her hand around the room. Fitz took it all in. The stacks of school exercise books, the drawings on the wall; the neat dressing table with the teddy bear they'd picked together to celebrate Katie's birth; next to it, the old leaded glass ornament cabinet his mother had given Katie to keep her rapidly growing collection of furry gorillas in; the posters on the ceiling; Nirvana, Twin Peaks, Astronomy Today.

'This is what you're giving up. What you're kicking away. Our lives.' Opening the cupboard, the dresser, stuffing clothes into Katie's bag. 'You're kicking it all away, Fitz. For a bloody bet on a bloody horse, or a bloody dog. Are we worth so little to you?'

No you're worth more than anything to me, all of you. You know that Judith, I know you do.

But somehow the words never quite made it to his mouth. Something blocked them. Perhaps it was the knowledge that his daughter was growing up. Nirvana? Twin Peaks? Had he lost them already and just never realised it?

'Where will you go?'

'I'm staying with Jo and Mike. I've left the address for Mark. It's on the telly. He shouldn't miss it there.'

Even those simple words seemed to be a subtle dig at Fitz. *He's your son. Get him sorted.*

'But you should know, Fitz, while Dad's on holiday I'm thinking about going back to Mum's.'

But you never talk to your mother, haven't in years.

'That's Leeds.'

'How observant. You remembered.'

He sat on the edge of the bed, rubbed his face with the back of one hand. Judith stared at him for a moment, then zipped Katie's bag shut and left the room. He made no attempt to follow her, merely rubbed his chin slowly with the fingers of his left hand. He heard the thump of cases being rocked down the staircase, the click of the front door, the muted thud of a car door, sound of a car engine starting up.

He made it to the window in time to see her car pull out of the drive and onto the road.

Look back. Please. If you look back it'll come right in the end. Please. Judith, Please.

But of course she didn't. She was too busy watching the road ahead.

And then he seemed to hear her voice, echoing distantly through the cloud of exhaust fumes: *That was something you should have been doing, Fitz. Watching the road ahead. You should have been doing it for a long time.*

For Penhaligon the rest of the afternoon passed in tedium. Bilborough was in a real strop, even Beck had got impatient with him at one point. That had fuelled the tension. The word on overtime still hadn't arrived by end of play, so they'd all stayed late anyway. What the hell. It wasn't as if she had a humungous social life. She drove home at five MPH over the limit all the way. Shoved the motor in the car park, slammed the door. At the last minute, as she was about to insert her key into the front door, she heard the telephone ringing inside. She rolled her eyes, gritted her teeth. She withdrew the key, deciding to go for a walk instead.

The flats were only a quarter of a mile from the canal that ran through town. She ducked through the loose planks in the fence the kids from the estate had made last summer rather than use the proper gate located further down the road to enter the waste ground edging the canal. Ten minutes later she was standing on the towpath, staring down past a brick embankment at the scummy water, wondering what the hell her life was coming to. Thirty two this August. Christ. She had friends younger than her that were married with kids. She didn't dare have kids.

A canal boat slooshed lazily past, flat sunlight glazing the windows a deep bronze. The figure on the rudder aimed a big grin at her and waved. She waved back and that made her feel slightly better. Seemed there was still some good old fashioned niceness in the world.

The boat's engine faded slowly into the distance. The water rocked sluggishly in its wake, back and forth, back and forth, glistening like treacle in the sunlight. Treacle covered with a sticky layer of dirt.

She sat at the edge of the embankment, feet dangling over the edge, watched a gaggle of kids charge along the opposite bank on brightly coloured mountain bikes. The tinny sound of music from a walkman echoed across the water, and did a little jig inside her head.

It was warm. It was drowsy. It was a little overcast; a typical Manchester summer evening.

A dragonfly buzzed around her face, zoomed away into the sunset.

Ten, twenty, thirty, forty, fifty or more, the Bloody Red Baron was runnin' up a score . . .

Now where had that thought come from? Out of the sun, that's where. And it was true as well. If you changed the names. Changed the names to protect the guilty. To protect Sweeney.

Tomorrow. Tomorrow she'd have the results from the post mortem and she'd be able to make a case Bilborough couldn't ignore. Woman or not, recently promoted or not. He wouldn't be able to drop this; she'd make him see she was right.

She watched the kids cycle away down the towpath and wondered how many of them would make it past twenty. Thought she was doing alright to have beaten the odds so far herself. Beaten the dirt.

Dad.

In view of the circumstances it would be a wise move to bring in the children for checks; standard checks, there'll probably be nothing at all to worry about.

But all the same she knew there was a fifty-fifty chance the dirt was inside her too; hiding inside her. Waiting.

The kids vanished, the sun slipped behind a bank of pale cloud, Penhaligon clambered wearily to her feet, followed her shadow back across the waste ground to the flat.

Later, she banged out a rough jazz triplet on the Zildjians as the telly lit up the room with inane rubbish. Around ten thirty the phone rang again; she drowned it with the bass drum until the neighbours banged on the wall. The phone was still ringing. It rang for nearly ten more minutes but she ignored it. When it stopped she took the phone off the hook, killed the telly, undressed, crawled into bed. She was asleep the moment her head hit the pillow.

And she dreamed. She dreamed of a thundering train, an open door banging to and fro in the wind, a dead girl and a killer with her mother's face.

And in a hospital bed five miles away a man lay asleep, his subconscious prowling the dark corners of his mind, an animal caged by the drip feed pushing into his hand, caged but not subdued.

Not nearly subdued.

– much blood. Blood all over him, and her body was jerking beneath him, an insistent rhythm, and his hands were at her throat, and they were covered in blood, so much –

THREE

Wednesday

Bilborough let Beck take Sweeney down.

The look of surprise on his face, the eyes wide, almost stupefied above the pale cheeks as Beck led the two constables forward to meet him in the hospital corridor made Bilborough wince. Chong and Turner were there; neither protested, there was no time; Beck was on the killer, all over him, cuffs glinting, cautioning him, the words designed for mutual protection smashing into his face like punches. And Bilborough knew that for Beck words could never be enough. He wanted the words to hurt, wanted a shot at payback for the dead girls, no matter how out of line it was. And despite Beck's desire the caution was letter perfect. Bilborough was inclined to let it stand. Beck represented his heavy guns; the time for subtlety was long dead.

'I'm arresting you on the suspicion of the murder of Jacqui Appleby –'

'But you know I can't –'

'– do not have to say anything but anything you do say –'

'– remember anything about the –'

'– will be taken down in evidence –'

'– please –'

'– you understand?'

'– please!'

'I said: do you understand?' The words quiet, the anger behind them screaming like a wild animal from which Sweeney cowered.

'Yes.' Shellshock. Numb from the barrage of words.

'It's in your own interest you're not photographed by the press. Do you understand?'

'Yes.' Resigned. Out on his feet. Surprise turning to fear.

Beck took a coat from one of the constables, slapped it over the killer's head, tightened the sleeves around his throat to hold it in place. It was almost a relief for Bilborough when his view of the killer's face, slack with shock, eyes wide and filled with tears, was cut off.

Then the hospital doors banged open to a hot press of bodies, a storm of cameras, of questions, lenses pointing, voices raised in acquisition, accusation, *give it to us, give him to us, anything, everything, we want him, we want him now.*

Bilborough said nothing as Beck parted the crowd, forced Sweeney through the passage to the car. A photographer got too close, Beck's arm was up and the man went sprawling, the camera falling to lie shattered amid a storm of jostling feet and curses and threats of legal action. Beck ignored them all with equanimity after that, got the car door open, got his hand on Sweeney's head, got him down and in, followed him onto the back seat as Bilborough hit the passenger seat in front and slammed the door between him and the animals.

And then the car was off, shoving its own path through the crowd, lenses and faces and hands pressed up against the windows, the glass rattling with demands and the clack of cameras and the whirr of tape recorders, all melting together and muting to a dull moan of disappointment and fading into the distance as the engine coughed and the car took them away.

And it hadn't even started.

The driver took the car around a corner, siren blaring, and Bilborough twisted in his seat to look back as Beck whipped away the coat from Sweeney's head, his shocked face, staring eyes and he was away again, with nothing to hold him back this time, nothing at all.

'Right you sick, perverted bastard. Now's the time to start talking. Because if you don't I'm gonna smash your lying face through that bastard glass, see if I don't –'

And then Bilborough was speaking as well, smooth, calm,

all part of the act, except for Beck it wasn't an act and Bilborough knew that, used it, 'Leave him Jimmy. Leave him. I trust this man so just leave him, OK?' *Trust me, I'm your friend. Trust me and we'll get through this together.* Find his eyes, hold them, his killer's eyes, his next-door-neighbour's eyes, hold them, silence him with your own –

'I had a niece that age. It could have been my niece you butchered, you sick, twisted gobshite –'

'Not yet, Jimmy. Now's not the time. There'll be a time but it's not yet, OK? Jimmy? OK? That's an order. Do you hear me?'

And Sweeney was crouching back into the seat, hunched away from Beck, and the detective was following, hands at the killer's throat, pressing his face back against the window glass. And the driver took another corner at forty and now Beck's face was an inch away from Sweeney's, and Beck's spittle was on Sweeney's cheek, and the siren was hammering at the other side of the glass, and Sweeney was caught in the middle, crushed in a vice of sound –

'– want him in a room just the two of us I want to see him do to me what he did to her I want to see how brave he is then, how fucking brave he is –'

'– oh God oh merciful Lord help me I can't –'

'– when he's face to face with –'

'– bear this I can't –'

'– a man, a real –'

'– please stop –'

'– man not some poor defenceless –'

'– please please please please –'

And Bilborough stepped in again, *I'm here. I'm your only hope. I'm calm, rational, look at me.* 'Now listen. You're finished. You're going to be remanded. You know what that means? For someone like you? Hundreds of blokes, hundreds of them, just like Jimmy here, all wanting to cut off your balls because they think you're an animal –'

'– had my way I'd turn you over to the families, the families of the women you butchered because they'd know exactly what to do with you, you twisted pervert, you sick fucking gobshite animal you –'

'– got one chance and that's someone like me, a DCI, looking after you. Someone pulling strings, and I can't do that if you carry on with this amnesia stuff because –'

'– name of God what makes an animal like you tick, eh? Killing women, butchering them? You didn't rape them, didn't rob them –'

'– I know you're lying, you know you're lying, the whole world knows you're lying, so –'

'– what's going on in that head? In that –'

'– my advice to you is to –'

'– dirty festering pit you call a –'

'– confess, you –'

'– head so just tell us what we want to –'

'– understand? Confess –'

'– hear and confess –'

'– confess –'

'– confess –'

And then Bilborough put the capper on it: 'I know what you're thinking. You're thinking you've got a chance of getting away with it. Well, you've got no chance. We've got footprints, blood, scratches on your face, witnesses. You've got absolutely no chance in hell –'

And Sweeney knew it, Bilborough could see it in his eyes, eyes that registered no pain as his head thumped against the glass as the car made another turn, no pain as Beck's grip tightened around his throat, only fear; fear of Beck, of him, of the outside, the world; pushing in, knowing him, opening him up.

And then they were at Anson Road, and he was out of the car, following Beck as he pushed and prodded Sweeney through corridor after corridor, manhandling him past a gallery of accusing faces as if he were no more than cattle, down the stairs to the basement and into the trough, the holding cell for the nightly drunks and loonies, ripping away his tie and belt, his shoelaces, shoving him down onto the plastic covered bench that was the room's only furniture, fixing him with a contemptuous stare as he slammed the door and banged shut the metal plate across the observation window.

And then a moment of peace. A moment in which the other officers dispersed leaving Bilborough outside the cell with Beck, as the detective struggled to regain control of his temper.

'I don't know about him, Jimmy, but you terrified me.'

Beck smiled thinly. 'How long are you going to keep him in there?'

Bilborough shrugged. 'Oh hell, I don't know. Couple of hours. Let him appreciate the difference between a hospital and the nick. Maybe Giggs and Jonesy'll come up with the cutter in the meantime.'

'Yeah, and maybe pigs'll fly.' Beck shrugged. 'How's the missus anyway?'

Bilborough looked up. 'Does everyone know she's – we're – having a baby?'

'Can't keep any secrets from your friendly neighbourhood copper.'

'I'm beginning to think it's a conspiracy between you lot and the missus.'

Beck grinned. 'So. Pint lunchtime? Bit of a celebration?'

Bilborough headed back up the corridor to incident. 'Thanks all the same Jimmy but I need a clear head on this one. I'll celebrate when I send Sweeney down.'

'Whatever.' Beck shrugged, lit his roll-up, tried and failed for a smoke ring as he fell into step.

Bilborough began to martial his thoughts as they approached the duty room. 'Has anyone been over the statements that were taken from the people on the train?'

'Mmm . . . don't know.'

'Well that'll need to be done. We'll need to double check all the descriptions, all the details we've got. Don't want to look like pillocks in court, do we?'

'Nope.'

'Good. What else . . . oh yeah. How did you get on finding a voice analyst to go over the tape we made in the hospital?'

'That's covered. Bloke's name's Kev something or other. Said he'd have a report within the hour, and that was two hours ago. With any luck he'll be waiting for us now.'

'Well thank all the little angels for small mercies.'

Kev was lounging in incident, a narrow faced man wearing horn rimmed glasses and a perpetually interested look. He was studying the bustle around him, the ringing phones, the charts, the banter. His eyes never stopped moving. He rose as Bilborough approached him.

'Riley. Kevin. Voice man.'

Bilborough shook his hand. 'What have you got for me Kev?'

'Not a lot. All interesting though. Take a minute to set up the gear. Your office OK?'

'Sure,' Bilborough nodded, turned back to face the room as Kev entered his office. 'Jonesy. Got a job for you.'

The detective looked up, replaced the phone he was about to use.

'It's OK, you'll need that. Get onto BR. Book yourself on the next intercity to Glasgow with a box of razors.'

Jones blinked. 'You want me to spend the afternoon chucking cut throat razors out of a moving train?'

'What better way to see how far they travelled?'

'I'm gonna look a right pillock, aren't I?'

'No more than normal, now do it.'

Jones shrugged. 'Beats working I suppose.' He picked up the phone and began to dial.

Bilborough waved a sheaf of papers at Giggs. 'Who took these statements? As if I didn't know.'

Giggs blew out his cheeks. 'I guess that was me.'

'Now look, I'll –' Bilborough became aware Kev was waving to him through the window that separated the duty room from his office. 'I'll see you later.' Signalling acknowledgement to Kev, Bilborough turned to Beck. 'Search the train.'

'We've done that.' Giggs. Just a little too earnest.

'There's nothing there, boss.' Giggs nodded as Jones backed him up.

Bilborough felt his temper rise, struggled to control it. 'Do it again. This time use more men. Take it apart. Turn it into your Chinese puzzle. I want the murder weapon.'

Giggs shrugged. 'You're the boss, boss.'

In the office, Bilborough's desk had been taken over by

a portable tape recorder in a leather case. 'OK, Kev. Tell me.'

Kev pressed play and Sweeney's voice came out of the tiny speaker. 'My being like this is annoying you, I know, but it's destroying me.'

Kev stopped the tape. Took off his glasses as Bilborough sat at his desk. 'Originally Irish, brought up around here. I'd say he spent a year or two abroad; Spain, Italy, Portugal, something like that . . . and the last ten or so years down south.'

Terrific. I ask for a voice analyst I get a geographer.

'Is that it?'

'No. Listen again.'

A warble as the tape rewound and then, 'My being like this is annoying you, I know, but it's destroying me.'

'According to the tape the man considers himself a manual labourer. "*My* being like this . . . ?" Not, "It's annoying you I know *me* being like this." '

Bilborough lifted his eyes from the tape recorder to Kev.

' "*My* being like this is annoying you I know." It's strictly grammatical. This man's no casual labourer. He's educated.' Kev replaced his glasses with a smug look. 'This man knows how to handle his participles.'

Bilborough pursed his lips thoughtfully. 'Just because he's educated doesn't mean he can't be a labourer.'

Kev frowned, shook his head. 'Doesn't ring true. People absorb accents. They do it all the time, without even knowing it. Best friend of mine spent two weeks on holiday in Canada and came back speaking like a lumberjack. It happens, believe me. If your man had spent serious time as a manual worker, I'd know it. On the other hand, what your man does have is a very precise speech pattern. Very precise. Not the kind that's drummed into you at school. This was a man who relishes the language. Understands it. Loves it.'

Bilborough sat back in his chair, lips curved in a thoughtful frown. 'Should this affect the way we look at him?'

Kev rubbed the side of his glasses. 'That's up to you.' He began to pack up his tape recorder.

Bilborough followed Kev into the duty room, said goodbye to him at the door. Jones passed him as he turned back into the room.

'Book me on the 12:55 intercity,' he said.

Bilborough nodded. 'Keep a receipt for the razors.'

'On my pay I hardly have a choice.'

Bilborough found Beck going over some of the statements with Chandra. 'Jimmy.'

Beck looked up, grinned when he saw what was coming. 'Alright. Let's do the bastard.'

But it wasn't going to be that easy.

Interview room one was a tiled enclosure twelve feet square, painted an off white colour. There were no windows, nothing to distract the occupants. The light was from two sets of neon tubes, one of which flickered irritatingly. The only furniture consisted of three chairs, set around a wooden table on which rested a notepad and pencil, and a domestic twin-deck cassette recorder housed in a wooden box. The recorder was connected electronically to a warning buzzer which sounded whenever the play/record function was activated.

The buzzer sounded now as Bilborough inserted two cassettes and started the machine up.

Sweeney, perched uneasily on the seat opposite Bilborough looked up as Bilborough spoke the time and date of the interview for the tape. 'Time 11:05, Wednesday the fifth. Interview in connection with the murder of Jacqui Appleby. Present are myself, DCI Bilborough, DS Beck and . . .'

He broke off, stared at Sweeney. *Do you want me to say it? Do you want me to call you by the name the media will know you by shortly?* The killer leaned back in his chair, said nothing.

'. . . unidentified suspect.'

He watched Sweeney's lips compress as Beck paced backwards and forwards behind him. He saw the tendons on Sweeney's neck tighten with the urge to look round, but he held himself in check. He blinked slowly, as if the light were too bright. That was calculated; bright light equalled tired suspects equalled better, quicker responses.

He signalled to Beck to get the ball rolling.

Beck sucked on his roll-up, bent low over Sweeney and

blew a smoke ring in the suspect's face. 'Do you smoke?'

Sweeney leaned away from Beck, forward across the table. 'I don't know.'

Beck followed him, exhaling another breath of smoke. 'Can you smell it?'

'Yes.'

Bilborough studied the killer minutely. His hands were on the table, clasped together, the left vanishing into a plaster cast which in turn vanished beneath his jacket. They were shaking minutely but that could mean anything under the circumstances.

'Doesn't it make you want to smoke?'

'No.'

Beck straightened. 'Then you've never smoked.' Somehow the words came out like an accusation. Beck was good at this. Bilborough pursed his lips as the Detective came around the table, pulled up the third chair and sat beside Bilborough, directly opposite Sweeney. Both men stared at the suspect, who turned slowly towards Beck.

'Good. Your lungs get enough dirt in them as it is without adding to it.'

Bilborough frowned thoughtfully. Judging by Sweeney's tone of voice there were reserves of strength there. Should have left him to stew a bit longer. Maybe overnight.

Beck went on, 'You think it's a disgusting habit?'

'It's dirt. You're breathing in dirt. It'll get inside you.' He paused. 'Yes, I think it's disgusting.'

Beck leaned forward, concentration narrowing to a fine point. 'But not quite as bad as murdering young women?'

Sweeney looked away, closed his eyes as if imagining – no, remembering – what he'd done to Jacqui, to Patricia.

Bilborough kept his voice soft, 'You play all naive, innocent. But you're sharp, educated.' *And push.* 'Am I right?'

Sweeney opened his eyes, stared straight at Bilborough. 'I can't remember.'

Bilborough leaned back in his chair, steepled his fingers thoughtfully; let Beck take over again.

'Why did you go into her compartment?'

'I can't remember.'

'Plenty of space?'

'Perhaps.'

'There was plenty of space elsewhere. The train wasn't full.'

Sweeney said nothing, his face composed, the stitches on his forehead and cheek standing out dark against the pale skin. Beneath his crumpled jacket, his left arm twitched in its sling, the cast rustling gently against the fabric of the suit.

'Did you go in there because you saw a young girl on her own showing a bit of leg?'

'Yes.' But the answer came fast. Too fast for Bilborough.

'You remember?'

A glance. 'No. I'm just agreeing with everything you say.'

Beck blew more smoke from his mouth. 'Amnesia's no defence.'

No response.

'It makes no difference to me whether you lie or tell the truth. You'll still get life.'

'Why are you interviewing me then?'

Beck's lips compressed to a thin line. Bilborough caught his eye, glanced at the tape deck. Beck leaned back in his chair, sucked on his roll-up.

Bilborough kept his voice calm. 'You trust me?'

'Of course. You're a policeman.'

Beck smiled thinly at that.

Bilborough nodded. 'That's a good answer. If you had a lawyer here he'd tell you to cooperate.'

Sweeney leaned forward until his chin was inches from the table. He rocked back and forth and a small moaning noise came from him.

'I am cooperating.'

'Sure.' Beck. Hard. Angled in there; see the light through the chink and go for it.

'If only you could see that!'

'Sure.' Prise it open, burrow in there.

'I just can't remember, I've told you that, I don't know how many times. I can't remember! Why don't you believe me? I can't remember! I can't . . .' And he was down, head

97

down on the table, sobbing, huge racking sobs that bubbled up from his chest, pumped out into the room.

Beck made a disgusted noise. Jerked a thumb at the tape.

Bilborough told the tape the interview was terminated and switched it off.

'OK, Jimmy. Back to the cell with him. We'll go on with this later.'

When Bilborough got back to incident the Applebys were waiting in his office. Penhaligon greeted him in the duty room. 'They got here a few minutes ago, sir. I said they could wait.'

Bilborough sighed, rubbed his face tiredly. 'Never rains, does it? Any idea what they want?'

'No, sir.'

'Fine.' Bilborough headed for his office. 'Couple of cups of tea?'

'Yes, sir. Right away, sir.' Her voice was even, very smooth. Bilborough sighed again, inwardly. Why was everything such an effort with Penhaligon? Shelving the matter once again for later consideration, Bilborough entered his office.

Simon Appleby rose to greet him. 'DS Penhaligon tells us you've caught him.'

Bilborough nodded. 'We believe we have.'

'Have you charged him?'

Bilborough allowed his gaze to slip sideways, taking in Ann Appleby's face, the hope there, the hope he was about to crush. 'Not yet, no.'

'Will you charge him?' Simon again, meticulous. What did he do for a living? Accountancy? Bank work of some kind?

'As soon as we find the murder weapon.'

'And if you don't find it?' That same even, measured tone. The kind of tone Bilborough might have imagined a condemned man to speak with when all hope had fled. He felt his temper boiling up, overflowing. This had to stop. They had the man. They *had* him.

Ann said the words he couldn't. 'You'll have to release him.'

Simon's eyes shot sideways to fasten on those of his wife. It was quite apparent to Bilborough this possibility had never crossed his mind. Bilborough wondered briefly how they would cope with this. Then he put the thought to the back of his mind. Sweeney wasn't going to be released. He was sure of that. He was going down.

'We still have twenty four hours. That's the length of time we're allowed to hold him without charging him. And we're doing everything possible.'

Ann appeared to stare at her knees. She said nothing.

Simon stood perfectly still. 'Well. I suppose we'll be going then.'

And that was when Penhaligon put her head round the door with a tray of mugs. 'Mr and Mrs Appleby. Can I offer you some tea?'

Bilborough turned to Penhaligon and felt like yelling at her. He worked hard to suppress the anger inside, the inadequacy of the system, a system that could potentially allow a murderer to go free. He stared at the steam rising from the mugs and felt his anger boiling with a potent heat of its own.

Simon took two mugs, set one on the desk beside Ann. 'Actually, we've come about something else.'

'Oh?'

What else could they possibly want?

'There's a man. A psychologist. A Doctor Edward Fitzgerald. Ann – that is we'd – like him involved.'

Bilborough sat heavily in his chair and reached for his tea.

It scalded his tongue.

'Did Doctor Fitzgerald ask you to approach me concerning his involvement?'

'Oh no.' Simon's voice held a note of surprise. The man really did appear to be ridiculously naive.

'Doctor Fitzgerald has no official connection with this investigation. He has no official standing with the police force.'

'We know that but all the same . . .' Ann's voice was hollow, something inside was all used up, gone away. 'I have a card.' She began to rummage inside her purse.

Bilborough stopped her with a gesture. 'It's alright, Mrs Appleby, I have one. Thanks.'

'I understand in certain circumstances the police are allowed to contract outside help, professional help, in dealing with certain crimes.'

'That's true, but . . .' How to put it into words. Fitz was a loner. A chancer. He seemed to be a good psychologist, true, but not someone he wanted hanging around his duty room. His team had enough worries without a loose cannon blasting away at all and sundry. And how would it appear to the hierarchies? No. They had Sweeney, they'd got him on their own and they'd take him down on their own.

'If it's a matter of lack of funding, we have some savings; we'd be prepared to employ Doctor Fitzgerald on a private basis, if you would allow him access –'

Bilborough was shaking his head. 'That would quite simply be out of the question. Members of the public are never allowed access to police investigations.'

Ann looked at Bilborough. Her eyes were clear and determined. 'DCI Bilborough, I want him involved. Please.'

Her eyes locked onto his.

'Please.'

He had to look away. Tried not to imagine that look appearing on Catriona's face if by some awful chance they lost the baby.

He dug in his drawer and took out the card Fitz had left for him.

'Alright,' he said. 'He's in.'

And when the Applebys had gone Bilborough looked at the phone for a long time before picking it up, waited even longer before dialling.

'Doctor Fitzgerald? Yeah. Bilborough. I'm sending a car for you.'

He put the phone down, reached for his tea.

It was cold.

Fitz was yelling at Mark when the phone rang. Actually screaming would be a better word. It wasn't the smell in his son's room that had annoyed him, or the socks he'd tossed contemptuously from the attic-conversion window, it wasn't even the fact that Mark had simply been lying there all day, all bloody day with his hand easing the waistband of his shorts and his head buried in some magazine, it was more than that. It was knowledge. It was the bloody truth again, changing the rules, upsetting the game.

The game that began mid morning with a visit to the Salford Project where Judith headed up a team of fundraisers. Lise had greeted Fitz with a slightly less warm tone of voice than when they'd met outside the florist. So she knew now did she? What had Judith told her? Fitz had wanted in, had pushed. Lise had smiled her best receptionist smile and refused. Fitz had done an end run around the desk in time to see Judith vanishing into an office with a bunch of executives. He'd bitten his lip as she had deliberately not met his gaze, allowed Lise to escort him to the foyer, where he'd taken a seat, picked up a magazine, planted himself there like a British Oak and let his eyes tell Lise *see if I'll move. See if you can make me move before she'll talk to me.*

And after three hours she'd come, and she'd looked down at him sitting there, magazine in one hand, stack of empty plastic coffee cups on the magazine table and she'd said, 'Who were the flowers for, Fitz?'

And he'd been so surprised that he'd said nothing, and after a moment and a pitying glance, Judith had vanished back into the bowels of the Salford Project.

And Fitz had gone home where, for lack of any clear thoughts about what to do next, he had slouched around the house for an hour or so before finding himself in his son's room. God alone knows what he'd thought to find there, not absolution, certainly not understanding. But what did await him, the sight of his son stretched out on a bed that obviously hadn't been made in a month, and the knowledge that it could so easily be him in that position, was just enough to tip his temper, precariously balanced these last few days, over the edge.

And so he was screaming.

'– past three in the afternoon and you're still –'

'– because there's no –'

'– in your pit! Get –'

'– point in getting up because there's –'

'– up you idle git you –'

'– sod all to do, nothing –'

'– the hell do you ever expect to –'

'– to get up for –'

'– do anything with your bloody life if you don't –'

And then the anger, the anger of youth, the fear of youth. 'Dad, you're a joke. You know that? A joke? Mum thinks so. That's why she laughs so much. You're a joke!'

A pause and then his own voice, mirroring the anger, the fear that Mark was right, that his son had inherited whatever genetic quirk enabled him to perceive the truth in others, always in others but never in himself. 'You're lying on your bed with your hand on your dick all afternoon and for all the sense you're talking you might as well give up any hope of getting a job. Any hope at all, do you hear me?'

'You're sad. Do you think I'm listening to you?'

'Get out of your pit or I'm going downstairs to get a bucket of cold water and I mean it. A bucket of cold water!'

'Do you think I'm listening to you? You're just a joke . . .'

And Fitz had moved towards Mark then, cruised towards him, surged towards him, and Mark's eyes had opened with lazy disbelief and Fitz had raised his arm, the hand clenched into a fist and that was when he became aware that the phone was ringing.

And half an hour later the car had arrived with a WPC at the wheel. Fitz didn't say goodbye to Mark, just slammed the front door on the way out. He was too exhausted even to take a poke at the police driver, the highly polished attitude, the highly polished uniform buttons . . . it was all simply too much. And besides, there was another thought crowding into his head. Another thought that came with the soft roar of the engine, the subtle smell of the air freshener tab attached to the dashboard of the car. The killer. Bilborough wanted him to see the killer.

'Your boss,' he said to the driver as they sped along the high street leading into town. 'Can't crack it can he? That's why he wants me along?'

The driver shot Fitz a little grin. 'For a start Bilborough isn't my boss, I'm just a driver. Secondly, no-one tells me anything around Anson Road.'

'But you know, right? You've got ways, you keep your ear to the ground? Am I right?'

The driver returned her eyes to the road. 'I'm not disagreeing with you mate,' she said. 'I'm not saying anything, right?'

Fitz grinned, and if his troubles weren't exactly forgotten then at least they were shoved to the back of his mind, locked away in a cupboard in there to search through later. The truth was beckoning again. He was in.

And it felt great.

Incident was in turmoil as he barrelled through the double doors. A full team meeting was in progress. That morning the unit had obviously been functioning on about half the normal staffing levels. Now the room was crowded. Ten or so detectives, a few of whom Fitz recognised, were grouped around in chairs or perched on desks. Bilborough was addressing a full scale gathering of the flock. Beck had one foot up on another chair as he casually sealed the edges of a roll-up and jammed it into his mouth, where it stuck out from underneath his moustache. Fitz grinned; Beck liked to think of himself as hard; if only he could see himself as others saw him, could see inside himself . . . Giggs and Jones were seated either side of a large scale map; Giggs was absently folding a piece of stationery as he listened to Bilborough drone on. Penhaligon was sitting upright on the far side of the room, back straight, eyes front, paying attention. A casual observer would have assumed she were brown-nosing; Fitz thought differently. There was something about that woman, something sharp, like a diamond in a velvet case . . . she turned at that moment, proving his point by being the first to notice his arrival in the duty room. He threw her a grin, a little wave; she looked away, her face carefully neutral. He shrugged, gave a little shake of his head as if to indicate he wasn't really hurt by her ignoring him. A little over-intimacy was always good for a laugh.

Bilborough noticed Fitz then, nodded a greeting. Fitz settled onto the edge of an unoccupied desk while he waited for the DCI to finish.

'Right then, next item; Jonesy? Razors?'

Jones looked up from the map. 'One pound twenty five pence per unit, boss, and that includes a ten per cent discount for bulk. Cheap at half the price. A box of 'em cost me an arm and a leg.'

Giggs grinned, kept folding his paper. 'I think they want to know how far you could throw them, mate,' he said in a conspiratorial whisper that had everyone in the duty room sniggering except Bilborough, a fact that Fitz noticed with some interest.

'Oh, sure, sorry. Furthest we travelled was eighteen metres and that was with a good following wind.'

Another round of sniggers, which Bilborough cut short with a sharp gesture. 'Right. Widen the search to eighteen metres either side of the track.'

Jones blinked. 'Boss? There's twenty five miles of track. There's more chance of Giggs answering the great question of life, the universe and everything than there is of finding that razor.'

Bilborough ignored the humour, kept his voice cold. 'I know that. Now find the bastard thing.' He made as if to turn to Fitz, then instead picked up a metal waste paper bin, walked across the room and placed it on the map between Giggs and Jones. 'Very nice Giggs. What is that you're making? A turkey?'

'Actually it's a velociraptor, boss. You can tell because they had bigger claws and . . .'

Bilborough said nothing, merely waited for Giggs to wind down. When they finally got the point, Bilborough tapped the bin against the desk. Giggs reluctantly dropped the half finished model inside. Bilborough didn't once look at Giggs. He was staring at Jones the whole time and his message was plain. Leaving the bin on the desk between the two detectives Bilborough turned back to Fitz, nodded towards his office.

'Coffee?' Bilborough offered as the door closed behind them.

'I'd prefer something stronger,' Fitz stared around the office as he sat, taking in the sparse decorations, the immaculate desk, the certificate of commendation on the wall. He let his eyes wander leisurely back to Bilborough.

'Never on duty, Fitz. But I guarantee this: after we send him down the drinks'll be on me.'

'In the mean time . . . strict adherence to the rules.' Fitz gauged Bilborough's response to his little dig. So far the DCI wasn't doing too badly. 'Except for me, right? I'm hardly in the rule book am I?'

'I have a budget. I can allocate it as I see fit in order to close the case.'

Fitz nodded, interested. 'How much of a budget are we talking here? Couple of hundred?'

Bilborough uttered a short laugh. 'They're not even authorising overtime.'

Fitz pursed his lips. 'What then?'

'Don't worry, Fitz. I'll see you right.'

Fitz's stomach began to churn with a familiar fire. He said unhesitatingly, 'I want a hundred and twenty. Fifty now. And I'll put him away for you.'

Bilborough frowned.

'And don't give me any crap about accounts.' Fitz shrugged when Bilborough smiled thinly. 'It's been a bad week.'

'Let's hope it gets worse. For Sweeney anyway.'

Fitz nodded in agreement. Inside he was holding a judgement in reserve. In his experience amnesia could be a devil. Bilborough wasn't helping; he was eager. Far too eager. That was dangerous. The officers in the duty room seemed on the level, pretty much. But you never could tell. If Giggs and Jones were an example then he may have to do an end run around the manual but there was little point in letting Bilborough know that. He was as much a part of the problem, in his own way.

'What have we got then?' he asked.

'To all intents and purposes we've got him bang to rights. We have four separate witnesses that will place him at the scene; the descriptions have been checked and are solid. The blood on his clothes matched Jacqui's.'

'But he's lost his memory, right?'

'So he says. Complete amnesia backwards from the time of the murder.'

'The time he fell off the train.'

'Jumped from the train.'

Fitz nodded thoughtfully at Bilborough's automatic correction.

'ID?'

Bilborough shook his head. 'Nothing. No wallet, chequebook, not even a library card. We're checking along the tracks for ID and the murder weapon.'

Fitz sniffed. 'I can see why you'd want a psychologist involved.'

Bilborough said nothing. Fitz noted the response with interest.

'So what have you got for me, Fitz?'

'The fifty quid?'

'Take a cheque?'

You must be joking.

'I'd prefer cash.'

Bilborough checked his wallet. 'I've got forty.'

'That'll do as a retainer.' Fitz reached out for the money.

Bilborough hesitated. 'Just so long as we get a result.'

Fitz sighed. 'Complete amnesia is as rare as common sense in the Houses of Parliament. It almost never occurs. There's always something, some spark buried in the quagmire of the mind. An old girlfriend, parents' names, a house number or street name; something buried in the subconscious, accessible by random association or similar tests; something that may tell us what we need to know. I can find it, get it out for you.'

'You can give us Sweeney?'

I can give you the truth.

'On a silver platter.'

Bilborough handed Fitz the money. 'I'll get you the rest by lunchtime tomorrow.'

'There's a cashpoint on the high street.' Just a little push.

'Tomorrow, Fitz.'

Fitz nodded.

Bilborough sat back in his chair. 'What next?'

'I'll do a standard SMaRT on him.' At Bilborough's prompting look, he continued, 'That's a subconscious memory retention test. It'll give us a good initial profile.'

'Can he fake the results?'

'It's possible. But the test is a subtle one, even if it is basic.'

'Where do we start.'

'Well we can start with your notebook. I'll draw up some questions.'

'Good. Anything else you need?'

'An ashtray. And some of that coffee you mentioned.'

'I'll arrange it. You can use interview room one when you're ready. Oh – do you mind if DS Penhaligon sits in? I'd like her to get some experience of this sort of work.'

Fitz shrugged, feigned indifference. 'Fine with me.'

This should prove interesting. Different, but interesting.

He looked at Bilborough. 'Oh yeah, one more thing.'

Bilborough slid an ashtray across the desk. 'What's that then?'

'Got any cigarettes?'

Fitz studied the interview room in the moment before the killer was brought in. It was white, flat, almost invasive in its blandness. Everywhere you looked the white stared back at you. You couldn't get away from it. The room was perfect for what Fitz had in mind.

His questions had been taken to the man, half an hour passed, the answers had been brought back to Fitz. He had skimmed through the pages, made a cursory study of the prisoner's handwriting, asked for him to be brought to the interview room.

Penhaligon had come with him to the room, taken a chair and sat against the wall, as far from Fitz and the table as was possible. She was there as observer, not participant so that was understandable. But Fitz thought there was something else there, something under the veneer of her impassive expression; she'd said just three words to him in the ten minutes before the prisoner was brought in, and they were in response to a direct question from him. Professionalism? He doubted it. There was something else. Something . . . anger perhaps. He wondered who it could be directed at. Bilborough was the obvious choice.

He sat himself at the desk, the pages containing the prisoner's answers ranged neatly before him.

There was a knock at the door. Two constables brought in the prisoner, seated him, left the room. The door closed behind them and the game began.

'Hello.' Fitz studied the man sitting opposite him. Dark suit, crumpled. Shirt open at the collar, no tie or belt; of course they would have taken those from him. Fitz wondered if these were the man's own clothes, or replacements while the blood stained originals were being examined by forensics. He let his gaze range freely over the man's face and hands, the cuts and grazes, the bruising, the cast on his left arm. The man met his gaze. Not comfortable, not frightened. Somewhere in between.

Fitz took off his watch, studied it, shook it slightly. 'What time do you make it?'

The man looked immediately to a wall; then back again, another wall. Twisting in his seat, he eventually spied the clock where it was positioned on the wall behind him; he would not be able to see it during the course of a normal interview. 'Ten past five.'

Fitz set his watch to the correct time, slipped it back onto his wrist. The man's answer was interesting. 'How's the arm?'

The man held up his left hand, the bare wrist emerging from the moulded cast. 'It tickles. Right up inside where I can't reach.'

Fitz clicked his tongue sympathetically. 'Bust my leg when I was a kid. Fell over at school. Had it in plaster for fourteen weeks. That's as much as an adult, you know. Young bones are supposed to heal more quickly than old bones. You know?'

The man moved his head, not a nod or a shake, simple acknowledgement.

'My leg itched all the time. I tried to scratch it with a pen; got the cap stuck down there. Didn't stop the itch. I was too embarrassed to tell anyone; by the time they took off the cast I had a pen-top shaped scar on the back of my leg. Took six months to fade.'

Again the movement. A nod of the head, a shuffle in the seat. *That's right. You get comfortable. That's how it works best.*

'You see what happens when you conceal the truth? You see what happens? You get scarred.'

Nothing from the man. Time for a little push; an experiment, check out the lay of the land.

'They call me Fitz. What do they call you?'

'I don't know.'

' "Bloodthirsty murdering bastard?" '

'I don't know.' There was no change of expression, no inflection in the man's voice. That in itself was a surprise. Fitz took a cigarette from the packet Bilborough had given him. He offered the packet to the man.

'No thanks.'

'That's right, you don't, do you?'

'I can't remember. I don't feel the need to. I said that to the other policeman.'

Fitz nodded, jammed the high tar in his mouth, lit up. 'Good for you.'

He waited a moment, aware of Penhaligon sitting against the wall, imagining her mind clicking away like a journalist's camera, recording the event, hoovering up all the subtle nuances. He flicked ash from his cigarette into the ashtray, picked up the papers in front of him, stacked them, showed them to the man. 'You remember filling these in?'

'Yes.'

Fitz placed his spectacles on his nose, peered down at the sheets, read aloud, 'Who's the British Prime Minister?'

'I don't know. I had to guess.'

'You guessed wrong. I gave you three choices, you guessed wrong.'

'Sorry.'

'That's understandable . . .' Keep it warm, pleasant. Get his confidence. 'The President of the United States. Again three choices. You got it wrong.'

'I'm sorry.'

'It's understandable, really.' Shorter pause this time; still no discernible reaction from the prisoner. 'The leader of the Labour Party. Three choices, got it wrong. The standard rate of income tax; three choices, got it wrong.' Time for another push. The truth was in there somewhere. Fitz leaned forward, hunting, the words bait. 'The Chancellor of the Exchequer, the manager of the England Football Team, the author of *Catch Twenty Two* and the capital of Sweden, all wrong.'

A pause. Then, 'I'm sorry.'

Fitz leaned back in his chair, rubbed a finger along the bridge of his nose. 'You will be.' He took off his glasses, folded them into the case, tucked it into his inside pocket. 'You see, that's definitely *not* understandable. You close your eyes and stick a pin in and you'd be bound to get at least two answers right.'

Nothing from the prisoner. The game was hotting up.

'The odds against getting them all wrong are huge.'

That got a response. 'You think I did it on purpose.'

'Yes.'

'I didn't.'

Fitz said nothing.

'I didn't. Don't you believe me?'

Fitz leaned back in his chair, smiled slightly. 'Who cares?'

That got another response. Surprise. A movement of the head, a narrowing of the eyes. There was intelligence there. Did he think Fitz was laying traps for him? A verbal minefield? Fitz smiled inwardly. 'That's right. Who cares anyway?' He shrugged, extending the papers to Penhaligon, who leaned forward to take them. Fitz watched the prisoner as she moved; his eyes flickered towards her, a moment to take her in, study the face, the figure, the attitude, then back to Fitz as she sat back in her chair. And he went on, 'Nobody ever loses their memory. It just gets locked away like the mad woman in the attic. Occasionally you hear her scream

110

but you daren't unlock the door and have a look in. Am I right?'

The prisoner pursed his lips. 'I think there's a great sadness in your life.'

Fitz aimed a little smile at Penhaligon. There was, as he expected, no response. He sucked on his high tar, blew out smoke, gestured with the cylinder before placing it gently back on the edge of the ashtray. 'This crime of yours – in the grand scheme of things, is nothing. It's nature. Nature knows: men have to penetrate women or the species dies. Now with all that at stake do you really think nature cares how we do it?'

No response from the prisoner. Penhaligon was a different matter. Had she sat up just a little straighter? Was that movement of the legs an uncomfortable twitch?

'Whether we say please or thank you. Whether she's willing? Mmm?'

The man licked his lips. Out of the corner of his eye Fitz saw Penhaligon roll the papers he'd given her into a tube, tighter and tighter, unconsciously.

'Sex crimes,' he continued. 'A little of what nature requires, taken to excess. Murder too.' Casual, drop it into the conversation, gauge the response. 'Healthy aggression taken a little to excess.' There. That flickering of the eyes. Was that fear? Had he touched on a raw nerve here? Get in there, check it out. 'I'm saying I understand. Yes?'

'Yes.' Not fear; disgust.

Another drag on the high tar and Fitz was up, circling the table, trying for another angle on it, probing, digging; and the man was twisting to face him, turning back to the desk when Fitz passed behind, back to the desk and Penhaligon beyond. 'They'll crucify you for it of course. You know why? Because you've gone and done exactly what they've always wanted to do, deep down in their hearts: murdered. Butchered. Raped.'

Fitz studied the back of the man's head. Muscles were twitching there in his neck. Beyond, Penhaligon sat perfectly still in her chair, obviously determined not to show a reaction to his words.

111

'They'll look at you and they'll be looking deep into their own hearts and it will terrify them.' Now he was back again, in front of the desk, and there was a reaction from the prisoner, a big one. The blankness was fading. The eyes were closed; he was gone in some interior landscape. Was he remembering? 'They'll crucify you out of fear. Not out of decency or justice or anything like that. Out of fear.'

The man opened his eyes, looked up at Fitz. 'I disagree.'

Fitz sat, leaned forward. Something was happening here. Some force was being released into the room. There was a tempo, he could feel it, dictating the pace of the dialogue. The overture had finished; it was time for the symphony.

'You're walking down the corridor on the train. You go past her compartment. You look in through the window. She's sitting there. Young, beautiful, alone. Vulnerable. Everything a woman should be. She's reading a book. She's got her legs crossed. She's showing . . . oh, maybe an inch, maybe two, of thigh . . . warm, soft, smooth, white thigh. You pull open the door. Her eyes flicker but she doesn't look up from her book. You sit down opposite her. You look at her. She can feel you staring at her. She just stares even harder into her book but you know she's not really reading it. Her legs are shaking to the rhythm of the train and you want to put your hand up there on that soft white thigh, just to stop it from shaking, just to stop her from shaking. If you did that she'd look at you, she'd smile, she'd know. She'd just know.'

The man licked his lips. To one side Penhaligon shuffled in her chair. Fitz knew she wanted to get up, knew she wanted out. Just as the man wanted out; Fitz could see it in the rapid blinking of his eyes, the tenseness of the muscles around his mouth. On the table his hands were clasped together, tightly together, the knuckles whitening.

'So you get up and you open the window and your legs brush hers and she makes a little movement and she shows a little bit more thigh, perhaps. And you sit down beside her, closer this time and you can smell her – '

fear her terror, her

' – perfume, and the blood's pumping through her throat and it's making the little silver crucifix around her neck shake and catch the light a little, and she's everything a woman should be; alone, vulnerable.'

His hands were twisting together now, his eyes half closed, and Fitz could feel the heat coming off him in waves, the anger, the thrill of it, the thrill of violation, and now his eyes were shut again and he was remembering it, Fitz was taking him back there and he was remembering it, and the crescendo was drawing very near.

'You say something. She looks up from her book and gives you a yes or a no answer, then goes straight back to her book again. She's dismissed you. She's dismissed you the way every woman has always dismissed you. Well you'll show her. Even the train's urging you on. Even the train. Kill. It tells you. Kill the bitch. Kill the bitch. Kill the bitch. Kill the bitch. Kill the bitch. Kill the bitch. Kill the bitch.'

And now his voice was accelerating the tempo, forcing it to play to his rhythm, while the man squirmed on his chair, the rubber tips on the legs squeaking, and his hands tangled together like tree roots, and the heat from him was a palpable thing, pushing Fitz, pushing him away; so Fitz pushed right back, as hard as he could and the words came out of him as he knew they would, and they were his friends, these words, he understood them, they worked for him, they were his army, his footsoldiers, his friends.

'They're all the same aren't they? With their white thighs and their smooth white shoulders and necks but underneath it all they're blood and filth and stench and *hair* – tatty, matted, disfiguring hair, you think that don't you? As you're killing? As you kill? The hair, the girl, the bitch? Kill the bitch. Kill the bitch. Kill the bitch. Kill the bitch. Kill the bitch. Kill the bitch. Kill the bitch. Kill the bitch.'

A sound from the man. A moan. Pleasure? Pain? Both?

'Is that how it was?'

Push him. Now!

'Tell me! Is that how it was?'

The eyes tightly shut, mouth a thin line, face white, the bruises, the wounds stark against the pale skin.

Push, see the light, there, through the cracks in the mirror. There! There's the truth, hiding away in the corner, in the

113

darkness, chase it, get it out!

'Is that how it was?'

And the man opened his eyes. Gazed at Fitz. Made a little noise of disgust.

'It's you who needs the psychologist.'

And then his head was down on his one good arm, on the table, and he was crying.

Fitz let out a shuddering breath.

And there was a sound from beside him. Penhaligon. Jesus. Her chair scraped as she rose, headed past him for the door, handed him the papers as she went. The papers she'd wrung to the thickness of a pencil.

'We're ready to come out now.' Her voice was firm as she instructed the constables waiting outside to remove the prisoner. She glanced at Fitz just once before leaving the room, her face utterly expressionless.

Fitz sighed again. Some days the rules changed faster than he could keep up with.

He reached for his high tar.

It had burned to ash.

18:30–20:00

Penhaligon knew she should have reported back to Bilborough, but she didn't go straight back to the duty room. She went instead with the two constables to make sure the prisoner was placed back into his cell. At least, that's what she told herself she did. But in truth it was something else that took her down the iron bannistered staircase, along the drab corridor, past the duty station and into the lockups.

The two constables placed the prisoner – she wasn't about to fall into the trap of thinking of him as Sweeney despite Bilborough's confidence – back into the trough, the cell normally kept reserved for overnight drunks, teenage chancers and the like. She nodded her thanks as they went past her back up the corridor, after sealing the door, handing the key back to the duty officer as they went.

Penhaligon moved slowly down the corridor towards the

door. It was big, old fashioned, made of thick oak reinforced with steel bands. In the centre of the door at head height was a steel framed observation hatch. The hatch was fitted with a single pane of one-way glass about four inches square. Big enough to allow observation of the prisoner. Penhaligon slid back the hatch slowly, wincing as it squeaked, placed her eye close to the glass.

Through the glass she could see the bare tiled room. The prisoner had removed the thin plastic mattress from the bunk and placed it on the floor. He was kneeling on it. He was praying.

Penhaligon frowned. Who the hell was this man? She studied his side profile for a moment, watching his lips move silently, seeing the stitches shift as his forehead creased with concentration. She strained to hear the words he spoke. Would they provide a clue as to his identity? Would they indicate his innocence or guilt?

Young. Beautiful. Alone.

What was going through his mind? How had Fitz's words affected him? Was he covering up? Or was his disgust as genuine as hers?

Vulnerable.

Penhaligon sniffed, pursed her lips. Inside the cell, the prisoner clambered stiffly to his feet; he seemed physically exhausted, as if the words had been blows, as if he'd been assaulted.

Everything a woman should be.

And he looked at her then, right through the one way glass, and even though she knew he couldn't see her, she felt the depth of his gaze, could almost feel him crying out to her; not for mercy, for forgiveness, but for relief from Fitz, from Bilborough, from Beck; the nutters who were condemning him, who were supposed to be his judges.

She slammed the metal hatch shut quickly, turned to lean against the door. She pressed her back against it and struggled to regain her breath.

'Everything OK down there, Sergeant?' The voice of the duty officer sounded metallic and distant in the shining corridor.

'Fine. I'll be out in a sec.' Penhaligon levered herself away from the wall. Keeping her back straight and her face neutral, she walked quickly past the duty officer's desk.

Giggs smiled briefly at her as she entered incident. 'Your dad phoned. Bilborough took the call.'

'Ta Giggsy. I'll call him back later.' She nodded towards the glass pane separating the duty room from Bilborough's office, inside which the DCI and Fitz were deep in conversation. 'Debriefing.'

Giggs smile broadened. 'Just like in the war.'

She nodded, knocked on the office door, walked in. Fitz was on his feet, turning to leave. 'Ah, speak of the devil.'

Bilborough waved her into the room. 'OK?'

She nodded.

'Learn anything?'

Penhaligon looked at Fitz. *Bloody right I did.* 'It was a useful session. Thanks for letting me sit in, Doctor Fitzgerald.'

'Fitz.' Patient.

'Your dad phoned.' Bilborough. Slight reproval.

'So Giggsy said.'

'Everything OK?'

'Yes.'

'Well, I'll be leaving now.' Fitz again. Words aimed at Bilborough, eyes directed towards her.

'OK, Fitz. I'll have a think about what you said. We'll talk again tomorrow.'

'Fine.'

Penhaligon stared at Bilborough as Fitz left the office, only turned her head when he was gone, to watch him cruise through the duty room, exchanging quips with Giggs and Jonesy, aiming an interested stare at Beck before leaving the room altogether. She wondered what he would do now. Where he would go. Back to his office? His home? His wife?

Young. Beautiful. Alone.

He accused the prisoner of raping before he murdered. He knew there was no rape involved. Why had he done that? Had he spoken to Copeley? Did he know something they didn't?

116

Vulnerable.

He was obsessed. A driven man. After the conversation the prisoner looked as if he'd been in a fight. She almost expected bruises.

Everything a woman should be.

'– hello there. Penhaligon?' She became aware Bilborough was talking to her, had been for some moments. 'Are you with us?'

She turned. *No I'm with the bloody Woolwich.* 'Sir?' She raised her eyebrows, invited him to continue.

'Look. I think it's about time we had a little chat, don't you?'

'Sir?'

Bilborough sighed. 'Sit down will you?'

She sat. Waited.

'What's the problem?' Quiet. Friendly. Probing.

'Sir?'

'The problem. This last fortnight you've been wandering around here like a bear with a toothache. Something's bothering you. In my department, one of my staff is bothered, they come to me, we sort it out, OK?'

'Sir.'

'Well. What's the problem?'

You are.

'It's nothing, sir. Just a bit under the weather, that's all.'

Bilborough stared at her, steepled his fingers.

She sighed. 'It's nothing, really. It's . . . I can deal with it.'

Bilborough leaned back in his seat. 'Penhaligon, you're a good police officer. You come highly recommended by your old department head and the board loved you at the interview. But promotion brings new responsibilities, I know that. If there's ever anything you want to talk about . . . well. I'm here, OK?'

'Thank you, sir.'

'Alright. Now for heavens' sake cheer up, will you, they'll think I've fired you.'

She smiled thinly.

'Now about this interview. I've got the tape to listen to yet but I gather there wasn't much joy, right?'

117

'Not really, sir.'

'Tell me, what's your evaluation of Fitz's methods? Is he any good? Did he get any kind of result?'

You could say that.

'Yes.'

'Do you think he'll crack Sweeney?'

If it is Sweeney.

'He could crack anyone, sir.'

'Well. That's what I wanted to hear.' Bilborough stood, dismissive. Penhaligon stood too, hesitated.

'Sir . . . about my theory . . .'

'The killer being a woman? What about it?'

'I'd like permission to follow it up. There are a few simple checks I can do. It might even have been someone Jacqui knew.'

'Look. It's a good idea. In other circumstances it might even warrant looking into, but . . .'

'If it's the phone call you're worried about, well that was obviously a crank. I wouldn't let it cloud the issue.'

'And I wouldn't let a redundant theory cloud the issue of sending Sweeney down.'

Penhaligon pursed her lips, said nothing.

'Alright?'

'Yes, sir.'

Bilborough pursed his lips. 'Alright then, that's it. Might as well knock off for the night. Tell the others, will you?'

Somehow the thought of another evening at home held no appeal for Penhaligon. Another night in with the kit, the telly; maybe a phone call to Dad. If she could bear it.

It was with careful deliberation that she decided on her plans for the evening. First she drove to the mortuary. For once Copeley was dressed in a suit rather than blood lathered overalls.

'Should I take this lack of blood as a good omen?' Penhaligon asked with rather more of a smile in her voice than she expected.

'Only if you like the smell of embalming fluid. Come in DS Penhaligon. What can I do for you tonight? Something to add to the list to look for on Jacqui's corpse?'

Penhaligon nodded as she followed Copeley into the office. 'Any traces of perfume. And check the scratches on Jacqui's body for traces of nail varnish.'

'You're really keen on this idea of Sweeney being a woman aren't you?'

She nodded again.

'I'm not sure you're right you know.'

'Oh?'

'That's right. You're getting desperate with this perfume and nail varnish stuff. Coffee?'

Penhaligon was about to refuse when she realised how much she needed a cup. 'Thanks.' She grasped the mug Copeley supplied her with gratefully. 'You've no idea how much I need this.'

'Bilborough's not into your theory, is he?'

She shook her head slowly, took another sip of coffee.

'It's understandable, you know. He's a rising star. The new golden boy. Wild theories do not hand in hand go.'

'Is it so wild?'

Copeley gestured at the filing cabinets stacked up against one wall of his office. 'I've been in this business thirty four years. In those cabinets are records of more than seven thousand cases in which I have personally been the principal pathologist. I've performed post mortems by torchlight and been presented with corpses in winter that were frozen so you couldn't cut them with a saw let alone a knife. I've seen the end result of murder upon murder, for reason upon reason upon reason. And in my experience they all boil down to one thing: sex. All killings are ultimately linked in some way with sex. Either emotionally driven, as in such cases as jealousy or frustrated desire, or sexually motivated, as exemplified in the desire to possess, or to prevent others from possessing the object of desire.'

'Are you saying there was a sexual motivation in the case of Jacqui's murder?'

'Without having performed the post mortem it's hard to be precise. It's just that if it turns out there is a sexual motiva-tion, then it's less likely to be one associated with a killer of the same gender. In my experience.'

Penhaligon frowned. 'Don't you think you're being a little old fashioned?'

Copeley shrugged. 'It's possible. In any case, forensically speaking, if there are no traces of sexual fluids on the body, it's almost always impossible to determine the gender of the killer. Obviously women have killed women before and no doubt will do so again. But ... there's something about this ... about Jacqui ... all my instincts are telling me it's a normal, sexually repressed male killer we're dealing with here.'

'Normal!'

Copeley grinned. 'You have to understand that normal in my profession may have a slightly different definition than the one you're used to.'

'Or the one Bilborough's used to.'

'He's as much rooted in his own experience as anyone. And if you'll forgive me making a truthful observation he is a little ... narrow of vision, shall we say?'

Penhaligon pursed her lips, drained her coffee. Thought back to the interview, other conversations in which Fitz had taken part. 'Fitz agrees with all this ...' she realised aloud, 'Fat misogynistic bastard ...' She looked up. 'There must be something you can do to determine the gender of the killer.'

'Well. There is a test. It's not a new one, but it is complicated, and time consuming. And it requires a sample of the killer's blood from the scene of the crime, or from the body. No matter how small a trace the blood will normally contain some white cells. These can be cultured and, in sufficient quantity, can be analysed. A gene scan can determine the sex of the owner of the blood.'

Penhaligon frowned thoughtfully, excitement stirring in her chest. 'So, if we could get a sample of blood from Jacqui's body that wasn't hers, and do the test, then we'd be halfway to proving the prisoner's guilt or innocence?'

Copeley nodded. 'The trick is to find some blood on Jacqui that isn't hers.'

'Is that possible?'

'That depends on a lot of factors. But we'll know to-morrow.'

'That's when you're conducting the post mortem?'

'That's right. We're clearing the decks for action around one-thirty. We'll let you know, anyway.'

Penhaligon nodded her thanks and allowed Copeley to escort her from the building.

As she pulled out of the mortuary car park Penhaligon's mind was a fuzzy blur of excitement. She was sure she was on the trail of something; at the very least she ought to pursue her line of enquiry if only to prove it false. That was the thing that annoyed her most about Bilborough's attitude. For one who had come so far so fast in his career it seemed a bit arse about face not to check out every possibility.

Then again wasn't that just Bilborough all over? What was going on in his head? Was he so sure that he was right? Were he and Beck playing the odds together, hoping for a fast conviction, a solid tick in the book? Or could it be simpler than that? Could it just be that he was a sexist and didn't even realise it?

Penhaligon sighed as she braked to a halt outside the Appleby's house. This line of thinking was going to get her nowhere. Bilborough was her boss. She bucked him at her own risk. So she'd better make sure she came up with the goods.

She got out of the car and walked up the path, knocked on the door. Simon Appleby let her in.

'Hello, sorry to trouble you . . . I was wondering whether I could take another look at Jacqui's room.'

'I'll get Ann.'

'Thank you.'

Ann agreed, just as Penhaligon thought she would, the unspoken message in her eyes begging silently beneath her words of greeting: *Get the killer out of the way. I want to grieve for my daughter. Get him out of the way, please.*

Fitz hit the high street with a wallet full of fivers and a black rage churning inside. Nothing was right. What had happened to the game? Nothing was right. The prisoner should have crumbled before his onslaught as Jericho had crumbled before the trump. Because words had power. They were his weapons, his armour. He knew how to wield them in defence or attack. He knew. So why this vacuum where knowledge should have been? Why hadn't the prisoner opened up, spilled his innermost thoughts?

Fitz slapped the palm of his hand against a lamp post as he cruised past.

What had gone wrong? Why had he been wrong? The interview had hardly been regulation issue, but there ought to have been some result: all that had happened was that instead of cracking the mirror wide open, Fitz had found himself staring at a more perfect reflection of himself.

It's you who needs the psychologist.

Was that true?

Fitz blew out his cheeks, earning himself a giggle from a couple strolling by, entwined in each other. Was that all he was worth now, a giggle?

Well bugger that for a game of soldiers. He'd given Bilborough his evaluation. The prisoner would remember something if he kept at it, the mirror would break if he kept hammering away at the glass for long enough. Tomorrow; tomorrow was soon enough for success. The truth couldn't hide forever. And in the meantime . . . in the meantime, there were ways of bolstering the slim width of his wallet.

The betting shop unofficially known in the circle of punters as Eddie's was shut, but that didn't stop Fitz. An impatient tap on the blank green glass door beneath the words Chartered Turf Accountant brought a man with a vacuum cleaner whirring towards the door.

He shook his head when he saw Fitz. *We're closed.*

Fitz smiled. 'It's OK. Eddie's expecting me,' he called through the glass.

The vacuum cleaner man's mouth moved silently. *What?*

'It's OK.' Louder. 'Eddie's. Expecting. Me.'

'Pardon?' This time Fitz heard the words faintly above the buzz of the Hoover.

Open the door you old scroat and let me in, then you'll hear what I have to say.

Fitz was on the point of turning away when there was a movement behind the vacuum cleaner man. He turned, cocked his head to one side as if listening, then nodded. He switched off the vacuum cleaner and opened the door for Fitz.

Fitz moved inside with a nod.

Eddie was ensconced behind the glass window; both hands in the cash drawer, a gentle look on his threadbare features.

Fitz knew that look. When Eddie looked happy, he was invariably at his worst. He decided to chance it anyhow. 'How are you fixed, Eddie?'

Eddie's face relaxed a little further. 'Dumb question, Fitz.'

'How about cashing a cheque?'

The smile elongated; another moment, Fitz thought, and Eddie's features would ooze right off his skull. 'No chance, Fitz.'

Fitz sighed. One last shot. 'Am I speaking Urdu or something?'

Eddie just looked up and grinned. Fitz felt he could have pulled that grin through the glass and Eddie with it, stretched it out like a Tex Avery cartoon and let it splatter back against Eddie's head. Instead he turned, walked past the vacuum cleaner man, now humming happily along with the tools of his trade, left the shop.

Outside the shop a cold wind bit through his suit. He shook his head. Cold summer. Typical British weather. And the weather was inside his head too, cold, blustery, undefined thoughts rattling around in there like hail. And then through the fuzz of confusion a clear thought like the note of a bell on a mountain slope, and a shape to go with the thought.

Fitz lifted the phone from the cradle, groped in his pocket for the number Judith had left for Mark.

'Hello?' It was her voice. Clear as that mountain bell, pushing away the hail and slurry of indecision.

'It's me. Don't hang up, please.' And there was a force in him, spinning in him, gathering strength, and this was right, it felt right, he would tell her it all now: that he knew the game had changed, that he was learning the new rules, had it under control at last. 'I haven't had a bet or a drink for two days.'

And there was the moment, that ripe, shining moment when you were *right*.

And then her voice, no longer clear, but attenuated by distance and anger. 'That's because you haven't got any money, Fitz.'

And the phone was a dead piece of plastic in his hand, no longer an umbilicus to another life, the irritable whine of disconnection grating painfully inside his head and filling the awful silence down the line.

He held the phone tightly against his ear as traffic rumbled past, unwilling to let it go. Attachment. Dependency. The phone had been his connection to her, for a moment it had *been* her. Now the electronic whine served to sharpen his thoughts. He let out a breath. Judith wasn't going to let it go just like that. Not twenty years. She –

He placed the receiver back on the cradle, a crazy thought forming in his mind.

She was –

A bus rumbled past in a clatter of dirt and noise.

She was *probably playing the game herself.*

And that was it. Finally, here in the high street with traffic rumbling and filling the air with dirt, and kids cycling and screeching away up there on Penn Street by the bank and a dog barking at a taxi driver by the entrance to the mall, that was it. And he knew. He got it. The new game. The new rules. Judith's rules. She didn't want to leave him at all. She only wanted him to change. Just to change.

And Fitz was back in cruise mode. He jammed the last of Bilborough's high tars into his mouth, lit up, added to the dirt in the air, but didn't even notice because his mind was whirling with the sharp, glittering realisation that he knew what to do now. Knew what to do to get her back.

He only hoped he could do what it was she wanted.

And then it was arm out, flag down the bus, take an upstairs seat so he could watch the evening draw in, see enlightenment in every flickering streetlamp; and even the ticket inspector couldn't annoy him because he had a destination, a goal, a shining goal.

And then he was off the bus and along the street, rattling his fist against the door, and Ann Appleby was opening it, ushering him into the hall with a distant smile.

'Hello, Fitz.'

'Ann.'

A moment of quiet, a moment to study each other while Simon Appleby's voice came from the lounge where a one-sided conversation made it obvious he was speaking into the telephone. 'Could you tell me where you got this number? No, you couldn't have, we're ex-directory. How do you think we feel? Look, I'm putting the phone down. Have you got any children? Then you should know better!'

'Sorry to trouble you.'

Ann nodded absently. No. Not absently. Exactly the opposite, preoccupied, utterly full with thoughts and feelings and desires. And no way of expressing them. A woman close to the edge. Close to breaking strain.

He softened his voice even further. 'Would you mind if I had a look around Jacqui's bedroom?'

'No, of course.'

'Perfect.'

'DS Penhaligon's up there already.'

Fitz frowned, caught a little off balance, nodded. 'Thanks.'

'I'll see you up.'

'Thanks.'

And there was Simon, popping his head out of the lounge, a little wave, just a waggle of the fingers. *Hi there.* And Fitz sensed something from Ann as he followed her up the stairs to the first floor landing, a heat, a pressure, and then at the top of the stairs she turned to face him and he knew.

'I'll leave him. When it's all over and she's buried.'

'Why?' There was surprise in Fitz's voice, but deep down inside there was no surprise. Because he'd seen that look on Judith's face all too recently. And he knew what it meant.

'Because it's what she wanted.'

That was a surprise. 'Jacqui? But she loved you.'

'She pitied me. For staying with him.'

Fitz began to speak again but Ann was already turning to lead the way along the landing to the furthest door.

She paused with her fingers on the door handle. 'Everything's exactly as it was. She left all her stuff here. Books, videos she made. Safer than at the university.'

Fitz nodded. Waited. After a moment Ann opened the door and stood aside to let him enter. 'I'll leave you then.' She turned and went back downstairs.

Fitz entered the room.

And Penhaligon looked up at him from the bed, an island in a room full of letters and photos, books, videos and other junk, trinkets, parts of a life, all that remained of a life.

'Panhandle.' Keep it light.

'Penhaligon, Doctor Fitzgerald.' Irritation. Perhaps a little melancholy.

'Fitz.'

'Whatever.'

Was she here in her official capacity? If so it was an odd time to be conducting an investigation. 'Haven't the police already looked through all this stuff?'

'I thought I'd take a second look.'

'I see. Have you found anything? Any clues from the dead girl's past?'

Penhaligon got up from the bed, a video tape in one hand. She crossed the room, put the tape in the VCR machine sitting beside a portable telly on the dresser. Switched the television on.

On the screen was a miniature of the university grounds, the cropped lawns, old stone bordered by sculpted trees, the scene filled with wandering figures. As he watched one enlarged.

'That's me,' said Fitz.

The camera panned to take it all in, the grounds, the crowd of students, Fitz himself, and walking beside him, Jacqui.

Penhaligon turned up the volume. '– invite me to your clinic one day Fitz! You must get all sorts of nutters there.'

'At least they don't all point cameras at me.' A grin. And Jacqui took his arm, a sprite next to a wood giant, footsteps booming loud across the grass. And she was waving to the camera, bringing it in for a two shot, a close-up.

'What's your best feature?'

Fitz laughed. 'My best feature? Oh definitely my chin.'

'Oh yeah! Which one?'

And in the bedroom, an older Fitz moved his lips in a perfect mimic of the words. ' "No, really, if you want an honest answer, I'd have to say . . . my sense of humour. What about you?" '

And he was reaching for the video remote, firing it at the machine, and last summer jerked to a halt; freeze frame on a dead girl's face, her smile, mouth open to form the reply which would never come, and suddenly the game took on another twist, and Penhaligon, the room, the whole world seemed to warp around him, and he was falling into himself, into the gravity well of his memories.

Jacqui.

Penhaligon's voice brought him back to the here and now. 'Why did you say he'd raped Jacqui?'

'What?'

'The prisoner. The man they all think is Sweeney. Why did you tell him he'd committed rape?'

'Shock.' Fitz sat on the edge of the bed, studied Jacqui's open mouth, the perfect even teeth inside her smile. 'I wanted to see if I could shock him, change his state, either emotionally or physically.'

'Fitz, that's dangerous.'

'So's crossing the road.'

Penhaligon sighed. 'I'm not going to spend the rest of the evening bandying truisms with you.'

'Fine. Leave the tape on your way out.'

Penhaligon shook her head. 'Wrong way around. I'm staying. These tapes are interesting. I didn't realise you knew her so well.'

Fitz rubbed his hand across his face. 'Well, Inspector Clouseau, keep digging. You never know what dirt you'll find in there. She probably saw me as a father figure or something, maybe she even fancied me.'

He looked up as Penhaligon narrowed her eyes. Interesting. He could feel the coldness emanating from her. Now what had he said that could have engendered that reaction?'

'Hardly likely.'

He sighed. 'Perhaps we'd better call a truce.'

Penhaligon looked at him. He met her gaze frankly. And it

clicked into place. 'You're here out of hours aren't you? What's the matter? Got a theory Bilborough won't let you follow up?'

Silence.

Got you.

'That's it, isn't it? You've got a theory and he's got a killer – that's how he sees it anyway. Your theory would clear his suspect . . . it all makes sense.'

Penhaligon shot the VCR with the remote, took the tape out, boxed it.

'You're right. This is all useless. If there had been anything here we'd have found it the first time round.'

'Well then, Panhandle.' Fitz scooped a handful of photographs of Jacqui into his pocket, stood. 'Why don't you invite me back to your place so we can talk about it?'

Penhaligon put the video back on a nearby shelf. 'You must be joking.'

Fitz plastered a big grin across his face. 'It's alright, my wife won't suspect. She left me as a matter of fact.'

'Bad joke, Fitz.'

He sighed. 'They seem to be my forte lately.' He hesitated. 'Don't suppose you fancy a quick half? You look like you've got some sorrows of your own to drown.'

'No thanks. A bath and then bed, that's me. Early start tomorrow.'

He nodded. 'I understand.'

'Post mortem's at one-thirty.'

'It's a date.'

Penhaligon shook her head sadly and left the bedroom. Fitz lingered in the room long after the sounds of Ann showing her out and the door closing had faded. Then he picked up the tape Penhaligon had played and slipped it into his pocket, next to the photographs of Jacqui. Then he switched off the light, left the room, said his goodbyes to the Applebys and made his way home.

Mark was still out when he arrived home three quarters of an hour later. He put the video into the machine, poured himself a vodka while the tape rewound, had second thoughts and grabbed the whole bottle as the tape began to play.

The vodka and the tape unwound together in his mind; he fell asleep with a head full of memories: the smell of newly cut grass, the purity of a summer sky, the sound of a girl's laughter rippling lightly over his own like a stream trickling across a bed of stones.

He awoke once, hours later, to a darkened room, a rectangle of static smeared by eyes full of tears. Jacqui. Judith. The names blurred together in his mind like the shapes on the TV screen, melding confusingly until sleep claimed him again, and held him until morning.

– in death, blood dripping lazily from one perfect lash to splash against the pupil, and her last involuntary breath, driven from her by his weight on her body, bubbled out from the red lipped mouth gaping in her throat, the mouth closing even now as her eyes bulged gently in death –

FOUR

Thursday

09:00–14:30

Bilborough was determined to keep up the pressure on Sweeney. He called Fitz in first thing the next morning. Sweeney was yanked out of his cell by Beck, allowed no respite to perform a toilet or to have breakfast, but was instead taken back to the interview room, where Fitz waited for him with a bleak look and another sheaf of papers.

The papers turned out to be photographs. Somehow Fitz had managed to get hold of some photos of Jacqui Appleby; they ranged from her aged about eight to her aged about seventeen. Ten years of a life intercut with the scene of crime photographs Murphy had taken on the day of the murder. Fitz slapped them down in front of Sweeney, one after another, testament to a life savagely curtailed. And the look on the psychologist's face was downright scary; blank, his voice an expressionless echo of his features. Bilborough had to admit, when Fitz went for it, he really went for it.

As he placed the photographs on the table Fitz let his gaze sweep over the man facing him. Unshaven. Looked like he hadn't slept for a week. The wounds on his face stark and bloodless, the stitches in his forehead dark as the shadows around his eyes, his arm bent beneath his jacket, as much a prisoner in its cast as his memory was a prisoner in his head, a prisoner Fitz was determined to set free. No. Not a prisoner. A fugitive. One he was determined to track down and bring to book.

The photographs might be the key. He let half a dozen or

so fall on the table without saying a word.

Jacqui aged ten, balanced precariously on a pony.

Jacqui aged sixteen or so, kissing a boyfriend at a party, eyes closed, wearing an embarrassed grin.

Jacqui aged eight, arms spread, squealing with joy as she glided down a slide in her back garden.

Jacqui aged nineteen, arms spread, mouth gaping with horror, face lathered with blood, throat slashed to ribbons.

A close-up of her chest, skin flayed almost to the breastbone in some places.

Another profile of her face, eyes wide and empty in death.

Happiness and joy and love taken and violated, opened to the world and discarded.

Fitz took a moment to study the prisoner's face. He was breathing fast. Murphy's photographs had the clinical detachment of the professional photographer. The lighting was stark, every detail clear and precise, a hideous comparison to the warmth and life displayed in the photographs Fitz paired them with.

As the sixth shot went down on the table with a flat slapping noise, the prisoner flinched. Fitz homed in on that, concentrated on it. 'The first thought that comes into your head.'

'What?' Stunned, away somewhere, lost in the photographs.

'When I ask you a question. I want the first word that comes into your head. You understand? The first word.'

A nod. He seemed beyond words. Fitz pushed anyway. 'A colour.'

The man didn't reply, eyes locked on the latest photograph.

'I said: *a colour*.' Snap the words out. Force an answer.

'Red.'

And another pair of photographs on the table: Jacqui hanging ornaments from a Christmas tree; Jacqui sprawled across the blood soaked rubber matting of a train carriage.

'A holiday resort.'

'Blackpool.'

'A city.'

132

'London.'

' "Amo, amas, amat." '

' "Amamus, amatis, amant." '

Jacqui pointing, caught in the act of hurling a frisbee; Jacqui's arm outflung, her hands, her fingers sliced into a parallel set of red and white lines.

'A sport.'

'Rugby.'

'A river.'

'The Thames.'

'A woman's name.'

'Mary.'

And Jacqui's life flickered by, a frieze in black and white and scarlet. Her smiling. Her waving. Her hugging her mother. Her mouth gaping, fringed with blood, her fingers, pointing in mute accusation, her chest and legs slashed and bloodied.

'A man's name.'

Her mouth –

'Joseph.'

– eyes –

'A country.'

– shaven belly –

'England.'

– open throat –

'I knew her.'

'What!' The admission was jerked out of the prisoner, a mixture of pity and revulsion and surprise. Fitz recognised that look. Shellshock. He had him now.

'Jacqui. I knew her. Young. Beautiful. Energetic. Intelligent. Seeing all that in one human being depresses you doesn't it?'

Blank incomprehension. A mirror. But one whose surface was beginning to tremble. Fitz snarled out the words. He had the truth on the run now.

'It brings it home to you how pathetic you are, how worthless, how boring, how dead you are. How unattainable she is. Makes you want to grab it, snuff it out, kill it, destroy it. Is that how you felt?'

133

Eyes wide, imploring, but whether to stop or to continue?
An interesting point if he were to take the time to analyse it;
but there was no time. Or rather the time was now. Now.

'I understand. Is that how you felt? I've been there. I've
felt that.'

'I –'

And hit him again, the words like blows, raining on his
face, making him flinch, shut his eyes to avoid the horror.

'A country.'

'Italy.'

Jacqui laughing on College Green with a bunch of
friends –

'A number. Any number.'

'Two double one, nine, oh, two.'

– mouth open in a soundless scream of pain –

'An animal.'

'A dog.'

– cavorting joyfully with a huge setter in a garden –

'Alpha, beta, gamma, delta.'

'Epsilon, seta, eta, theta.'

– eyes wide, little pools of blood in her ravaged face –

'Who made you?'

– fingers crooked, one torn almost to the bone –

'God made me.'

– and her eyes –

'Why did God make you?'

– and her gaping mouths –

'God made me to know Him and love Him and serve Him
in this world, and to be happy with Him forever in the next.'

'A writer.'

'Dickens.'

And pace it now, soften just a little, now the cracks are
starting to show; put away the bludgeon, bring out the fine
tools. 'I know you've got a conscience. I know that deep
down you're a good man. I've been to the house twice.
Met the parents. Can you imagine what you've put them
through?'

And more pictures rained down in front of the prisoner,
and he was unable to look away, and Fitz began to pile on the

pressure, feeling the moment was close, so close.

'What they've been through? It's not grief. Grief is a process they can't even begin thanks to you.'

And more, the pile spreading across the table, spilling onto the floor, unstoppable, undeniable.

'It's desolation. Cold, bleak, numb desolation. The daughter they loved is dead.'

There. Hit him with it, smack him in the face with it, see him flinch from the truth, let it go, get it out of hiding!

'The daughter they loved is down in the morgue in a refrigerated cupboard.'

Watch him flinch from the words. But hold off now. Back to the gentle pressure. A subtle push.

'Let them bury her. People will say: he was a killer, he was a butcher, but he did one decent thing. He confessed so they could bury their daughter.'

Soft. Hold him with your eyes.

'It's the one last decent thing you can do.'

Softer. A gentle push.

'Please.'

A pause. The moment passed.

He'd pushed too hard.

He'd lost him.

As two uniformed constables led the prisoner out of the interview room, Fitz found himself thinking of Judith. How his perception of her had changed. Of his realisation that she didn't want to leave him, but that she simply wanted him to change. He hadn't been wrong exactly, but off base. He frowned. Something about the prisoner reminded him of Judith. What was it?

He allowed his gaze to slide sideways. Penhaligon was sitting against the wall, same place as before, hands in her lap. He hadn't even considered her presence during the interview, now he wondered what was going on in her head. How she had viewed the proceedings. If she approved of his methods.

Did he need her approval?

Where the hell had that thought come from?

He shook his head. None of that was important. What was

important was that his perception of things might be off base. What if he hadn't pushed Sweeney too far, hadn't lost him? What if there was nothing to lose? What if he wasn't hiding anything?

What if he wasn't guilty?

And suddenly the game warped again, and with it came the realisation that if the man was innocent, if he had really committed no crime, only he, Fitz, was likely to find out the truth. All Bilborough wanted was a fast conviction, a tick in the appropriate box. That was no good. It wasn't the truth. It was just a reflection of his own hopes and desires. Fitz could see a little further. Could see that there might in fact, be more to this man they were all thinking of as Sweeney. This man whom, in their own minds, Bilborough and his team, with the possible exception of Penhaligon, had already buried.

Fitz got to his feet, turned to Bilborough. The DCI looked expectantly at him. 'Have we got a result?'

I'll give you a result all right.

'We need to talk.'

Bilborough ushered Fitz and Penhaligon from the room. 'What?'

'First the background.'

'Background?'

Fitz nodded. 'Got a cigarette?'

'This is becoming a habit, Fitz.' There was no humour in Bilborough's voice.

'It became a habit twenty years ago.' Was that a hint of a curve to Penhaligon's lips? The merest suggestion of a smile?

'There's a machine in the corridor.'

'In a police station?' Fitz shook his head. 'What is the country coming to?'

Penhaligon said, ' "Amo, amas, amat?" '

Fitz aimed a look her way. 'It's Latin. "I love, you love, he loves." '

Penhaligon pursed her lips. 'I might have guessed.'

'What about that alpha beta stuff?' Bilborough. Determined not to be left out of the discussion.

Fitz pushed open the door to the duty room. 'You learn all

that crap when you're eleven. It never really leaves you. Same with the Catechism. He's a Catholic Grammar School boy.' Click of the tongue, faint disapproval. 'Same as me, God help him.'

'Now that is interesting, Fitz.' Penhaligon kept her face absolutely straight, but her voice held a smile a mile wide. Fitz narrowed his eyes and shot her another sideways glance, flapped his eyebrows a tad, just for effect. She didn't grin. Ah well.

Their way to Bilborough's office was blocked by Jones. 'That number. It's not a bank account or a national insurance number. We're checking out phone numbers but it doesn't look good.'

Bilborough nodded. 'Anyone else got any ideas?'

Fitz pursed his lips. 'A number from childhood?'

That got a round of blank faces. Beck broke the silence. 'Army number?' Fitz nodded. Predictable.

Bilborough nodded as well, turned back to Jones. 'Army, Navy, RAF. Get onto them.'

'Check.' Jones turned away, grabbed hold of Giggs by his collar. 'Come on Robin. To the Bat Phone.'

'Anyone else got the grain of a useful thought?'

Fitz noted the irritation in Bilborough's voice. Time for a little push. 'Go public.'

'Absolutely no chance.'

Another push. 'An appeal from the grieving mother . . . I'm right, aren't I, Panhandle?'

Penhaligon rolled her eyes. *Don't drag me into this, thank you very much!*

Fitz dryly nodded his thanks to Penhaligon for her non-existent support. 'Go public with his photograph. Does anyone recognise this man? You know the sort of thing.'

Bilborough ushered Fitz into his office, shut the door behind him as Penhaligon returned to her desk. When he spoke Fitz heard the impatience, the anger, the sheer frustration in his voice. 'Are you serious? The I.D. evidence wouldn't be worth a carrot. The defence would do a number on us.'

And Fitz was grinning now because he had it all in his

head, clear as a bell, clear as mirror glass. 'You wouldn't need a defence. Prove to him he did it and he'll confess.'

Bilborough sighed. 'You really believe that?'

'Yes!'

'Then you're a pillock.' Bilborough walked around his desk and sat heavily. 'Now what did we need to talk about?' *Have you got a result?*

Fitz looked away, looked through the glass dividing Bilborough's office from the duty room, raked his gaze across the organised chaos to where Penhaligon was talking on a phone. Looked back at Bilborough.

'I think he might be innocent.'

Bilborough opened his mouth, was half out of his chair before he realised he had nothing to say. He shut his mouth and sat down again. Fitz looked at the desk, the ashtray, the plastic trays full of papers, the clock, the ceiling, then back to Bilborough, lips widening into a smile as the DCI did a slow burn.

'You daren't even consider that, eh? You've got yourself a suspect so all your energy's concentrated into proving that he did it.'

Bilborough was gaping. Fish on a hook. Let him squirm a bit. Probably do him some good. God knows it felt good to Fitz to hammer home the point.

'You could prove he didn't do it but where would that get you? A classic policing error.'

Now Bilborough was fuming, Fitz could see it, saw the words boiling up from inside him, erupting from the surface. 'Piss off back to your clinic.'

Fitz sniffed. Looked Bilborough squarely in the face. 'He's never worn a watch you know.'

Bilborough blinked. 'What's that got to do with –' He stopped. Fitz knew what was going on inside his head. Rage. Affront. His pride had taken a knock and this new tack would keep him off balance, make him think. Hopefully.

'You ask him the time, he doesn't look at his wrist. He looks at the wall.'

Bilborough was subsiding into his chair. Fitz was making his point at last.

'I noticed that in the first interview. Even a couple of hours of sun would leave the beginnings of a tan and he doesn't have a white mark on his wrist.'

Bilborough said nothing. Fitz could see him working it through.

'What do we know about Sweeney?' The question was rhetorical; Fitz answered it himself anyway. 'He catches trains all the time. People who take trains wear watches.'

'And that's it? That proves he's innocent?'

Time to ease off. 'It proves he could be.'

Bilborough sighed. Fitz saw it all laid out like a picture book. The inside of his head. Clear as daylight. 'Go back to your clinic, Fitz.' But the words held no anger, only resignation. Bilborough couldn't refute Fitz's theory. It only remained to see how he would act on it.

There was a knock at the door. Penhaligon came in.

'Two double one nine oh two. A number from childhood?'

Bilborough made as if to speak but Fitz was there first, acknowledging the detective, urging her to continue.

'Four three nine six two one. My mum's Co-op number.' A grin.

Fitz's mind was whirling like the neon fruit on a one armed bandit. He was grinning madly. 'Double four double six two one. Panhandle, I love you.'

Bilborough was staring at Fitz and Penhaligon as if they were both mad. 'Well stop grinning and check the Co-op records. Find the bloody parents.'

Penhaligon shot Fitz a glance. *What a wonderful idea.*

Fitz just grinned and grinned. As Penhaligon left he turned to Bilborough and held out his hand. 'Eighty quid.'

Bilborough burrowed in his desk, came up with a slip of paper and a wage packet. 'Oh you even got cash you sweetie, you,' Fitz smiled as he signed the receipt with a flourish. Then he was away into the duty room with a brief nod when Bilborough reminded him of the post mortem that afternoon; catching up to Penhaligon, flipping her around with a look, a casual grin. 'A drink.'

'Do what?'

'A drink for the case breaker. As in: I'll buy you one.'

139

'Get away with you.'

'Aha. A good officer. Doing things by the book, well I can appreciate that. But Panhandle – and trust me on this – a drink is the correct procedure for this situation.'

A little grin, stand back, let her absorb the amused glances from Giggs and Jones and the others. Let her take her time.

'Fitz. I've got work to do.' She tapped the phone with a finger. 'Two double one nine oh two, remember?'

Fitz pursed his lips. 'Hm. I'm not entirely convinced, officer Panhandle. However –' a wry grin. 'I will accept a rain check on my most generous offer.'

'Good.' Penhaligon picked up the phone. 'See you at the Nuthatch.'

'Absolutely.' Fitz winked, turned, made a swift exit. As the doors banged shut behind him he heard her voice raised in mock anger.

'And it's *Penhaligon!*'

He grinned.

Outside the police station, Fitz turned left and headed towards the high street. On the corner as he reached the intersection was *The Robin Hood*, a small pub, unobtrusive, with reasonable looking food and even more reasonable looking Jack Daniels.

Fitz grinned at the barman as he ordered. 'You've no idea how much I deserve this,' he said.

Two double whiskys later he was comfortably ensconced in a fashionably battered armchair beside an open grate. No fire burned in the grate because it was a warm day, but the setting, combined with the alcohol he'd drunk, suffused Fitz with a warm glow. He felt very pleased with himself. He ordered another drink. A half hour passed. He looked at his watch. The post mortem was scheduled for one thirty; it was still an hour and a half away. As yet it was only lunchtime. At the Salford Project Judith would be sitting down to eat. At her school Katie would be doing the same. God knows what Mark would be doing. Probably wanking himself off in his bedroom, or asleep.

Fitz took out his wallet and counted the money Bilborough had given him. He thought about Eddie in the betting shop.

140

Thought about his face, thought of the fun he'd get out of seeing Eddie scowl when he won. He got up and left the pub, weaving slightly.

Outside on the high street a mild wind whipped dirt off the pavement into his face. Overhead the sun struggled to reassert itself through a thin layer of scudding cloud. Shoppers walked past Fitz as he headed for the bus stop, but he didn't register them. There was just him alone in the world. Him and the money and the bet and maybe, if he got it right, the moment. The moment that made everything else worthwhile.

And then the Arndale Centre was looming up in front of him, shiny in the sunlight, grey-green glass and ochre brick, stylish, modern, like the lego Katie used to play with when she'd been younger. At the thought another figure entered his rosy world. Katie. How long had it been since he'd heard her laugh? Seen her smile? Three days? Was that all? It seemed like forever.

Fitz stopped at Eddie's. Stared into the blank windows, saw his own reflection there. Shoved his hands into his pockets and fingered his wallet. Thought of winning. The buzz. Thought of Katie.

Then he turned away from the betting shop and continued walking along the street and into the Arndale.

Half an hour later, as he stood beside the wire mesh gates to the school Katie attended and watched as she ran into the building with the other kids, as she clutched the little package he'd bought for her, looking wonderingly at it, shaking it, trying to find out what was inside it, Fitz realised there were other ways to achieve the shining moment when life made sense, ways that didn't include gambling. Ways he'd forgotten until now.

He waved to Katie. She waved back and turned, smiling, to vanish into the school building.

He flagged down a taxi. The hell with the cost. For the time being at least he could afford it.

He arrived at the morgue sporting a lopsided and oddly peaceful smile which earned him a second glance from Penhaligon.

'Liquid lunch, Fitz?'

He allowed his smile to widen but said nothing. At that moment another car pulled into the car park and Bilborough stepped out. 'All set?' Without waiting for a reply he led the way into the building.

Copeley was waiting for them in the office. He was swaddled in a white plastic surgical smock. He gave them similar smocks to wear and gestured for them to precede him into the cold room.

Fitz saw his breath steaming in front of him as he pushed through the plastic swing doors into the room. It wasn't the first time he'd been in a mortuary. He noticed with interest that there seemed to be little difference between this and the one in Glasgow where he'd once held a summer job while studying for his degree. It was a little neater perhaps, a little more modern in appearance, but that was all. The room was large, approximately thirty feet square. One entire wall was taken up with a row of grey steel doors about three feet square. The end wall was glass, beyond it was a narrow observation chamber. A video camera was set up on a tripod in front of the glass, pointing towards the centre of the room where the body of Jacqui Appleby lay pale and cold on a theatre table. Sinks lined the right hand wall, along with a set of sterilising units and receptacles for instrument trays. The trays themselves were stacked on a wheeled trolley. A tall glass fronted cupboard held racks of surgical instruments in neat, gleaming rows. The floor was angled slightly, tiled in rubber, and had a channel running down the middle, in which were set several drains. All other surfaces were either painted steel or white ceramic. One wall held a roll chart of the human nervous system. It seemed to Fitz to be there more for decoration than any practical purpose. The rows of postcards pinned neatly to the bottom confirmed his supposition.

Copeley swept across the room, nodding to his assistant, who handed him a pair of surgical gloves. He pulled them on as the assistant wheeled a trolley containing a set of instruments towards the head of the table on which Jacqui lay.

'Thanks, Rudi.' Copeley pursed his lips as he snapped the gloves tight about his wrist, studied the face of the dead girl, let his eyes travel along her body to her feet and back again. He shook his head slowly. 'Beautiful isn't she.'

His statement was quite clearly rhetorical. Fitz made the distinction anyway. 'She was.'

Copeley lifted his eyes briefly to Fitz. Glanced at Penhaligon and winked. 'Is.'

Fitz frowned, said nothing.

'The wounds look impressive, don't they?' Copeley gestured towards the girl's neck, held in place by two moveable steel blocks, the ruff of blood crusting the second mouth there. 'But this is the one that killed her.'

Bilborough shuffled on his feet. Fitz glanced at him, wondered if it was the cold or the smell of the antiseptic that turned his face that pale colour. Perhaps it was just the harsh neon light. Fitz sniffed. He looked at Penhaligon. No change there.

Copeley went on, 'Typical razor wound. Neat. I'll show you what it did.' He lifted a scalpel from the tray of instruments, bent low across the girl to make a shallow incision in her throat. There was no blood as the skin opened. He placed the scalpel aside and took a reflexing tool, gently peeled back the top layers of skin, exposing the fatty tissue beneath. Fitz peered closer. This was standard stuff. The tissue displayed the expected bruising. Placing aside the reflexing tool, Copeley took up a fresh scalpel and began to work deeper into Jacqui's throat. As he worked he kept up a steady flow of words, quiet, unobtrusive. Background.

'There's a bonus to this job, I keep telling my mother. A belief in God.'

Fitz rolled his eyes. Grinned at Penhaligon. Copeley didn't notice. She frowned. In place of a grin? Bilborough was looking very pale. He swallowed hard as Copeley reflected layer after layer; skin, fatty tissue, muscle, gradually working in, as his words worked into their minds.

'Bacteria toiling away in their own little organs with no idea of the body as a whole. For them only the heart exists, or the liver or the spleen. And the organs themselves, all throbbing away, convinced this body they're in is the entire universe. And then one day, a knife cut, and they see with

143

blinding light the world outside the body . . . Rudi? Thanks.'
He placed the scalpel on the receiving tray and once again
took up the reflexing tool. 'Here you go. He's gone right
through the trachea and the cartilage, totally severed the
carotid artery. Death in seconds.'

He moved around the head of the table. Fitz stood aside to
let him pass.

'Although there's no real way of telling for sure, I reckon
he did it from behind. Cutting from left to right, so he might
be right handed.' He continued on around the table, gesturing
with his scalpel. 'Wounds to the breasts. Some of these look
like they were from behind so it's my guess she was alive at
the time. Alive and standing, see the way the blood has
travelled? And her hands, look at the damage to the backs
and knuckles. She's put them up to defend herself and he's
hacked away at them.' Selecting a larger grade scalpel, he
began to mark a line along Jacqui's chest, from her throat to
her pelvis. 'And then there's the body itself, the way it's put
together.' Reflect the skin, muscle tissue. 'The way it's put
together, the intricacy, the genius.' Put down the scalpel, take
up a bone saw. 'No accident this, it's the work of an almighty
God.' And *push*.

Jacqui's sternum cracked under Copeley's expertly ap-
plied pressure. The bone saw went back onto the tray and
Bilborough let out a slow breath. Penhaligon's expression
hadn't changed a bit.

Copeley looked up when Fitz didn't react to his words.
'No?'

*What God would allow a girl to die like this? A girl like
Jacqui? Of course there's no God, you moron, or if there is,
he's as twisted as the killer that he made in his own image.*

Fitz shook his head. 'No.'

Copeley shrugged. He used retractors to open the chest
cavity, working down along the length of Jacqui's body, into
the stomach.

Penhaligon was staring at Jacqui's groin. Copeley caught
the direction of her gaze and paused in his work. 'She was
dead when he shaved her pubic hair – by whatever method –
because there's not so much as a nick. Tender loving care.'

144

And there it was, plain as the sun in the sky, as the look Penhaligon directed towards Bilborough as she spoke: 'Or depilatory cream.'

If Bilborough chose to make a facial expression in response to Penhaligon's dig, then Fitz wasn't able to distinguish it from the sick look he'd worn since Copeley had made the first incision in Jacqui's neck.

That was when Bilborough's bleeper went off. He jerked as if electrocuted, hands burrowing under the surgical smock to find the source of the noise. Copeley didn't seem to notice.

Fitz glanced at Penhaligon and saw she was containing a grin at Bilborough's antics.

'They have a cure for that nowadays,' he said, completely deadpan.

Penhaligon's eyes widened and she mouthed the words, *cheap shot!*

Fitz nodded as Bilborough finally wrenched the unit free from his pocket and read the message on it. There was a cold light of triumph in his eyes as he spoke which obviously worried Penhaligon; Fitz considered that a good enough reason to be worried himself.

'That was Beck. They've got an I.D. on Sweeney. They've sussed him. His name's Kelly. Kelly. Now we're getting somewhere. We'll do the bastard yet. Kelly. Yes!'

Fitz looked narrowly at Bilborough. For one moment he looked like a die hard Man U fan two seconds after the winning goal. He knew it, too, because he caught himself after not much longer than that, and the professional look was back. He began to take off his smock. 'Please let us have any pertinent results as soon as you can,' he said to Copeley.

Copeley looked up at Fitz as Bilborough left the cold room. Fitz shrugged, followed Bilborough out as Penhaligon thanked Copeley for allowing them access to the post mortem.

15:00–17:30

Bilborough was in a thoroughly good mood. For once things seemed to be moving his way. The Co-op records department

145

had turned around the number in record time, producing a name, Kelly, Kathleen, and an address in Salford. Giggs and Jones had scooted out to conduct a door to door hoping to trace the actual whereabouts of the parents. By the middle of the afternoon they had returned to the duty room with a fairly detailed, if somewhat cold trail. Bilborough, along with Penhaligon and Fitz came out into the duty room to listen to Giggs begin the tale.

'The Kellys apparently lived in Salford for six years, until summer of 1973. The husband, Peter, had recently retired as branch manager of one of a nationwide chain of shoe shops.'

'Had?' Bilborough waited as the answer came.

'Popped his clogs in seventy three,' Jones grinned. 'Pun intended.'

'But not very good, Jonesy.' Giggs grinned before taking up the tale again. 'There was a neighbour, Mrs Irene Hobbs –'

'– senile old bat –'

'– and she says they planned to move before his death. She was going to move afterwards anyway. Bad memories, I suppose. Anyway, before she could make arrangements –'

'– she gave up the ghost too. Died in her sleep, apparently. They were buried together at a cemetery on the edge of Salford.'

Bilborough nodded. 'Bloody typical.'

Jones added, 'Inconsiderate, I'll grant you. But that's not the interesting bit.'

With perfect timing Giggs added, 'The interesting bit is they had a son. Thomas Francis Kelly. Description by the senile old bat next door fits that of our suspect. She even recognised a mug shot we showed her.'

Bilborough was looking more and more interested by the minute. 'Go on.'

'Well that's almost as far as we got. Thomas Francis Kelly vanished in 1974, shortly after his mother died. The house remained empty for a while, then was repo'd by the mortgage company and sold at auction.'

'And the boy?'

Giggs sighed. 'Well, this is where the fun started, boss.

146

Jonesy here banged on the other neighbour's door and it was answered by –' he referred to his notebook '– one Mrs Janet Forbes.' He grinned. 'Apparently Mrs Forbes harboured a bit of a dislike for Mrs Hobbs –'

'– screaming at each other like witches they were.' Jones shook his head in mock despair. 'As much as we could do to get two pennorth of sense out of either of them.'

Giggs nodded. 'That's right. But what we did learn was that Kelly junior had got himself a bit of a rep for being an oddball by the time he upped and vanished. Mrs Hobbs told us he was,' once again he referred to his notebook, ' "Round the bloody twist, that one; more than one slate loose if you ask me." '

Jones added, 'Mrs Forbes on the other hand swore blind Thomas Francis Kelly was a sweet, shy man who wouldn't harm a soul. She claimed he'd told her brother he was going to Rome to become a priest.'

Bilborough was leaning forward now, thoroughly immersed in the tale. 'And then?'

Giggs sighed. 'Then Mrs Hobbs told Mrs Forbes she was as gullible as a newborn babe and why didn't she keep her oar out of it, Mrs Forbes told Mrs Hobbs that she was an interfering, evil minded old witch who would go to hell for telling lies, and me and Jonesy left them to it rather than arrest them both for causing an affray.' He snapped his notebook shut with a flourish. 'And that's pretty much it. We can do a follow up later if you like.'

Bilborough leaned back in his chair. 'Bloody good work, both of you. Yeah. Follow up interviews, separately. Also check further up and down the street. See if we can get any more details. We'll need to check with the Seminary in Rome in order to confirm or deny the story.' He looked around the duty room. 'Who wants to talk to Jesus?'

Penhaligon said quietly, 'Just don't ask me to take the mother.' That got a round of scattered applause and an admiring look from Giggs. Even Bilborough grinned.

'Right then,' he said. 'Let's get on with it, shall we?' He turned to Fitz. 'I'm beginning to think I wasted that hundred and twenty.'

147

Fitz frowned. He shot a look at Giggs. 'What was the name of the cemetery, Giggsy?'

'Saint Mary's. On the outskirts of Salford.'

Fitz nodded. 'I'll find it.' He turned back to Bilborough. 'Fancy a trip out to the boondocks? I think it's time to confront our friend Kelly with a little piece of his past.'

Saint Mary's was a modest building established in the latter half of the previous century. Built close to one of Manchester's many canals the building had sagged slightly over the years. The graveyard was spread out across a similarly modest quarter acre of land along the side of the building facing the canal.

As Penhaligon followed Fitz, Kelly and Bilborough along the neatly kept gravel path leading to the nave, late afternoon sunlight slanted across the chapel to lay dusty yellow spokes across the headstones lying in irregular clumps throughout the graveyard. Their shadows stretched out in front of them, moving together across the neatly trimmed lawns, interspersed with clumps of grass that were growing around the headstones.

At the last minute, as they were a hundred yards or so from the chapel, Fitz headed off into the graveyard. Penhaligon saw Kelly hesitate at the edge of the path. As she watched, Fitz glanced back, noted the hesitation and urged him on with a gesture. Bilborough followed Fitz and Kelly more slowly, picking where he stepped carefully, as if afraid to disturb what lay beneath the ground.

'Oughtn't we to've asked the priest to show us to my parents' graves?' That was Kelly, precise as ever in his speech. That afternoon, while Giggs and Jones had been out conducting their door to door enquiry, a peripatetic nurse had arrived to change the cast on Kelly's arm, snipping away the old plaster with a glorified pair of shears, replacing it with a new wrapping of elasticated plastic. The bruises on his forehead had begun to fade, the scratches to heal. The nurse had changed the dressing on his forehead, smiling as she did so. Kelly responded to her with a grin of his own that was no surprise to Penhaligon. The nurse must have been the first person to show Kelly any kindness at all in the three days since he'd been found.

Fitz shook his head. 'The state of this church he'd 've probably charged us to walk on the grass.'

Penhaligon noted with some interest that Kelly frowned. She got the feeling he was on the point of disagreeing with Fitz, but at the last minute he said nothing, merely followed the psychologist across the rows of graves.

Penhaligon let her gaze wander around as they walked. Beyond the last row of gravestones was a high mesh fence behind which was the towpath for the canal. Sunlight glinted greasily off the thin line of water she could see beneath the far bank. She glanced at Bilborough. He returned her look but said nothing. As far as he was concerned there were better procedures to follow than tramping around some old graveyard in search of a killer's past. Penhaligon got the feeling he was only indulging Fitz because a conviction was now looking so certain. The hundred and twenty quid he'd authorised probably had something to do with it as well, she thought dryly. She became aware Bilborough was looking at her as if to say *what's so funny?* and she realised she must be grinning. With an effort she wiped the grin from her face, shaking her head a little to make sure Bilborough didn't follow up.

By now Fitz had stopped beside two graves. Kelly moved forwards to stand alongside him. He stared at them for a moment as she and Bilborough stayed motionless a pace or two behind him. Then he frowned, blinked, craned his head back to look momentarily up at the sky before falling to his knees in the grass between the graves. He mumbled something quietly. Fitz leaned in closer and asked for a repeat. After a moment Kelly looked sideways and up at him. 'I said: there are no flowers. There should be flowers. Surely there should be flowers, shouldn't there?'

Fitz nodded, not understanding, not sympathy, just acknowledgement. Kelly lowered his gaze to the graves, brought his hands together.

The headstone was fairly modern, black marble, but plain. Cheap. The inscription was simple. *In loving memory*.

Names. Dates of birth and death. Your basic headstone. Penhaligon glanced around the cemetery. At other points headstones were leaning slightly, in emulation of the chapel itself. One or two had fallen or been laid flat. The black marble-finished stones appeared randomly but often throughout the maze of older stones.

'Does it mean anything to you?' That was Fitz pushing again, not content to let Kelly take it in his own time. Needing a result as much as Bilborough in his own way. Penhaligon sighed as Kelly shook his head.

'No.'

'You know how important this is . . . Please think hard.'

Again a shake of the head. 'I try . . . I look around me and I see their names and I try to picture them in my head but all I get is a blank. Just grey. Just . . . nothing. I'm sorry. Just nothing.'

Fitz placed one hand on Kelly's arm. 'And there's nothing else. No associated memories?'

Kelly shook his head. Climbed slowly to his feet. 'There should be flowers. Can I get some flowers?'

Bilborough said, 'I'll have someone do it for you, OK?' His words were aimed at Kelly, but he was looking straight at Fitz. The meaning beneath his words was clear.

Fitz was about to say something when the church bell rang. The sound echoed sonorously across the graveyard, mingling with the sound of water lapping distantly at concrete and the cry of a distant bird, to fade as the wind rose among the hibiscus and high rhododendrons that formed cloistered areas within the graveyard.

And Kelly looked up at the sound. He'd registered it. It was in him, changing him. Fitz had seen the change too. Kelly was straighter. His eyes were no longer filled with the lost expression that had characterised him over the last three days. There was an intensity there. Something none of them had seen before. Even Bilborough had homed in on it. Perhaps he thought it would bring his arrest that much nearer. Perhaps it would.

'Can we go inside?' Kelly's voice rose a tone. Excitement? Expectation? Fear?

Bilborough shrugged. 'In for a penny . . .'

'Come on,' Fitz's words were less dismissive and they were spoken in a kinder voice. He led Kelly back onto the path and along it towards the church.

The sound of a choir singing *Faith of our Fathers* came to them as a whisper on the wind, a whisper that lifted into full song as they stepped across the vestibule, Kelly leading now, accelerating as if drawn to the sound of human voice lifted in praise. Then they were inside the nave and fluted stone columns rose around them, and the congregation were in full voice, and their words rang in the chapel like a storm through a forest of stone.

And it didn't take a genius to see the effect it was having on Kelly. As Penhaligon watched the sound hit him like a shotgun blast, drilled into him, blasted him back a step until the backs of his knees hit the leading edge of the nearest pew, and then he was folding into the seat, collapsing into it almost, and his face was alight, not just with joy, with a reflection of the congregation's love of Jesus Christ, but with memories. Real memories, alive right there on his face, she could see them, see his face become mobile, watch the stitches stretch in his forehead and the scratches wrinkle across his cheeks. She watched the memories come alive for him. Watched his lips move in time with the hymn.

Bilborough leaned closer to Fitz, whispered, 'He knows the words. He knows the bloody words . . .'

Fitz silenced the DCI with a gesture. 'Is this familiar to you?'

And Kelly was looking at him, and he was smiling, an angel's smile, despite the wounds; a smile of trust, of love, of thankfulness, but above all one of relief, every feature shone with it; it lit him from within.

'Oh yes. Yes. This is familiar to me.'

And then the congregation's voices died around them as the hymn came to an end, sank into the brickwork to leave an echoing silence into which the priest spoke.

'In the name of the Father, and of the Son and of the Holy Spirit –'

And Kelly was blinking rapidly, the relief gone, fear crowding back in –

'– grace of our Lord Jesus Christ and the love of God and –'

– flooding him, and he was shaking, his teeth chattering and –

– Fitz was leaning closer, a hand on Kelly's shoulder, squeezing gently –

'– OK, it's OK, it happens like this sometimes, it's perfectly alright, it's just a reaction, a reaction to your memories, to whatever you remember –'

And Kelly grabbed hold of Fitz's hand, gripped it until his knuckles whitened, and words came sliding out from between clenched teeth. '– English it's in English –'

Fitz frowned. 'It's been in English for twenty years.'

'– fellowship of the Holy Spirit be with –'

And Kelly was away, spitting words through chattering teeth, every muscle locked and shaking, eyes wide with fear of the unknown.

'– in English I don't understand why it's –'

And then he was –

'– flowers aren't there any flowers I must have but it's in English it's –'

– arching back across the pew, eyes closed, body shuddering, voice rising into the silence as the priest faltered, and the congregation were turning, all turning to stare as Fitz and Bilborough helped Kelly out of the chapel, back out into the dusty sunlight, the late afternoon warmth, to sit him on a nearby headstone until his fit had reduced to a shiver and then faded entirely.

And when he was recovered Fitz was waiting. 'What do you remember? *What do you remember?*'

There was blood. So much blood –

He took the blade –

– spurting –

– lifted it –

– out –

– face blank, eyes dead –

– out from beneath –
– *but churning inside, churning and* –
– the cloth –
– *brought it* –
– arcing out and –
– *down through the neck* –
– down –
– *through the cloth* –
– down –
– down –
– *down.*
– *and held the struggling body until all movement had ceased.*

They waited but Kelly didn't answer Fitz's question. Instead he remained sitting on the gravestone and looked up at Bilborough. 'You can only hold me so long can't you? This afternoon you have to charge me or let me go, isn't that right?'

Bilborough's eyes glowered. 'I can get an extension. The Chief Super could authorise –'

But Kelly was shaking his head. 'No.' Looking from Bilborough to Penhaligon to Fitz and back to Bilborough again. She saw the thought as clearly in his own mind as it was in her own, as it was in Bilborough's. 'If the Chief Superintendent could authorise extra time before I had to be charged I wouldn't be here now, would I? We wouldn't be doing this . . .' He fell silent, thoughtful, pensive. Finally looked back at Bilborough. 'I could walk out of this graveyard now and you wouldn't be able to stop me.'

Bilborough couldn't bring himself to reply.

And then, incredibly, Kelly smiled. 'But it's alright. You asked me once if I trusted you. I do trust you. I know you can't hold me. But I want to help you. Because if I did kill those girls I –' he hesitated. 'I must be punished. Do you understand?'

Bilborough said nothing. Fitz was nodding thoughtfully. Penhaligon kept herself in the background, watching closely, memorising the scene for later consideration.

'I have to be punished.'

Bilborough snapped. 'What are you trying to say?'

'I would like to be released into Doctor Fitzgerald's care. Voluntarily.' He glanced at Fitz. 'If that's alright with you?'

The Chief Superintendent at Anson Road was a thirty year man named William Allen. Bill Allen had a friendly looking face, all round curves and jolly dimples. Even his grey hair seemed faintly jolly; bits of it stuck up whenever he took off his cap. He seemed almost to take pride in its uncontrollability, for he never trimmed the awkward bits. He was not a large man, nor was he a small man. He carried his medium weight fairly well and, apart from his untoward lock of hair, never appeared on duty looking anything less than smartly turned out. His overall appearance was of a genial, friendly fellow, considerate, ingenuous.

Nothing could have been farther from the truth. Allen was a taskmaster. He was in charge and he knew it. During the course of his career, Bilborough had spoken to Allen any number of times. The man still terrified him. There was something about his bland faced jollity which, like the layer of fat over a sumo wrestler's muscle, concealed something that could pick you up and crush you flat in an instant. And yet when he wanted to be Allen could be the most charming man in the station. The civvies all loved him.

He was with the Applebys, waiting for Bilborough when he returned with Fitz and Penhaligon to Anson Road from Saint Mary's. Allen greeted Bilborough with a friendly smile. Bilborough knew enough of his boss to know that was a bad sign. Fortunately he'd taken a few moments to check with Beck before coming to his office. Beck had some more good news. Was it going to be good enough?

Allen came straight to the point. 'Time's run out on you, David. And you know I'm not one to beat about the bush. Especially not on a case as important as this one is.'

Bilborough nodded. 'You want to know what the situation is. Fair enough. I've just been informed we've heard from Rome. Thomas Francis Kelly went there, to Saint Peter's seminary in the Via Tranquillitata, in 1974 and left in 1976. "Doubts about his stability." '

At that moment there was a knock on the door. Giggs showed Ann and Simon Appleby into the office, grinned, left. Fitz stood to allow Ann to sit. Simon stood, nodding a greeting to Penhaligon.

Allen said, 'I've asked the Applebys to be present at this meeting.'

Bilborough pursed his lips, nodded. 'As I said, Thomas Francis Kelly was in Rome between 1974 and 1976. He left the seminary under a cloud of doubt. Now the problem is, there's no national insurance number for a Thomas Francis Kelly. There's no police record either, he's never owned a vehicle and, as far as we can tell, he's never been in a mental institution.'

Bilborough glanced at Ann Appleby, found himself drawn by the dark ringed eyes. She wasn't taking this very well. Then again, what did he expect? Fanfares?

And Allen was there, just as he expected, with the key question: 'Has anyone actually identified the suspect as Thomas Francis Kelly?'

Bilborough sighed, glanced at Penhaligon and Fitz, then back to the Super. 'Yes, sir. Giggs and Jones have taken statements from neighbours who have recognised the photographs we showed them.' Bilborough hesitated, glanced at Ann Appleby. 'But that still doesn't give us enough for a conviction.'

In the momentary silence, Ann's tiny, breathless 'Oh,' was a thunderclap of sound. Simon placed his hand on her shoulder. Bilborough noticed there was no moving together, no comfort there. Ann ignored her husband's touch as she might have ignored the touch of a drop of rain.

And there was Allen, filling the remainder of the silence with a single word: 'Well?'

Bilborough nodded slowly as he answered the question. 'We haven't got enough to charge him. And we can't hold him any longer. But –' a quick look at Fitz '– he has agreed to go into Fitz's care. Voluntarily.'

Allen shot a glance at the psychologist. Fitz shot the glance right back, perfect in every detail, a mirror. Allen looked back to Bilborough. 'Anything else?'

'Yes.' Bilborough looked at Ann. Studied the dark rings around her eyes. Fitz might have been able to divine her interior thoughts, but he was glad he was unable to. Such emotions as he suspected might exist there were almost too dreadful to contemplate. 'It's asking a lot, I know. But I'd like you to make a televised appeal for information.'

Ann sucked in a little breath. Just a little breath, but enough. Enough to tell the whole room how she felt. And Simon was stepping forward.

'I'll do it.'

Bilborough drove on, ruthlessly excising all feeling from his mind. 'I'd like you both to do it if that's possible.'

Ann began to speak, but Simon beat her to it. 'She's not up to it.'

That earned him a look from Ann, and Bilborough saw them move even further apart. And he also got an inkling of exactly what Ann Appleby was capable of.

Fitz drove home the point. 'That's just it.' He parried the glares from Simon and Allen, threw the challenge back out again. 'Isn't it?'

There were no takers. Simon met Fitz's eyes and looked away. Allen looked back towards Bilborough; the DCI felt Fitz's presence in the room, felt him taking over the meeting without saying a word.

'I'll do it.' Ann glanced sideways at Simon, who removed his hand from her shoulder. 'I'll do it if I can bury my daughter.' The distinction wasn't lost on him, even Bilborough could see that. *My* daughter.

But it wasn't going to be as easy as that. He looked over at Penhaligon but there was no help there. She was observing, just as he'd wanted her to do. The ball was in his court. 'Mrs Appleby, there are certain legal difficulties which –'

'I don't care about that.' Ann leaned forward, a strength in her voice. 'I can only take one step at a time and for me the first step is to bury my child.'

She still didn't see it. Bilborough explained. 'You need permission from the coroner. The accused has a right to an independent post-mortem.'

'You mean I've got to ask his permission?'

Allen glanced at Penhaligon. 'Get Mrs Appleby a glass of water would you please?'

Penhaligon narrowed her eyes but obeyed.

Bilborough sighed. It was going to be a long night.

18:00–21:30

At least they'd arranged for his clothes to be cleaned before they released him. For Kelly it was strange to be outside again. As far as he could comfortably remember his whole world had existed within the confines of the police station. The trough. The interview room. And although it had been no more than two days since he had last walked along a city street as anything other than a prisoner, he felt like falling to his knees and kissing the ground, sucking in a deep breath of fresh air. Forget the carbon monoxide, the sulphates, the acid rain, the dirt; the filthiest thing on the street was cleaner than the inside of the station because in there the first thing to go was freedom, a sense of identity. And yet that was confusing too; the idea of uniformity, of brotherhood, should be comforting to him, shouldn't it? Everyone together standing against the night? Against the world? Kelly frowned, felt Fitz's eyes on him as he walked uncertainly down the steps of the station, onto Anson Road, knew what he must be thinking: *get him out of that cell, that dungeon, get him out among real people if you ever want to see his memory intact.*

And Penhaligon, she was with them too, looking very peculiarly at Fitz. Kelly couldn't work that one out. They were totally at odds those two; Fitz's easy familiarity sat uncomfortably with the woman's obvious edginess, antagonism. Kelly fretted over the contradictions for a moment, then put the thoughts aside. All that mattered for now was that he was out, and the air was fresher, the sunset a little more gloriously coloured, the pavement delightfully hard against the soles of his feet. Even the elasticated cast on his arm seemed more absurd than frightening, even a little comical, sticking out from underneath his jacket like that, the ache in his arm dulling against the buzz of the moment.

Then he felt Fitz's hand on his shoulder. 'Don't drift away just yet, will you? Panhandle's offered us a lift.'

Kelly looked around. 'Where to?'

'You'll see.'

Kelly shrugged slightly, nodded.

Fitz studied him closely. 'All seems a little hyper real doesn't it? Like an airbrush painting? Every detail, every little grain of dirt standing out in sharp relief.'

Kelly nodded slowly. Fitz was an easy man to trust. When someone knew that much about you then there was no way you could ever doubt them. And Fitz knew it.

Kelly became aware Penhaligon was waiting impatiently some way back along the pavement. Fitz gave a little sideways shake of his head in her direction. *Mustn't keep the chauffeur waiting.*

In the car the tension began to climb sharply. Kelly became aware that there was something happening between these two, the psychologist, the detective, perhaps something they were themselves only peripherally aware of, if at all. Penhaligon started the car, pumping the revs, making the engine growl aggressively. Fitz glanced at her from the front passenger seat. 'Home, James,' he said with that same sideways waggle of his head that obviously meant his words should be taken lightly.

Penhaligon slapped a sheaf of papers into his hand. 'This is a copy of the Mental Health Act. I suggest you read it.'

Fitz peered back at Kelly and grinned. 'Just can't get the staff these days . . .'

Penhaligon shoved the car into gear and pulled out without checking her mirror.

Fitz went on, and his voice held no hint of humour now. 'Don't take it out on us.'

'What?' Sharp. Aggressive. Kelly noticed Penhaligon kept her eyes firmly on the road. Afraid of what she might see in Fitz's eyes if she looked at him? Or simply pissed off by his casual condescension?

'Your boss treats you like a skivvy. Tough. But don't take it out on us.'

Penhaligon slammed the car into third almost hard enough

to break the gearstick, stamped on the accelerator. There was a hint of a smile at the corner of Fitz's mouth but he didn't say anything.

'I need directions.' Penhaligon again, her voice tightly controlled, almost pinched.

Fitz glanced out of the window. 'We're going to the dogs.' Added in a deceptively casual tone, 'So ... how many brothers do you have?'

Penhaligon ignored the question, scooted the Volvo around a slower vehicle and back into the left hand lane, indicated, took a left turn. 'This man was released into your care on the understanding that you –'

'He was not released into my care. He placed himself in my care. Voluntarily.' Kelly barely had time to decide how he felt about being discussed in his own presence before Fitz was off again. 'I'd say four, am I right? Brothers I mean.'

Penhaligon pursed her lips, changed down as they approached the stadium. 'Three. You're not really going in there?'

Fitz ignored the question. 'No other sisters though? You're the only girl, right?'

Penhaligon spoke again, her voice harsh, and this time Kelly was stung. 'You'll lose him. First chance he gets he'll do a bunk.'

'I'll take that chance. But you are the only girl. Am I right?'

Kelly was amazed that she let him push her so hard. What kind of woman was she? What kind of *man* was he? What was going on between them? Kelly frowned. If he had his way all this sort of nonsense would stop. Nobody should treat anyone like this. He'd done it yesterday as well; used his interview as an excuse to wind Penhaligon up. Wind her up? Torture her more like. Kelly felt an overwhelming rage surge through him, felt himself flush with anger. This was the man he found so easy to trust? Into whose care he had surrendered himself? What had he been thinking of? Fitz should be made to do penance for his arrogance. And as for the woman ...

'Right.' To Kelly's amazement, Penhaligon was agreeing

with Fitz, nodding as she steered the Volvo into a parking bay.

Fitz said thoughtfully, 'That explains everything.'

'What?' Penhaligon put the car into neutral and yanked savagely on the handbrake. 'What does it explain?'

'The chip on your shoulder. The constant need to assert yourself. Penis envy. There's the boys outside playing football and you're stuck indoors doing the ironing.' Fitz eased the passenger door open, his voice slipping out into the gathering evening, drawing curious looks from a trickle of punters heading for the stadium. 'Angry, resentful, classic case. Penis envy. Freud; Clement not Sigmund.' And Fitz was out of the car, opening the door for Kelly, ushering him out, closing the doors even as Penhaligon fired up the engine and backed the Volvo out of the parking bay in a cloud of fumes. 'Thanks for the lift Panhandle . . .'

Fitz watched the Volvo slam away into the twilight, shrugged, turned to Kelly and jerked his head towards the stadium. 'Shall we?'

Anger fading into bemusement, more than a little shellshocked by the exchange he had just witnessed, Kelly followed Fitz towards the entrance to the stadium.

Kelly spent the next hour watching Fitz lay bet after bet, winning a little, losing a little more. He didn't speak. That was a pity because Kelly desperately needed to talk to someone. He needed a friend. Needed a way back into his mind. Fitz might have been that person. That way back. But no. He simply kept up a running monologue about the dogs, the form, the odds, and without exception it all went over Kelly's head. Had he never gambled, he wondered? Or was it just that he couldn't remember gambling? After an hour he mentioned the fact that he was hungry, hoping Fitz might take it as a sign to leave. Fitz had bought him a hotdog lathered in ketchup and watched him as he ate it, slowly. Had he been a vegetarian? Was the smell of the meat familiar? Did it provoke a particular reaction? The answer to all these questions was, no. It was simply food, neither good nor bad; warmth in his belly and energy in the gathering night, that was all.

When Kelly had finished the hotdog and washed it down with coffee from a plastic cup Fitz had led the way back into the bleachers where he had studied more form, placed more bets, while leaving Kelly to stand in the hustle and bustle of the crowd in the glare of the floods reflected in through the observation windows by the posters and hoardings pasted all around the track.

In truth Kelly was surprised to find he was quite happy to be apart from Fitz, at least for a few moments. There were things in his head he needed to sort out. The hotdog had settled uneasily on his stomach and this, combined with the giddy feeling of being out of the police station, and the noise and bustle and smell of the crowd, combined to make him feel lightheaded, even dizzy.

Then down on the tracks the traps clattered open. The crowd roared, a gestalt creature stamping its hundreds of legs and screaming approval with its dozens of mouths. Even Fitz lost his identity in the crowd, on his feet, nose pressed up against the glass, roaring and stamping with the rest. And Kelly had to turn away from it all. In moments the race would be over and the aftermath would wash over him, a sullen tide of emotion. The crowd would split into its many fragments, the gestalt creature decomposing before his eyes, to melt into the wash of humanity, one or two bright sparks, the winners, crowing amongst the dejection, the emptiness, the determination, no, the obsession to bet again, perhaps to win.

Kelly felt his stomach churn. The lights blinded him, gold bled through his eyes and into his mind. Gold like sunlight, like *sunlight dappled through a juddering train window, and the crowd screaming, no, screeching like a dying girl, and the light exploding inside his head and driving him back against the motion of the train, to tilt, to fall as the train rocked –*

And Kelly was running, feet pounding against the concrete, the roar of the crowd as nothing compared to the violent pounding of blood in his ears, his throat, behind his eyes, in there with the light, the golden light, the vision of death, the memory of –

161

Kelly stopped when he almost ran into a man. Small. Pinched face. No hair. Narrowed eyes. Looking at him. Looking at him *as if he knew him!*

And then the man was off, gone in a whirl of greatcoat and greasy trainers, feet slapping the ground like a panting animal, fading into the crowd. Kelly shook his head. He was sick to his stomach but the feeling only heightened his perception. The man had recognised him. Here, in the most unlikely place in all creation, he'd met someone who might be able to tell him about his past. Without thinking, Kelly began to run again. Through the bleachers, past the teller's booths, down a long flight of wooden stairs, out into the car park, out into the night. Behind him the crowd roared again, but that animal couldn't keep up with him. He was flying. Flying through the night. And his breath was roaring in his throat and his ears and his heart was a swollen thing in his chest hammering the blood through him, and *oh God it was good to be alive, was good to feel the air blasting across his face and hands, to taste the night glory on his lips, inside his mouth and* ahead of him trainers slapped concrete in a faint rhythm. A rhythm that slowed, stopped as the man with the pinched expression turned to face him, face gaunt in the sodium yellow light from the distant floods.

And Kelly was down then, back on the ground, feet aching, lungs clawing at the dirty night air, heart beating a ragged rhythm in his chest. 'I won't hurt you . . . I promise. I only want to know . . .' *Know about myself. Who am I? Where have we met? Please. Please listen to me. I won't hurt you. Look at me, I couldn't hurt you!*

And then the man was coming forward, shadows lengthening across his face as he moved, eyes glinting in the night. Thief's eyes. Night eyes.

'Please –'

And Kelly realised his mistake. They were alone here at the farthest edge of the car park. Alone. And now more flashes of memory lit up the night like fireworks. Those eyes, crouching over him in the bushes, examining him. – *'ere mate're you dead? Jesus look at all that blood, yeah you're dead alright, you ain't movin' s'much as a muscle –*

162

'I only want to know who I –'

And the eyes loomed closer in front of a golden sun filled with memories of a screaming girl, a blood lathered –

Something smashed into the bridge of his nose, a great weight that exploded into his head, blew his eyes apart into a thousand squealing fragments of pain, and he was on his knees, and the blood he could see, that he could feel on himself was real, no memory this but a solid reality –

'– please –'

Another great weight smashed into his side, burned along his ribcage, paralysed his lungs. Gasping he sank to the ground, his breath escaping in a low wheeze as, distantly, the sound of trainers slapping against concrete faded into the night.

The pain burrowed further into him, little flashes bursting all through his body. *Flash. Flash.* Shellshock. Blood. Concrete pressed up against his face. Dirt, grainy concrete, *flash*, blood; black in the yellow light, *flash, flash* –

Fitz fought his way through the crowd. Gone. Mary mother of Christ. Gone. Penhaligon was right. Took him in, tried to sort him out. One look. One bloody look the other way, that was all it had taken. And he was off on the lam. First opportunity. Oh Penhaligon was going to love this. She was going to laugh his balls off. But that was nothing to what Bilborough was going to do, what Allen, the bloody Chief Super was going to do. Visions of lawsuits and professional standards committees loomed in front of his mind. Another cross in the box. How many more before Fitz goes under? Poor Fitz. It's the drink you know. Can't handle it. And the gambling. And the wife. Can't handle her either. As it were.

Fitz spun in a tight circle, his bulk clearing a space for him among the crowd. Down on the tracks the traps were being loaded up again, shotguns with a full load of canine shells. An apt analogy. They might as well be real weapons. He'd certainly blown away any professional ethics that might have been left intact around here.

Around him the crowd ebbed and flowed, tugged him this way and that. With no other recourse he followed the current past the teller booths towards the main exit leading to the tracks. Down the stairs. Gone. Fucking gone. Unbelievable. How was he going to explain this? *Bilborough? Yeah, it's Fitz. I've lost Kelly but don't worry. I'm at the dogs so I'll have him paged: bing bong; would the suspected serial killer Thomas Francis Kelly please come to the main entrance where his psychologist is waiting to arrange his incarceration, thank you, bing bong.*

The row of phone boxes loomed in front of him, distorted out of all proportion by the night and the floods, the shadows stretching from their bases as black as the look he could imagine on Bilborough's face when he told him the wonderful news.

He looked around, bit his lip, walked a few yards this way and that; unsure for the first time in a long time about what to do next. The feeling was a nightmare. He was in a nightmare. Had Kelly really legged it? Maybe he'd got into a fight. Had a fugue, perhaps even a stroke. Christ even now he could be lying somewhere bleeding from the nose while any opportunity to find the truth trickled away into the night forever.

Fitz became aware a number of people were watching him. *Oh great that's all I need. Yoo hoo! Hi there! It's me, your friendly neighbourhood loony, pacing up and down outside the dogs with an expression on his face that says gone inside, in his head, where it matters, gone away somewhere the sun doesn't* –

'Oh fuck it.' Fitz raised his voice. 'Anyone seen a suspected serial killer? Thin face, bruised, grey suit, crumpled? May even now be tracking his next victim?'

The people began to move past Fitz, eyes locked on the middle distance.

'I'm serious you know. You could help prevent a murder or prove a man's innocence.'

But they were gone.

'Oh fuck it,' Fitz said again. He turned to the nearest phone, took the handset from the cradle, dialled. A voice answered. 'Beck? Fitz. Get Bilborough for me. Then you'll probably want to leave the room for about ten minutes.'

And that was when the shadows beyond the phone boxes

moved. Or rather when something buried deep within them moved. Fitz turned during the momentary silence before Bilborough came to the phone. And he was there. Kelly. Looming out of the night like a bloody spirit. Clothes crumpled, dirt and blood splattered liberally across his face and hands and sleeves.

On the phone Bilborough's voice said, 'Fitz. Bilborough. I'm in the middle of a bloody PR meeting, what the hell do you –'

Fitz put the phone back on the cradle, cutting off Bilborough in mid flow. Kelly was level with the box now, face glazed by the floods reflecting from the glass. Fitz came out of the box, grabbed Kelly, spun him around.

'You look like shit.'

Kelly looked at Fitz. Looked through him. 'He knew me.'

'What?'

'He knew me. I saw a man. He knew me. He ran so I followed him. He knew me.'

Fitz studied Kelly's bloodied cheeks. The wound on his forehead had split open and slow blood oozed from behind the stitches. His skin was pale and grazed, grimed with dirt. A bruise was beginning to form across the bridge of his nose, which was swelling rapidly. Blood lathered his mouth and the front of his shirt and his hands.

'He butted you?'

Kelly nodded painfully, his eyes narrowing, the pupils shrinking. Shock. Any minute now the pain would hit and then Fitz would know all about it.

'Looks like you could do with a drink.'

'I . . . don't drink.'

Fitz clucked his tongue in sympathy. 'Shame.'

Family Fortunes was running on the television as Fitz ushered Kelly into the sitting room. Mark was in his usual position, scrunched into the far end of the couch, knees hoisted to chin level, poking through rips in his jeans, glazed expression plastered across his face. Fitz noted the glazed look, made a mental note to check the ashtray for evidence of spliffs later. Mark was deep into the game show. He'd be deep into a party political broadcast if that was what was on, judging by the state of him.

Mark nodded vaguely as they came in. Fitz took Kelly out of the sitting room and through into the kitchen leaving the telly wittering on quietly in the background. He pointed along the hall. 'There's a packet of Band-Aid and some Germaline in the bathroom cabinet. You want a drink?'

'Do you have any tea?'

Fitz studied the row of caddies Judith kept shelved neatly beside the breadbin. 'Only about as much as the East India Company. Take your pick.'

Kelly looked at the teacaddies, suddenly recoiled from them. Fitz noticed the movement immediately. 'You remember something?'

Kelly nodded. 'I think . . .'

Fitz waited.

'. . . I don't drink tea or coffee.'

Fitz studied Kelly. How far could he be pushed? 'You don't drink it because you don't like it?'

Kelly shook his head. 'No. It smells lovely. But . . .'

'You're allergic to caffeine.'

Kelly blinked. 'Perhaps I'll just have water.'

'There's decaff if you want it.'

'Just water's fine, thanks.'

Fitz nodded. 'Bathroom's through there.' He indicated the hall.

Kelly turned and vanished through the door Fitz indicated. He raised his voice and called out, 'Mark! Tea?'

'Do what?' His son's voice slurred quietly. Fitz pursed his lips and frowned in annoyance.

'Do you want a cup of tea?'

'Oh . . . Yeah. Wouldn't mind.'

Fitz made the tea, took it on a tray into the sitting room. Mark was still hunched up on the far end of the couch. Fitz didn't bother to sniff the air for traces of tobacco. He handed a mug of tea to Mark, who took it without a word, balanced it on the arm of the sofa.

'You have that over and you'll clean it up.'

Mark let his eyes drift away from the television to Fitz,

166

then back again to where the nine o'clock news was beginning. Fitz sighed, picked up the TV remote and upped the volume a little.

'Blimey, Dad. You deaf or what?'

Fitz's lips narrowed to a thin line but he said nothing.

Mark recoiled a little from Fitz's look. 'I'm fine!'

Fitz began a sarcastic reply, stopped as his attention was drawn to the television, currently showing a picture-in-picture shot of Ann Appleby sitting at a desk in front of a keyed-in background shot of Jacqui. Her face was a wretched mask. Fitz could almost hear the pain, fear, disbelief screaming in her, demanding release, louder than any shout.

'– and the police would like any information, no matter how trivial you think it is. Do you know anybody who was away from home on the day Patricia Garth was murdered – Monday April 3rd – and the day my daughter was murdered, May 8th?'

And Fitz was drawn in by her eyes.

Beside him, Mark winced, hugged his knees to his chest. His expression showed fear and pity, but he seemed unable to look away from Ann's face. 'Do us a favour Dad. Turn it off. This is horrible.'

'Shut up!' The words came out louder than Fitz had intended, sharper.

Mark blinked.

'Your tea's going cold.'

'Oh yeah. Right.' Mark made no move to drink the tea.

On the screen Ann was speaking again, 'Have you ever felt threatened by a man on a railway station or on a train? If so please phone this number.'

The sitting room door opened and Kelly walked in. He'd washed his face and covered the bridge of his nose with a plaster. He sat, perched on the very edge of a chair, eyes glued to the set.

'This man's clothing must have been heavily bloodstained. Both Patricia and my daughter put up a fight so it might've been torn as well . . .'

Fitz swallowed. Ann was trying hard to hold back the tears, struggling on in the face of the studio lights, the stupid executives, the bloody make-up women and directors, with only Simon and Bilborough for support. He shuddered. Christ.

'Does this mean anything to anybody? Monday April the 3rd, May the 8th, a man with torn, blood-stained clothing? If so please, please contact the police. This man could be highly dangerous.'

'Christ, I feel sick.'

Fitz turned to look at Mark, who shuffled back on the couch. His elbow hit the mug of tea, sending it flying all over the carpet.

'Christ, Mark! Now clean it up.'

Mark was shaking his head, blinking rapidly. 'Sorry. Sorry . . . I just feel –'

'Just learn to handle it if you're going to do it at all!' Fitz's words shot out like bullets, smashed into Mark, knocked him even further up the couch. Fitz shook his head, went into the kitchen for a tea towel and some stain remover. When he came back Ann's picture had been replaced by a mug shot of Kelly. He shifted his gaze from the television to the man perched on the edge of one of his living room chairs and back to the screen.

A voice-over announcer said, 'And finally, do you know this man? Police are anxious to trace his whereabouts. It's possible he's known as Thomas Francis Kelly. Police think he comes from the north west. It's known he spent some time abroad and for the last five or ten years has been living in the south of England. Do you recognise him?'

And as Fitz turned to begin the process of mopping up the spilt tea, he saw Mark looking from Kelly to the screen, finally making the connection.

Fitz squirted stain remover at the carpet as the teenager got up and left the room. Mark didn't say anything. He didn't have to. Fitz had seen the look on his face. Fear. Pure and simple. And something else. Accusation. Fitz had to acknowledge the truth of that. In bringing Kelly home he, Fitz, had been responsible for placing the fear on his son's face.

On the screen the announcer was saying, '– giving you that number again in an update after the news. I'd like to finish with a reminder that violent crime really is a rare occurrence and the chance of any of you becoming involved in –'

Fitz scowled. Bollocks. It was all bollocks. Tell the faces they're safe and warm in their comfortable semis. Put a mirror between them and the truth so all they could see was their own complacency and then tell them it was normal. It was sick. He turned to stare at Kelly. He hadn't moved, was still perched on the edge of his chair. He turned to look at Fitz and his eyes were an open book. *It's my fault, isn't it?*

Fitz finished wiping up the tea, went into the bathroom and wrung out the tea towel, dumped it in the dirty laundry basket. A big pile of clothes in there now Judith was gone. Who'd have thought it could have got so big so quickly?

And then came the sound of a key in the front door.

Fitz poked his head out of the bathroom. A familiar figure was letting herself into the hallway.

'Judith.' You're back. *You've come back. Thank God.*

She didn't say his name. Didn't smile. Simply handed him the Lego Gorilla set he'd bought for Katie that afternoon.

'If you could've seen her face,' Judith's voice when she eventually spoke was cold, tight. 'If you could've seen what my taking this away from her did to her.'

So why take it away?

'I don't understand. Judith what are you –'

'I don't believe that for one moment. Stop bribing my daughter!'

Fitz staggered as if Judith had punched him. 'I –'

'And don't give me that innocent look. You had it all figured out. Katie's missing you like hell already. When she came home with this she was practically in tears. "When are we going home, Mum? When can I see Dad, Mum?" It worked like a dream. Push her and she'll push me, that's what you thought wasn't it? Well it won't work like that Fitz. I won't be pushed!'

Fitz reeled against the wall, punch drunk from the words.

'Anyway, you haven't any money.'

'I have money. I've got a job with the police.'

'Oh I see. And what's that? Helping to convict a bunch of

gamblers who've defrauded on their mortgage and had their houses repossessed?'

'Actually it's a murder case. A killer with amnesia.' Fitz scratched his head, waited for another onslaught from Judith. When she simply stared silently at him and said nothing he continued, 'I have to find out whether he's telling the truth or not. I think he may be innocent you see. It's an important case. Um . . . why don't you come through. Have a cup of tea. We can talk about it. You can meet Kelly. He's a lot like me in many ways. Catholic school boy . . .' Fitz tailed off. Judith's expression didn't change one iota.

'You've invited a possible murderer into my house?'

'Well, as I said I think he's –'

'And as if that's not enough you invite me to come and sit down and have tea with him.' Judith shook her head pityingly. 'Oh Fitz. You're really not dealing with this whole situation very well at all are you?'

Inside Fitz was yelling and screaming. But no words came out. It was as if Judith had stamped on his vocal chords and ripped them from his body.

'Nothing to say Fitz?'

Fitz opened his mouth to answer and at that exact moment beside him on the hall table the telephone rang. He didn't look at it; he remained staring at Judith. *Look at her, hold her with your eyes, let her see how hurt you are, let her get inside you, get past the confusion, the anger, get at the truth.*

Instead she looked at the telephone. It kept ringing. She looked back at Fitz. 'I'm taking Katie to Mum's on Saturday. The 12:30 to Leeds. I don't want you to meet us at the platform. I don't want you to come and see us off. I need a couple of weeks to myself.'

The telephone kept ringing, ruining any sense Fitz might have made of Judith's words. Exasperated he wrenched the handset off the cradle and placed it to his ear. 'Fitz.'

Judith sighed, turned to leave, had her hand on the door when Fitz called her back. 'Wait!' Then, to the telephone, 'No, not you. Yes of course I'll speak to him.' And, 'Judith, look hang on a minute can't you? You can't just tell me you're going off to sunny Leeds on the Orient Express without –'

170

And back to the phone, 'What? Yeah. Bilborough? Fitz. What? What! Christ. I'll get a pen. Hang on.' He put the phone down on the table, looked up at Judith. 'Do you have a pen?'

A sudden flash of hatred sparked across Judith's face. She didn't say anything, just opened the door and walked out through the porch into the night.

'Judith, wait! You don't understand. They put his face on the news. They got a call from his wife. His wife!'

Judith rounded on him. 'The way you're carrying on Fitz you'll be damn lucky if you ever get the same.' She strode down the garden path. Fitz took a few steps after her, remembered the phone, hesitated, went back into the hall as a car door slammed and the engine started running.

He searched in his pockets for a pen and a piece of paper, eventually found an old betting slip and a stub of pencil. He picked up the phone. 'Bilborough? Your timing sucks a very large one, do you know that?'

22:00–Midnight

Penhaligon showed up with more information about half an hour later. When she told Kelly the news his face stayed blank for a moment, then suffused with an incredible joy. Watching, Fitz didn't need to analyse this reaction, Katie could have told him what was going on in Kelly's head.

Kelly leaned back in Fitz's armchair and let out a long breath. 'Her name's Emma? My wife's name's Emma?'

Penhaligon nodded.

'Does this mean anything?' Fitz gave a little push just to see what the response would be. Kelly sighed again. Frowned. 'I get a picture of a woman . . . in her thirties, straight brown hair, gentle eyes . . . it could be anyone. My mother when she was young. A sister.'

Fitz said, 'You don't have a sister.'

Kelly met Fitz's gaze with one of his own. 'I didn't think I had a wife.'

Fitz turned to Penhaligon. 'Is this on the level? How do you know it's not a crank call?'

Penhaligon shrugged. 'Giggsy's checking it out. In the meantime we might as well act on it.'

Not exactly standard police procedure, but under the circumstances I agree completely. Even if the woman turns out to be a red herring we might learn something.

Fitz watched Kelly's reaction to his suggestion. Kelly leant forward until he was perched on the edge of the armchair. 'I have to see her. I have to see my wife. Can you give me her address? Can I go there?'

Fitz and Penhaligon exchanged looks. Penhaligon said, 'It's a Sheffield address. I'll take you.'

'No,' Fitz shook his head. 'We'll take the train, if it's all the same to you.'

He glanced at Penhaligon; she'd already got the point. Put Kelly on a train and something might come back. Fitz's only reservation was that they might find out more than they wanted. He said as much to Penhaligon as Kelly went to have his second wash of the evening, before they went to the station.

Penhaligon shrugged. 'I'm a police officer,' she said, keeping her voice perfectly neutral. 'And we can never have too much information.'

Fitz threw her a quirky grin. 'Big Sister is watching you,' he misquoted gently.

Penhaligon compressed her lips, half turned away, unable to repress a smile.

'Well,' Fitz went on. 'I'm glad to see you still have enough perspective to keep a sense of humour about your job.'

Penhaligon's smile faded abruptly. 'Sometimes, Fitz, you don't know anything about anyone,' she said coldly.

Fitz bit back an answer as Kelly came back into the room, face scrubbed and gleaming. 'I used some of your deodorant, was that OK?'

'Fine.'

Kelly looked from Fitz to Penhaligon and back again, then shrugged as the detective led the way out to her car.

Penhaligon bought the tickets and ushered her two charges onto the train with barely a minute to spare. The ten twenty-three overnight service to Edinburgh had chugged out of the station and into the night before they'd even found their seats. Following Fitz and Kelly along the aisles, through carriage after carriage, Penhaligon found herself oddly disturbed. She frowned, trying to analyse the feeling. She was a professional. A good copper. No scratch that: a *damn* good copper. And damn good coppers didn't get freaked out in a moving train. She shook her head, a slight movement, as Fitz stood aside to allow her to reach her seat. She retied her hair as she sat, and settled back with a sigh as Kelly sat opposite her.

Fitz was still standing. 'Drink?'

Penhaligon frowned at the psychologist.

'Of course,' Fitz corrected himself, 'Never on duty, am I right?'

She nodded, careful to keep her face blank. The truth was, she fancied a drink like nobody's business.

'Never mind. Little touch of Bilborough-itis never hurt anyone. It's probably good for the soul, am I right?' Without waiting for an answer, Fitz vanished along the aisle to the buffet car. She found herself studying Kelly. He was staring out of the window into the night. The deep blue and umber blur of the sky and nearer, the dark streaks of buildings, houses, factories, chimneys. What was he thinking, she wondered. Was he looking forward to this meeting? Was he excited? Apart from that one flash of intense joy he'd shown in Fitz's sitting room when she'd first told him the news, he'd said nothing, shown nothing. If pressed she might even say he looked a little guilty. But guilty about what? That he was about to confront his past? Learn who he was? Perhaps he was guilty because he knew something he wasn't telling that he was afraid would now be brought to light. Penhaligon frowned. Was Kelly the killer? Were Bilborough and Beck right, damn their misogynistic hearts? Was Kelly Sweeney?

Penhaligon settled back into her seat, crossed her legs. Kelly noticed she was staring at him, and turned to meet her gaze. He didn't need to speak. The accusation was plain in his eyes.

You think I did it. Killed those girls; Jacqui, Patricia. You think I did it.

173

Penhaligon frowned. Beneath her the train swayed gently, back and forth, rumble and clunk, rumble and clunk. She felt like telling Kelly nothing was ever that clear cut. Police training told her that the simplest theory was nearly always the correct one. But she knew that might not necessarily be true. At least she knew she must always allow for the possibility that it might not be true. *I'm not condemning you. I won't hang you without proof. I'll believe you're innocent until you're shown to be guilty. But if you lie to me –*

Kelly looked away then. Had he divined her thoughts? Or had he merely interpreted her looks and body language in his own way, imposed his own fears on another, as she had just done?

She shook her head again, rubbed her fingers across the bridge of her nose.

'I saw the broadcast.'

She looked at Kelly.

'I was at Fitz's. I think I scared his son. Mark, isn't it?'

'I don't know Fitz's family that well.'

'I think it's Mark. He never really introduced me. I think Mark was a bit stoned.'

Interesting. 'What makes you say that?'

'He just looked and acted mildly stoned.'

'Kelly . . .' Penhaligon chose her words carefully. 'If you can't remember anything about your past, how do you know what someone's behaviour is like when they're stoned?'

'I –' A hesitation, the immediate reply bitten off. Penhaligon watched a range of emotions chase themselves across Kelly's face. Confusion, guilt, puzzlement, a kind of searching look.

She said nothing, let him arrow in on the fact, the memory.

'I . . . remember the poster on her bedroom wall. It was of the Earth . . . it looked like the face of a monkey. I saw a monkey's face in it . . .'

'Beck told me you've never smoked.' That was Fitz, back with a handful of small whisky bottles and a couple of plastic glasses. He'd caught the tail end of the conversation and had listened thoughtfully before sitting down.

174

Kelly's face collapsed back into apathy again. 'That's right.'

'If you injected the chances are we'd know it. Chemical traces in the blood, needle marks, withdrawal symptoms, you name it. You don't smoke. You don't shoot up.'

Kelly nodded slowly, head bobbing in time with the motion of the train. He let out a slow breath. 'Do you think I'm trying too hard to remember? That I'm remembering things which never really happened?'

Fitz shrugged, offered Kelly a glass and a bottle. 'Tell me about your mother.'

Kelly took the offered glass and bottle. 'You're making fun of me.'

Fitz wobbled his head, smiled ingenuously. *No harm done, right? Just my little joke.* But Penhaligon had noticed the glance he'd aimed in her direction. Why had he said that? Looked at her like that? What had Kelly's mother to do with anything? She felt herself frowning, made a great effort to smooth her face, stop the anger rising in her. No, not anger, well, not *just* anger. Other feelings too. A confusing mixture. She glared back at Fitz but he was now looking at Kelly, making small talk.

He gestured with the whisky bottle, then poured the alcohol into his glass. 'Well that was nice and quick. Only thirty-five serious alcoholics in the queue.

Penhaligon watched as Kelly put his bottle and glass down on the table between the seats. The bottle was unopened. 'Why do you drink so much?'

'I like it.' Fitz glanced at Penhaligon as he replied. She frowned, tried to stop an irrational blush reaction that seemed to come from nowhere.

Fitz took a sip of his own drink, then a drag on his cigarette.

'And smoke so much?' What was Kelly doing here? Pushing Fitz back, the way Fitz pushed everyone else? That might be dangerous. But Fitz was smiling, even if the smile never reached his eyes. 'I like it.'

'And you gamble as well.'

'Yes. I like it.'

Penhaligon glanced out of the window, out at the streaky sky, the gathering clouds, felt her gaze drawn back to Fitz and Kelly. Well. To Fitz.

And then Kelly laid it out for them. 'What is this sadness? This void in your life?'

And suddenly, it was Fitz on the defensive. Covering it well, she could see, but definitely on the retreat. 'I'm sorry. "This void in my life?" "This void in *my* life?"' And the space between the words, the look he gave Kelly, all these said, *What the hell business is it of yours how I conduct my life!*

Interesting.

There was a momentary pause. Penhaligon studied Fitz as he drank his whisky and opened another bottle. The casual chat of other people in the carriage wafted to them on smoky air. Somewhere, distantly, a baby began to cry.

And then Kelly's voice, drifting over all of this, a close-up against the audio background, and Penhaligon found herself pulling focus on his words. 'When I meet my wife, the void in my life will be filled.'

The words broke the spell. Fitz put down his glass after taking only one sip, all business again. 'You really think that do you?'

Kelly frowned, looked back out of the window.

'Cherry Hill Farm?'

Kelly nodded at Penhaligon. 'That's what you said.'

'Does it mean anything to you?'

Kelly shook his head. 'I'll know it when I get there.' His voice was firm, but Penhaligon could hear the doubt there. Fitz did too.

'How long have you been married for?'

Kelly didn't answer.

And Fitz was pushing again. 'Women, eh?' he said in a too-loud voice. He took another sip of whisky. Penhaligon wondered briefly whether the act was deliberate. If it was an act.

Kelly was looking at Fitz, face puzzled, trying to make some sense of the words. Fitz helped him out.

'You know,' he smiled with drunken exaggeratedness.

'Show your picture on the telly, come right out with it. This man is suspected of murder. I'm surprised they didn't all fall for you, not just the one. I bet right now they're phoning in their droves.'

Kelly studied Fitz with a look bordering on anger. Just the first edge, but it would grow. Just as Penhaligon could feel it growing in herself.

'Dirty Den. Mean anything to you?'

Kelly shook his head, sipped at the whisky.

'EastEnders? Neighbours? Home and Away?'

'No.'

Fitz sat up a little straighter in his seat. 'Well, I have this idea, see. A soap, right? And all the actors, not the characters, mind you, all the actors are convicted murderers.' Penhaligon noticed a little glance come her way then. 'Fifteen million viewers, all of them women, no problem. All drooling at the mouth. Mothers. Daughters. Sisters.' He looked at Kelly, back to Penhaligon, back to Kelly. 'Women, eh?'

Penhaligon felt the anger rising in her again. Opened her mouth to speak, but Kelly was there first.

'I'm sure Judith will come back to you.'

Penhaligon allowed herself a thin smile at Fitz's reaction. Kelly was spot on – and Fitz knew it.

Her smile widened when Kelly began to hum. The tune was familiar . . . she couldn't quite place it . . . Fitz took a bad tempered slug of whisky . . . and then Kelly was in full voice.

' " . . . and you sing, Laura, on a train that is passing through . . ."

' " . . . those eyes, how familiar they seem . . ."

' " . . . she gave her very first kiss to you . . ."

' " . . . that was Laura . . . " '

And then Penhaligon saw that heads were turning, conversations fading; even the baby stopped crying because Kelly's voice was so beautiful, a powerful tenor soaring through the carriage, through her mind. Beautiful.

A Police Constable named Daniel Brady was waiting at Sheffield with a car which took them beyond the outskirts of the town, even further into the night. When they reached Cherry Hill Fitz saw the property was a converted farmhouse located on a quarter-acre of well kept gardens. Hibiscus straddled the front fence, a pair of lime trees bordered the main gate. Although not as large a property as it had once been, and situated in what might amount to only one per cent of its original acreage, the property still held its value. Even that might be improved if the hedges were cut back, the limes trimmed, perhaps even pollarded to ensure new growth.

He studied Kelly. Did the man have visions of acres of good grazing, cows, sheep; delinquent chickens chasing each other across a yard filled with hoes and tractors?

Kelly simply gazed out the window of the police car with the same equanimity with which he observed the rest of the world.

Fitz frowned. Unusual. Kelly should be displaying some signs by now. Whether it be excitement, apprehension, fear, happiness. There should be some flicker there. But no. Apart from that one moment in his sitting room an hour and a half before when Kelly's face had lit up with overwhelming joy, there had been nothing. Just the mirrors. Fitz puzzled over that for a moment. Perhaps amnesia wasn't all he was dealing with here. Perhaps there was a mild form of psychosis. Perhaps Kelly was withdrawing, or wanted to withdraw, wanted to hide from the world. Fitz pursed his lips thoughtfully. That would certainly fit in with the evidence they had so far. Young man, parents die, runs away to Rome, drops so far out of normal society you'd need a telescope to spot him.

And now he was back. As the Rover drew to a halt Fitz wondered what really happened to Kelly out there. Why he'd come back. Were they about to find out?

Lights shone in the windows of the main building. Another police car was parked in the gravel path leading up to the house. Fitz got out of the car first, opened the door for Kelly. Penhaligon walked in front with Brady, leading the way up to the front door.

Brady raised the knocker and rapped firmly. The door was opened almost immediately by another uniformed officer who introduced herself as Judy McKerrel. She gestured for them to move into the main room of the farmhouse.

Fitz stood aside to let Kelly walk past him into the room.

The woman waiting for them stood as they came in, eyes locked on Kelly. She was about five seven, slim, neither attractive nor unattractive; had obviously made no effort to smarten her appearance for Kelly's arrival. Straight dark blond hair framed a nondescript face. She wore no make-up that Fitz could see. Her clothes were simple, elegant, not the most expensive nor the cheapest. She stood quite still. Staring at Kelly. And Kelly was staring back. Neither said anything for a moment. The moment of silence continued as Fitz took the opportunity to look around the room. The furnishings fitted the picture he was beginning to form here. Once elegant but old, a little threadbare. An old fashioned radiogram stood against one wall, its scratched cabinet polished to a high gloss. A television squatted incongruously in one corner. Hanging baskets sported flowers and greenery.

It was Kelly that spoke first. 'Your name is Emma.'

He took a step towards the woman. Fitz returned his attention to Kelly's face. It twisted as the man struggled to interpret the data his brain was receiving.

Penhaligon drew Brady and McKerrel to one side. They watched quietly as well.

Kelly took another step closer. Held his hand out. The woman looked at the hand. Looked up. Spoke, suddenly. 'Would you like a cup of tea?'

And suddenly a spike of apprehension drove into Fitz's head. He turned, walked forward even as Kelly nodded. He too held out a hand.

'They call me Fitz. I'm your husband's psychologist.'

The woman blinked, took Fitz's hand. 'Mrs Royle.'

Fitz affected surprise. 'We're divorced. Have been for a number of years. Didn't they tell you? I remarried.'

Kelly's face crumpled. Fitz was peripherally aware of this, drove on anyway.

'Indeed. Mrs Royle. So you recognise this man do you?'

'I said I did, didn't I? Otherwise why would I have phoned?'

'This man. Thomas Francis Kelly?'

'Yes.'

'Your husband of . . . ?' He shrugged. 'Ten years? Longer?'

'Actually we were married for eight years.'

'Before or after Thomas Kelly lived abroad?'

'Oh, after.'

'And, just as a point of interest, Mrs Royle, could you tell me where your then husband, Mister Kelly spent his years abroad?'

The woman pursed her lips. 'No, I'm afraid I can't. You see the years he spent abroad were very traumatic for Thomas. He never liked to talk about them and I didn't like to pry.' She cast a look at Fitz. 'I respected his privacy.'

'Because you loved him.'

'Yes.'

'I see.' Fitz chewed thoughtfully on his lower lip.

Beside him Kelly hovered nervously. 'Fitz . . . ? What's going on here?'

Fitz gave a little shake of his head. 'Mrs Royle, you say you loved your husband. Yet you never made any effort to help him overcome the trauma he must have suffered while he was abroad.' He lifted a finger cutting off her protest. 'Oh yes, I understand that you say you loved your husband. Loved him enough not to pry. That does seem a little odd to me but . . . I suppose it's understandable. What I don't understand is how you could be married to a man for eight years and not realise he had an allergy to caffeine, a fact I learned earlier this evening.'

Mrs Royle closed her mouth.

'You did just offer to make tea for us, did you not?'

'I meant decaffeinated tea.'

Fitz sniffed. Penhaligon smiled, stepped forward. 'Don't worry. I'll get the tea.' There was no accusation in her voice. Fitz nodded.

'Mrs Royle, what was your husband's favourite meal?'

'Actually he liked good old-fashioned home cooking. Pies. He liked his vegetables too.'

'He had large helpings?'

'Yes.'

'Seconds?'

'Sometimes.'

'And did he drink?'

'On occasion.'

'What did he drink?'

'Oh you know . . . the usual.'

'And what was that?'

'Whisky.'

'Glenfiddich?'

'Jack Daniels actually.'

Brady edged a little closer. 'Mister Fitzgerald, is this really –'

Fitz hit him with a look. 'Doctor. It's Doctor Fitzgerald.' Push. Brady folded. Fitz turned back to Mrs Royle. She was quite still and calm, standing with her back to the kitchen where the sound of Penhaligon rummaging around could clearly be heard. Fitz took out a high tar and lit up. He offered the packet to Mrs Royle. She refused.

'Did your husband smoke?'

'No.'

Fitz frowned.

'Actually he gave it up. We both did.'

He took another drag, exhaled. 'And you are quite sure about all this information?'

'Well, as sure as anyone could be after two or three years of separation.'

Fitz pursed his lips. 'Which was it?' he asked suddenly.

'I beg your pardon?'

'You said you'd been apart two or three years. Which was it? Two? Or three?'

'Um . . . three.'

Fitz nodded. 'Mrs Royle, your husband, Thomas Francis Kelly, went to Rome. To the seminary. He learned to be a priest. He learned very well. He doesn't drink. He has a highly developed sense of morals. He is not greedy. Gluttony is a sin, you know.'

Mrs Royle blinked, said nothing.

'On the journey up here, I offered Thomas Francis Kelly a drink. A whisky as a matter of fact. He refused. Apparently,' here he glanced at Kelly, 'it too is a sin.'

Penhaligon came back into the room with a box. She shook it in Fitz's direction. 'Decaffeinated tea.'

Mrs Royle smiled.

Fitz smiled back, took a drag on the high tar. 'Shall I tell you what else is a sin?'

'If you feel you must.'

'The state record system. It's terrible. You can't find anything in there. More bloody holes than the Tory Government's manifesto. In particular, there are no references to the marriage or divorce of a Thomas Francis Kelly or Emma Royle, nee Kelly, nee whatever your name was.'

Fitz took an ashtray off the Welsh dresser and tapped his cigarette into it. He sat on the couch facing Mrs Royle.

'You live alone. By choice, probably. You see the neighbours occasionally. You don't really like them. You don't have a job. You've never found one that suited you. Your parents died some years ago, left you a little money, but that's nearly all gone now. You're not greedy. You're not selfish. But you are lonely. And you're frightened of the world. Frightened to go out there, to see what it's like. The thought of it terrifies you. The thought of us being here terrifies you. But it exhilarates you too, doesn't it? It does. I know it does, I can smell it does. It's something new to think about. Something else apart from the hanging baskets and the old seventy-eights on the 'gram and Jimmy bloody Saville on the radio.'

He flicked a look at Penhaligon. She was quiet. She knew something was going down and she was keeping out of the way. He looked back at Mrs Royle, who sat very suddenly in the nearest armchair. She licked her lips. Her confidence had evaporated with her smile.

'You don't have any pets do you?'

'No.'

'Did you ever have any?'

'Yes.'

'What?'

'A labrador.'

'While you were married to Thomas Francis Kelly?'

'She died . . .' Mrs Royle rubbed the side of her nose. 'I

182

was never married to Thomas Francis Kelly.'

Fitz sighed, took a triumphant drag on his high tar. 'I know.'

He looked at Kelly. The man was quite still, staring at Mrs Royle. His face was quite expressionless.

Mrs Royle put her face in her hands. 'I've done something terrible, haven't I?'

Fitz stubbed out his cigarette. 'A cry for help is hardly a crime.'

Mrs Royle looked up at Kelly then, just for a moment before hiding her face once more in her hands. 'I'm sorry. What you must've thought . . . I'm so sorry . . .'

And Kelly was turning to look at Fitz, and his face wasn't blank any more. It was suffused with a dreadful anger. *You took her away from me, Fitz! You took her away from me!*

Outside Penhaligon caught Fitz by the arm as he prepared to follow Kelly into the Rover driven by Brady. McKerrel had decided to caution Mrs Royle rather than arrest her.

'She doesn't live alone.'

'Do what?'

'Mrs Royle. You stubbed your cigarette out in her ashtray. She doesn't smoke. She doesn't live alone. You were wrong.'

'I was right.' Fitz turned to Penhaligon and allowed her to see something of his own feelings. 'Even if she does live with someone, she still lives alone.' He tapped the side of his head. 'In here.'

Penhaligon opened her mouth, then shut it without saying anything.

'You're saying they don't get on.'

Fitz nodded. *Well done, Panhandle. You're getting the point.* He got into the car, found his mind drawing disturbing parallels between his own marriage and that of Mrs Royle. *And maybe, finally, so am I.*

– the truth, lathered with blood, hands jerking wildly before him, and there was the razor, the cut throat razor in his hand and before him was the truth; wild, inescapable, savage as the pain in his hands, his face, and then he was running, running in dreamlike silence from the girl, her mutilated body, running from the truth –

FIVE

Friday

Penhaligon woke from a restless, dream haunted sleep to a
pounding headache, the kind that comes when the radiators
are left on and the windows are left closed all night. A
claustrophobia headache, one that makes you feel like the
world is boxing you in, just sticking a label on you and
jamming you in a little bottle and leaving you up there on the
shelf with all the other no-hopers. You could see out through
the glass but could never reach the outside world. It was in
sight, frustratingly close, but forever out of reach.

Two mugs of double strength Red Mountain coffee didn't
shift the headache. A palm full of olbas oil rubbed into the
back of her neck, two aspirin, and ten minutes on the balcony
of her flat for a solid dose of fresh air had a similar lack of
effect.

She made breakfast but then couldn't bring herself to eat
it. She showered, paced the flat, uncertain what was wrong,
unable to pin down the cause of her steadily increasing bad
temper.

She arrived at Anson Road after a stupidly fast drive in
anything but a cheerful mood.

The duty room was half full. Bilborough was already
ensconced in his office, ferreting through a mound of papers;
orders, directives, memos from the Chief Super no doubt.
Giggs greeted her with a grin and held out the handset of a
telephone. 'For you,' he said. 'It's your dad.'

185

'Christ,' Penhaligon sighed, sat at her desk. 'Thanks Giggsy. Chuck it over here, yeah?'

Giggs transferred the call.

'Hi, Dad.'

'Hello, Jane.' Her father's voice sounded thin and distant. Well, it was distant, wasn't it? Even further than the telephone made it sound. Had been for ages. 'I've been trying to reach you. I haven't had a lot of luck.'

That's because I've disconnected the phone.

'Yes. I've ... I've been having some problems with the line.'

'I've called you at work as well. You didn't call back.'

That's because I can't handle it. Can't handle the way you let them run your life. They've put you in a box already you stupid bastard. Don't let them!

'I've been a bit busy Dad. Big case going on here. I'm in it up to my ears.'

Oh sure. 'Take the parents Penhaligon. Take the mother. It'll be better coming from you, Penhaligon. You're good at it. Take the parents.'

'Well I just called to say ...' her father hesitated. Penhaligon became aware Giggs was looking at her. Nothing obvious, just a little sideways glance. *Everything OK?* She looked away. Turned to the wall. The filing cabinets. Anything rather than let Giggsy know what was going through her head.

'Sorry, Dad. What was that?'

'I said, I just called for a chat, really. Nothing special.'

'Oh.'

'Are you OK?'

No Dad, it's awful. My life's turned upside down since the weekend. I'm having nightmares, the case is for shit, my boss is a sexist wanker and the psychologist on the case is a misogynistic bastard and all that on top of the wonderful knowledge that my father is –

'Yeah, Dad. I'm fine. Really.'

'Are you sure?'

'Yeah.'

'Well ... Mum sends her love.'

You stupid bastard, Mum doesn't love anybody. Neither do you. You're only phoning now because you're –

A light flashed on the telephone indicating another call was waiting to be answered.

'Dad, I've got to go, I have another call waiting. I . . . look, I'll call you later, alright?'

She put the phone down without waiting for a reply. Shoved her elbows on her desk and rested her chin on her hands. The phone began to ring immediately the receiver hit the cradle. Penhaligon let it ring for a moment. Giggs was looking at her openly now, but no-one else seemed to have noticed her agitation. Thank Christ for small mercies.

Giggs said, 'You want me to take it?'

She shook her head. 'You could dig up some headache tablets for me though if you like.'

'Sure.' He nodded, began to rummage in his desk drawers.

Penhaligon became aware that Bilborough had looked up from his mountain of paperwork, was studying her through his office window. She tried to remember if it was possible to hear the duty room phones ringing from in there. Oh hell. Who gave a blind bollock anyway?

She picked up the receiver, punched the button to accept the call.

She heard a man's voice speaking. Mild, perhaps introverted, a flutter that could indicate nervousness or excitement. And there were background noises as well. A rumbling. And a funny sound that might almost have been someone speaking, except she couldn't quite tell because the man's voice swept over the background noises and swamped them almost entirely.

'I have to speak to DCI Bilborough. I can't give you my name.'

Penhaligon sighed. Another crank. 'DCI Bilborough's out of the office right now.'

A hesitation. The sound of breathing in the silence. Then, 'I know who Sweeney is.'

The blood pounded in her temples. Christ, where was Giggsy with that bloody aspirin? 'I'm DS Penhaligon. I'm authorised to take your call.'

187

Another hesitation on the line. Then, 'I'm a Catholic priest.'

Oh great, a religious nutter.

'This has got to be confidential.'

Hasn't it always?

'Of course, sir.'

'Yes well . . . Look. Are you sure DCI Bilborough's not there? The thing is, it's a bit of a delicate matter.'

For a woman?

'I can take the call, sir. I'll log it and pass it on to DCI Bilborough as soon as he arrives back in the office. Now if you'll just tell me what you have to say. Why don't we start with your name?'

'I said, I can't tell you that!' Anger. A hint of fear?

'Well then. What can you tell me?'

The man's voice lifted a notch. 'I'm not a crank you know.'

No, no, of course you're not, Adolf.

'Of course, sir.'

'Well then,' another hesitation. The breathing got faster. Was this guy a perv? 'Two months ago, a man came to me and confessed to the murder of Astrid Reynolds.'

Penhaligon sat up at that. She remembered the disappearance of Astrid Reynolds vividly – she'd had to cope with the parents on that one too – and it was even worse when there was no body, because there was always that element of hope; hope that the missing girl would show up again, when all Penhaligon's instincts were telling her that simply wasn't going to be the case. And Astrid's case had never been made public. So almost as soon as the man's words had blipped out of the telephone and into her ear, she was signalling Giggs to set a trace in motion while she engaged the caller in a little smalltalk. 'Who was this man who spoke to you, sir?'

A sigh from the telephone. 'I don't know his name. But I'm looking at his picture in the paper right now.'

'Which paper, sir?'

'Yesterday's *Evening News*, late edition, page four. Man in his middle thirties, missing person.'

188

'You're sure about this, sir?'

'Look. It's got to be confidential. I've heard all this in confession.'

Penhaligon rubbed her eyes tiredly. 'Did he tell you where Astrid's body is now?'

'Promise me it's confidential.'

That lie was easy. Standard police procedure. 'It's confidential.'

A long silence from the phone, filled by a kind of clanging noise. Penhaligon shifted restlessly in her seat. On Giggs's desk a small hill of origami models taken from his drawers during the detective's search for aspirin wobbled alarmingly as the telephone wire brushed against it, Giggs himself was whispering urgently into the phone, organising the trace.

Eventually the voice on the other end of Penhaligon's phone said, 'She's at the bottom of Clayton Wharf.'

Christ. That's only a mile from where I live!

'And you say you knew about this two months ago?' Stay calm. In control. One hint of excitement, any emotion, and you've lost him.

'Yes.'

Two desks away, Giggs looked up from his phone. He turned, mouthed the words, *It's local,* made a circular motion with his fingers: *Keep the bastard talking.*

The voice on the phone said, 'I'm putting the phone down.'

Penhaligon jumped into the silence. 'I've promised you confidentiality. I just want to know why you've waited this long.'

'Are you a Catholic?'

Not if it was the last religion on Earth.

'Uh . . . it's one of a number of religions I've . . . recently come into contact with.'

'But you don't practise?'

'No, not as such.'

'Then you wouldn't understand.'

'I might. I'll try. Look, I tell you what, you try to explain. I'll try to understand.'

'He's killed again, hasn't he?' The voice on the phone

189

softened, seemed to come nearer, to crawl into her ear, into her head. 'The same way.'

'What way would that be, sir? Did he tell you? You must be able to give us a few more details.'

There was a long silence. No not quite silence. Something was ... no, someone was ... Penhaligon waved her arm around, trying to get a bit of quiet.

'He's killed again hasn't he?' The voice was a bad tape recording in her head, the stuff of nightmares. 'Killed again the same way?'

'Possibly.'

'God forgive me.'

The line went dead.

Penhaligon slapped the phone down. 'Giggsy?'

'One minute, they're just getting a fix.'

'Doesn't matter. There was sound on the line. A voice. A tannoy.'

She looked up at the ceiling, down again, aware she had the whole room's attention. 'He's at the station.'

And Giggs was there to confirm her supposition, slamming the phone down and toppling the stack of origami models across the desk blotter. 'Platform fourteen.'

Bilborough had come out of his office for the last few moments of the call. 'Well? What are you waiting for? Jimmy,' he turned to Beck. 'Go with her will you?'

Penhaligon caught Giggs's eye as she got up from her desk. He grinned. *Makes a change from the parents, eh?* He tossed her a box of neurofen he'd taken from his desk drawer, hastily swept the origami models back into it.

Penhaligon caught the box with a grin. She stuffed the box in her jacket pocket, even though she didn't think she'd be needing them. The headache had already begun to recede.

Something told Penhaligon there was no point in rushing to the station. She drove like a bastard anyway, running red lights with the siren blaring, only killing it as she slid the Volvo into the station forecourt, a shade ahead of the police Rover carrying Beck and a couple of uniforms.

190

And she was right. By the time they reached platform fourteen ten minutes had passed since she'd put down the phone in Anson Road. She glared around the station, took in the numbers of people, mid morning commuters, early shoppers, families starting their weekends early, all getting ripped off on the Friday white travel day, and shook her head in despair. The only way they'd catch the bloke now would be if by some miracle he'd been stupid enough to make another call after the one he'd made to Anson Road.

She led the way along platform fourteen, Beck at her side, his face set in its usual scowl, roll-up tucked behind one ear. There was only one phone box on the platform. Penhaligon sighed. Maybe ... but Beck was already off, opening the door and taking the phone from the person inside, placing it back on the cradle, his reactions automatic, and the uniforms were backing him up, leaving just Penhaligon to hesitate.

When Beck realised the person he'd ushered insistently from the phone box was a woman the look on his face was priceless, almost a match for that of the woman herself.

In her twenties, wearing torn leggings and an old greatcoat covered in painted designs; braided hair full of beads and a head full of dope, the phone box stank of it. She stared at Beck with a mixture of stupid surprise and outrage, as if to say, *What the hell, got video cameras in the bloody phone boxes now have you?*

Beck sighed in disgust as she shook free of his grip.

One of the uniforms eyed the joint in the woman's hands, said to Beck, 'She's in possession, Guv. You want to take her in?'

Beck shook his head. 'Don't be stupid. Total waste of time. Avon and Somerset'll get her for something serious at Glastonbury.'

The uniform nodded sagely, 'If the bloody government don't make that illegal too, eh, Guv?' This observation earned him black looks from both Beck and the woman.

Beck opened the door to the telephone box. 'I'm sorry about that, ma'am. Genuine mistake. You can go about your business.'

The woman thrust her face aggressively forward. 'And

191

how am I supposed to do that when you've just wasted my last ten pence?'

Beck just sighed and Penhaligon didn't need to hear the words he muttered contemptuously under his breath. *Oh fuck off.* He turned away as the woman hit on one of the uniforms for some loose change.

Penhaligon took it all in peripherally. But her attention was fixed on something else; nothing concrete, more like an idea, or at least, the germ of an idea.

'What's bugging you then?' Beck. Bad tempered, embarrassed at his mistake.

Penhaligon frowned thoughtfully, gazed around at the bustling crowd. 'Why would a priest phone the police from the platform of a railway station?'

'Perhaps he just picked up the paper this morning.'

Penhaligon shook her head. 'No. He said he saw the picture in last night's evening edition.'

Penhaligon left Beck staring thoughtfully at a nearby newspaper vendor as she began to walk back to the cars but there was no answer there.

An hour later Penhaligon parked her car at Clayton Wharf, got out, studied the lay of the land.

The wharf was no different from any stretch of canal in the city. A little lonelier perhaps, bordered by the usual towpaths and narrow strips of waste ground. One path was particularly narrow, made of brick, and abutted directly onto a high wall made of damp brick which had been slowly crumbling into the water for at least fifty years. At one time the wall had been pierced with openings through which cargoes could be offloaded, moved to the courtyard beyond and then distributed to the buildings beyond. Now the openings were sealed by only slightly newer brick, the rotted stumps of wooden derricks hung limply over the water while beyond the wall a new industrial estate had sprung up, low units containing a graphics house, a DIY wholesalers, a magazine distributor and the local car pound. The top of the wall had been levelled and banked with earth, landscaped to form a lunchtime respite for the workers in the estate: the same workers who were now held back by a dozen uniformed constables, and half a mile of *no admittance* tape.

Penhaligon climbed a grassy embankment to the path that ran along the top of the wall, eyes glued to the ground even though the chances of finding any form of evidence after such a long time was almost negligible. Along the banks of the canal, handlers with dogs were strung out in a long line, also sniffing for evidence. They weren't likely to be successful, but Bilborough was taking no chances. This one was going by the book.

Penhaligon was disturbed by a sound. A motor launch. That would be the frogmen, dropping a new team into the canal to dredge. She sighed, wondering if they'd find anything. Anyone. She stopped for a moment to watch them flip backwards into the scummy water. A few of the lunchtime crowd gathering beyond the taped off boundary clapped. What did they think this was, a circus?

Penhaligon began to walk again, wanting to put as much distance as the local environs permitted between herself and the crowd.

As she walked she envisaged the setting at night; the cold glare of one yellow sodium lamp, casting rings of light through the branches of a few artfully placed trees, the dark buildings lurking beyond the grassy slope, the gentle lapping of the water only twenty-odd feet below the path, beyond the tubular steel safety rail.

What had Astrid Reynolds been doing here?

She fit the pattern: twenty-two years old. Attractive, perhaps beautiful. Intelligent if her records were anything to go by. Liked by her friends. No enemies as such, though Penhaligon found it easy to imagine that, at school particularly, Astrid, like Jacqui and Patricia before her, had been the subject of more than the average amount of jealousy from girls who weren't so well liked.

Penhaligon sighed, and as she sighed the imagined night closed in around her, and she pictured herself as Astrid, walking along here, perhaps for a secret meeting with a friend or lover. But no-one turned up. They're late. What should she do? Leave, or hang around? Give it a few minutes. Just a few.

Perhaps they'll turn up. Just a few minutes in the dark. That was all, then home.

Then the footsteps, the friendly greeting followed by silence, followed by – what? A chase? A scream? Or just a silent struggle, no strength left to cry for help, just flight or fight, fight or die. And then the soft hiss of a blade through the air, through skin, a flood of blood, perhaps a short sigh of surprise or pain, a moment of silence to register the swiftly approaching end of life, and then a spastic struggle fading into the night as life drained out of her with the blood –

Penhaligon looked up, there was a shout from one of the frogmen. The launch cruised slowly over to where the figure had ripped off his breathing mask and was waving in the air for attention.

Penhaligon watched as more figures crowded around. After a few minutes something roughly the size of a person was brought to the surface and eased onto the launch. Penhaligon looked closer. A wrapped body, rotted by the water? The frogmen all began to laugh suddenly. Penhaligon realised she was looking at an old roll of carpet loaded with silt and weed.

What they'd fished from the canal was the forensic equivalent of an old boot.

The frogmen dumped the offending item onto the towpath and resumed their search.

Penhaligon leaned against the steel railings bordering the walkway and cast her mind back over the last two months, back to the time that Astrid Reynolds had been reported missing.

It had been the week her father had been diagnosed as having inherited the disease Huntington's Chorea.

Because of her partial estrangement from her parents and brothers, Penhaligon had only been peripherally aware of her father's illness. The usual tests had been carried out, all negative. Then one bright medical spark had the idea of testing for Huntington's. A month later the result had come back: positive.

She kicked absently at a stone, watched it arc into the water, watched the ripples spread and fade. She was like that,

194

a ripple spreading from her father's illness, but unlike the wave in the water there would be no natural fade with time.

Huntington's was a wasting disease, one which melted the flesh from its victims. Its other symptoms were akin to those of motor neurone disease, but it acted much more slowly, over the course of years rather than months. The problem was by the time any symptoms were displayed the victim was usually well into his middle age with a family, children. And that was the horror of Huntington's. Unlike motor neurone disease it was inheritable – invariably fatal to the male line, and inheritable through the female line, in which it was non fatal.

There was a fifty per cent chance that she herself was a carrier. She couldn't have children. Didn't dare risk it. Didn't even dare risk the test. Because what if the disease was inside her, coiled up in her DNA somewhere, hiding, dirt under the carpet, unreachable?

At that point there was another commotion from the vicinity of the launch. Another bundle was hoisted aboard. This one white and bloated, wrapped in scraps of discoloured fabric and the tattered remains of human hair.

That was it then. They'd found her. Astrid.

Penhaligon retraced her steps along the walkway and down onto the towpath proper, where the frogmen had set up a cache of equipment, extra tanks of air, excavating tools and the like. The launch was already moored there; less than a hundred yards away from the car park for the industrial estate. As she watched Bilborough's car drew up and parked. The DCI got out, closely followed by Beck, Copeley and Murphy, the pathologist and photographer carrying a minimum of on-site equipment.

Beck wandered over to the launch while Bilborough glanced around, spied Penhaligon, came over. 'Is it her?'

Of course not, Bilbo, it's a murder victim's convention down there; they're pulling them up in their droves.

'Seems likely, sir.'

Bilborough nodded. 'Listen . . . that was nice work on the phone earlier.'

Penhaligon was thrown for a moment. 'Er . . . thanks. We

left a few uniforms at the station asking around for descriptions of anyone using the phone about the time the call was made.'

Bilborough nodded again. 'As I said. Good work. Now. Let's hope what they've pulled out of here doesn't turn out to be an old boot.'

Penhaligon pursed her lips but said nothing. Sometimes Bilborough's sensitivity vanished so far into minus figures it might have been rocket powered.

Copeley was gently peeling back the rotted tatters of cloth surrounding the body as they approached. Penhaligon swallowed hard. What the water made of Astrid looked like it could have come out of a cheap horror flick. The real horror was that this almost shapeless mass of ragged, bloated flesh had once been a beautiful young woman named Astrid Reynolds.

'Did she drown?' That was Beck. Digging for information as usual.

Copeley frowned, studied the body. 'There's a lot of surface damage. A blood test to determine the red cell count and level of potassium would tell us that; drowning in fresh water always messes up the blood salt balance.' He looked up. 'That's what causes death you know. Not oxygen starvation. Upset the blood salts that regulate heartbeat and – bingo – no heartbeat.' He knelt beside the body, ran gloved hands over the puffy flesh of the face and neck. 'But she didn't drown.'

'Oh?'

Copeley turned the head of the corpse slightly, the flesh already beginning to crumble. The wound was almost swallowed by the bloated flesh of the neck, but under Copeley's ministrations it became clearer. A wound that must once have been straight edged. A razor wound. They'd found another of Sweeney's victims.

Penhaligon could have predicted Bilborough's next words. To Beck and Penhaligon he said, 'Jimmy. Let the parents know, will you? Penhaligon – go with him. When you've done that get round to Fitz's. Bring that bastard Kelly in.'

Fitz poured Yorkshire pudding mix into a bowl and began to whisk. He used a hand whisk, not because there was no power mixer in the kitchen, but simply because he liked to whisk. The repetitive movement exorcised tensions in his muscles without interrupting his steady flow of thought. Fitz liked to cook; if he wasn't particularly good or bad, at least he was consistent. And oddly, it was the one thing about himself that he rarely, if ever, examined. Judith had often commented that if he'd only concentrate on the culinary arts instead of gambling he'd probably have made a more than fair chef. Then again, perhaps Judith's interest in his undeveloped talent was one of the things that drove him to ignore it.

Behind Fitz, Kelly was peeling and chopping spuds. Fitz spared him a sideways glance. He was making an almighty hash of it. Then again after a night like they'd had last night perhaps it was only to be expected.

When Fitz had brought Kelly home he'd gone immediately to his room and, presumably, to sleep. Fitz could only wonder what his dreams had been like. When he'd awoken the next morning, and wandered down to make breakfast, Fitz found Kelly in the garden. He had opened the French windows and was sitting cross-legged on the garden lawn, just sitting there, still and quiet, staring at a collection of sparrows that were pecking at the grass about ten or fifteen feet away from him. He'd been up for hours by the look in his eyes. A haunted look ringed by darkness indicative of how little sleep he'd had.

Fitz would have given his right arm to know what those dreams had been about.

'How do you like your eggs?' he'd asked.

There had been a moment's hesitation from Kelly before his eyes locked to Fitz, his gaze pulling out almost completely from his interior landscape. 'Why did she do it?'

Fitz had sighed. It was going to be one of those days. 'Why does anyone do anything?' He studied Kelly, sitting cross-legged on the grass. 'Why did you leave the country? Go to Rome?'

'I suppose I wanted to be a priest.'

'You remember that?'

Kelly frowned. Shook his head.

'What about why you left. Do you remember that?'

'I was . . . unsatisfied.' Kelly rubbed one hand absently across his grazed cheeks. 'With my life. I . . .' He gestured with the other hand, Fitz saw there was the remains of a crust of bread in it. 'I took it from the breadbin. It was past its sell by date. Do you mind?'

Fitz shook his head. Taking the crust, he broke it into pieces, threw them at the sparrows. The birds took flight, frightened by the hail of food.

Kelly watched the birds peck and squabble over the choicest crumbs. 'Manna from heaven.'

Fitz looked at him. 'It's just bread.'

'To us, that might be true.' Kelly gave a tremulous kind of half-smile. ' "And the Lord said unto Moses: Behold I will rain bread from heaven for you: let the people go forth and gather what is sufficient for every day: that I may prove them whether they walk my law or not." ' He paused, eyes lost in the distance, before continuing. ' "So it came to pass in the evening that quails coming up, covered the camp: And in the morning a dew lay round about the camp, like unto the hoar frost on the ground. And when the Children of Israel saw it they knew not what it was. And Moses said to them: this is the bread, which the Lord hath given you to eat." '

As Kelly came to the end of his recital, Fitz was nodding slowly. 'Do you suppose they were scared?'

A puzzled look stretched across Kelly's face. 'What?'

'The people who were there. Do you think they were scared?'

Kelly frowned. 'I don't understand your point. Of course they were scared. They were fleeing for their lives.'

Fitz shook his head. 'The point I'm trying to make is that it was a pretty improbable occurrence, right? All those people, no food or water, then all of a sudden, bingo! Old Moses pushes a few cosmic buttons, hits the heavenly jackpot and the manna falls like . . . well, you get the point.'

'I suppose so.'

'But the Bible never lies, right?'

'I suppose not.'

'So how do you explain the discrepancy?'

Kelly hesitated.

'You don't know.' It wasn't a question and Kelly knew it. He shrugged. 'I . . . suppose I don't.'

Fitz grinned, lightened the mood abruptly. 'What the hell; it's probably all a load of old hogwash anyway, right? Written by a couple of guys with an eye for a good yarn and a fast return.'

Kelly stared at him. 'You're laughing at me.'

Fitz shook his head.

'What then?'

'It's just interesting that's all.'

'What is?'

'That someone who spent a decade of their life in Rome learning to be a priest could admit to having a less than total belief in the one thing that forms the core of his faith.'

Kelly's eyes narrowed. 'How do you know that's true?'

'Ask any priest, even the average churchgoer. They'll reason away the Bible's inconsistencies with any number of explanations. It was an analogy. It was metaphorical. Any number of explanations. Yet when I asked, you had none. You merely accepted the possibility that the foundation of the Christian ethic could be inconsistent, even untrue.'

Kelly's breathing quickened. 'Do you think that's important?'

Fitz threw the last piece of bread to the end of the garden. 'I think it's time for breakfast.' Seeing there were no more missiles coming their way, the sparrows began to return. 'Scrambled eggs on toast alright for you?'

Kelly laughed. It was the last reaction Fitz had expected, but it was at least interesting.

After that one spell of humour Kelly had lapsed again into a depression which lasted the following two hours. Fitz had taken a stroll down to Eddie's, where he'd lost a little, won a little more, and returned home an hour later in a fair-to-middling mood. Mark had been on his way out as Fitz had re-entered the house. Taking a chance Fitz had smiled at his

199

son. Mark had looked coldly at him. *How could you leave me alone in the house with a murderer? A serial killer?*

Fitz's good humour melted away along with his smile. 'Lunch will be at two-thirty.'

'Fine.' Mark had slammed the door on his way out.

Now Fitz finished stirring the Yorkshire pudding mix as the front door slammed indicating Mark's return to the house. Fitz continued whisking as he followed his son's progress through the house by the noise he made: the slam of the front door, the thud as a rucksack hit the bottom of the stairs, the clump of footsteps into the sitting room and through into the kitchen. Mark stopped in the doorway. Fitz glanced up – and that was when he realised something was wrong.

'When's it gonna be ready –' That was as far as Mark got before trailing off. He stared at Fitz – no, not at Fitz, past him.

Fitz turned. Kelly was standing quite still, one hand gripping the other, the potato knife clutched in white-knuckled fingers. Both Kelly's hands and the knife were covered in blood. More blood dripped from the blade into the saucepan containing the peeled potatoes.

Fitz became aware Mark was backing away. He raised a hand. *Stay still!* Mark froze.

Fitz looked back at Kelly. The man was hunched over slightly, favouring the wounded hand. The blood seemed to be coming from a thin cut in the base of his thumb. Kelly turned then, slowly, as if mesmerised, until the knife was pointing directly at Fitz.

'Blood.' Kelly's voice was quiet, almost weak. Almost.

Behind Fitz, Mark made a noise, a kind of sigh, a mixture of surprise and anger. Fitz ignored his son, concentrated on Kelly. Something was going on here. They might be in line for a breakthrough if he handled this right.

'They asked me to kill the chicken.'

'Who's "they?" '

'I put a sack over it.'

'Dad . . .'

'Be quiet, Mark!'

200

'It was struggling . . .'

'Who's "*they*?"'

And Kelly was away, eyes half closed, focused on an interior landscape only he could see. 'I bought the axe down, through its neck, through the sack. It twitched. Pulsed. With every pulse the blood spread. I held it down, dying, pulsing . . .'

Fitz became aware Mark was moving, backing away. Good. Let him go. Kelly was remembering. And the truth was somewhere close. It was in the room, in here with him, in Kelly. Now. All it needed was a little push, a nudge in the right direction and –

The doorbell rang.

Immediately Kelly was upright, moving, eyes wide, droplets of blood flying from the knife to splatter against the oven, the floor. He lunged towards Fitz, knife gleaming. Fitz remained perfectly still. *Don't move. That's the truth, right there in the room. Move and you'll scare it off. Move and you'll never –*

Kelly stopped with the knife six inches from Fitz's chest. *Go on. Say it. Tell me; everything, anything. I'm here, I'm waiting. Tell me!*

And Mark was back at a run, two familiar figures pushing past him into the kitchen even as Kelly reversed the knife and held it to Fitz, eyes filled with horror, fear, total realisation.

'Put the knife down, you twisted pervert.' That was Beck. 'Or I promise you I'll break your other bloody arm.' Beck took Kelly out to the car, taking care to make sure he didn't get any blood on his skin or clothing.

Fitz stared at Penhaligon. 'He was on the verge of remembering. He actually did remember something. Something from his past.'

Penhaligon was unable to meet Fitz's accusation. She looked away. Then, 'Bilborough's orders. Another girl's been found.'

'A new one?'

Penhaligon shook her head. 'Two months old, maybe a bit more. Astrid Reynolds.'

'Then it doesn't prove anything, you know that!'

'There was a phone call.'

'A phone call? Saints preserve us from Santa's little helpers.' There was more. 'Kelly's beginning to crack.' A push. 'I'm close. I know I'm close. You know I'm close.'

Penhaligon said, 'Talk to Bilborough.'

Fitz sighed. 'Give us a bloody lift then, eh?'

The drive to Anson Road was a nightmare. Kelly said nothing, just seemed to sink further into a bleak depression. Penhaligon drove like a mad woman. Beck was a threatening presence beside Kelly in the back, leering, crowding into his personal space. Fitz glanced around once or twice. Threw a glare or two at Beck. The detective ignored Fitz with the same intensity that he intimidated Kelly.

When they arrived at Anson Road, Beck took Kelly to the cells. Penhaligon went with them. Fitz thanked heavens for small mercies. Without Penhaligon's presence, there was no telling what Beck might do to extract a confession from Kelly.

Fitz himself headed upstairs to incident, strode through the duty room and barged into Bilborough's office without knocking.

'I must see him again,' he said, hands spread across the desk, towering over Bilborough as he sat behind it. Pushing.

Bilborough frowned. Thought about his reply. Fitz could see the sarcasm, the anger all tangled up inside, struggling to get out. Instead, when he spoke, Bilborough's voice was quiet, with only a thin edge of sharpness to mar the calm. 'I'm sorry, Fitz. You're wrong about Kelly. He's as guilty as sin. We've got evidence that he's admitted to killing Astrid Reynolds.'

Crap!

'It's circumstantial, you know that. You don't have a witness. A phone call won't get you a conviction.'

'A confession will.'

Christ, Bilborough, you're a bloody-minded idiot sometimes, do you know that?

'Please. Just once more. He was on the verge of remembering something. Don't blow it now, please.'

Bilborough hesitated. Sighed. Fitz smiled. *Gotcha!*

His smile faded as Bilborough said, 'You're wrong about Kelly, Fitz. You've been wrong all the way down the line. You're out.'

Fitz straightened. 'And that's your final word?'

Bilborough nodded.

'Right then.' Fitz turned to leave. *I'll have to use other avenues.*

Bilborough didn't rise to show him out. He looked worried though. *Fine. Let him look worried. I'll give him reason to worry.*

Fitz stumped through incident, drawing looks from everyone there. Giggs threw him a sympathetic shrug and Fitz nodded slightly in return. Beyond incident, in the corridor, his temper began to build. The wanker. The wanker. What did he think he was playing at. Out? Him, Fitz, out? So close to cracking it? Cracking Kelly? Getting at the truth? Wanker. Wanker!

He realised he must be muttering the words aloud when a uniformed constable carrying a box of documents along the corridor gave him a narrow look. Fitz smiled ingenuously at the man. 'Bilborough,' he said. That one word spoke volumes. He thought he saw a look of relief on the constable's face when he realised Fitz wasn't looking for a reply, and he was going to be able to slip past Fitz and hurry on up the corridor without being engaged in conversation.

When the doors to the lift opened he cruised in. The only other occupant of the lift turned and looked at him. Penhaligon.

Fitz shoved the button for the ground floor.

After a moment he pursed his lips thoughtfully. He gave Penhaligon a sideways look. She met his gaze squarely. *Whatever the game is, I'm not playing*, her face seemed to say. *So bugger off.*

Fitz tilted his head to one side. *Other avenues.*

Penhaligon seemed about to put her expression into words. Before she could do so, Fitz reached out and slapped the emergency stop button on the lift control panel. The lift shuddered to a halt between floors. Somewhere in the building an alarm bell began to ring.

203

Penhaligon sighed, closed her eyes momentarily. In a perfectly controlled voice, as if this sort of thing happened to her every day, she said, 'I'll scream.'

Fitz smiled. *Keep it light.* 'I'm not after your body, Panhandle.'

She stared at him. 'Penhaligon.' Her voice dripped ice.

And he was away, gently at first, but building in intensity, building because she had to see his point, had to see it his way. 'Look I want a list of suspects aged thirty-five to forty-five, who are single and catholic. I want a car. And I want you as a driver because I'll need your I.D.'

Penhaligon laughed. 'If this lift isn't moving in ten seconds I start screaming.' She began to count.

Fitz's smile slipped a notch. 'Come on, what's the difference? You're on the case anyway!'

Penhaligon didn't react to Fitz's words, merely continued counting. She reached five. Six. Seven.

'You'll solve the case. You'll catch the killer. You'll get all these wonderful brownie points.'

Penhaligon said, 'Eight. Nine.' She looked at Fitz. 'Ten.'

He stared back, imploringly. *Come on, Panhandle. See it my way, I know you can do it.*

Her face utterly expressionless, Penhaligon began to scream in a tight, controlled manner. More like a siren than a woman.

Fitz screwed up his face. In the narrow confines of the lift the sound was deafening.

'Look, Bilborough's wrong. I know he's wrong. You know he's wrong.'

That earned a flicker of interest from Penhaligon. It didn't stop her screaming though. And from the stairwell wrapped around the lift shaft came the sound of running feet, officers responding to the alarm, and to Penhaligon's screams.

'Please do this for me. I'll repay you. I promise. Look. I have to do this. Please. *Please.*'

Penhaligon kept right on screaming.

Amazed to find himself genuinely begging Penhaligon for her help, Fitz sighed. He punched a button on the panel and the lift began to descend once more.

Immediately Penhaligon stopped screaming. Without changing expression, she looked at him and asked, 'Why?'

Fitz was on the point of answering when the lift reached the ground floor. The doors shuddered open, revealing a crowd of uniforms; faces, all staring at them with expressions ranging from curiosity to alarm.

Instantly Penhaligon was away, out of the lift and off along the corridor. The words 'Just testing,' drifted back over her shoulder, deadpan.

As one, the staring faces turned to follow Penhaligon, then rotated back towards Fitz. He, too, cruised through them, not following Penhaligon, instead heading for the main entrance to the station. He smiled a thin smile as he reached the middle of the crowd of officers, sure he had their complete attention.

'Multiple orgasms,' he said loudly, clearly, and with more than a hint of smugness.

When Penhaligon left Fitz in the lift, she turned a corner and went straight back up the stairs to incident. Her mind whirling with thoughts. What the hell was going on here? What was Bilborough playing at? Was Fitz on the case or was the fat bastard trying some kind of end run around the police heirarchy? If he was and he was using her, he could go and jump in a canal as far as she was concerned.

By the time she'd reached the third floor for the second time in ten minutes part of her anger at Fitz's attitude had faded. She was inclined to think rationally about his plea. From his point of view it was easy to see where the problems lay. Bilborough. When you examined it with any thought at all it all boiled back down to Bilborough.

As she entered incident Penhaligon found herself wondering exactly how competent the DCI was. How he'd got where he was, and how he was planning to move on the rest of the case.

She got an answer to her last question almost immediately.

Bilborough spied her through the window and waved her into his office, where he and Beck were talking in low voices. He looked up as she entered.

'I'm going to interview Kelly myself. Jimmy's going to be the second officer present. You'll be observing. So if you could get the prisoner sorted for me? Get him into the interview room?'

'Sir.'

Penhaligon did an about face and got out of there before her composure broke down and she told Bilborough exactly what she thought of him.

Bilborough brought the recording of her telephone conversation with the priest to the interview room. Kelly was already there when he arrived with Beck. He hadn't said a word to her. Somehow she was rather relieved about that. She didn't really know what to say to him. You were supposed to stay impartial in situations like this. Impartial, unemotional.

Somehow, faced with Kelly, looking into his eyes, that all went straight out of the window. And what was left was confusion.

What was it about this bloody case that affected her so? Sometimes she felt if she saw Kelly's self-effacing smile one more time she'd go stark staring cuckoo.

Bilborough put the tape recorder down on the table between himself and Beck, in front of Kelly. Slipped two cassettes into the recorder which would tape their conversations, started the interview.

Kelly responded mutely to all Bilborough's questions. Then he played the tape.

And the voice on the telephone said, 'He's killed again, hasn't he? Killed in the same way?'

And her own voice said, 'Possibly.'

And the voice again: 'God forgive me.'

Bilborough stopped the tape. She watched Kelly for a reaction. If it turned out that he had been a priest it had been a good idea to play him the tape. How would he take to the accusation from another priest that he was the killer, was Sweeney?

Kelly licked his lips. Sniffed. Blew his nose. Said nothing. Not that he needed to. Bilborough was already on him, voice deceptively calm.

'So? Are you a Catholic? Do you understand me? Are you a Catholic?'

'I think so.' Slowly. Some hesitation there. Was he trying to avoid the question? He must know that was impossible surely?

Bilborough went on, 'Well? Do you think a Catholic priest would lie?'

Kelly shook his head slowly.

'Could you answer rather than shake your head?' Bilborough nodded towards the tape recorder. 'Do you think a Catholic priest would lie?'

'No.' If Penhaligon expected to hear desperation, despair, she was mistaken. Kelly's voice was tired, flat, but still essentially emotionless.

Bilborough leaned forward, said, 'Then you did it. You killed those girls.'

Penhaligon sat up in her chair. Kelly was nodding! Was he going to admit it? Bilborough leaned even closer. She could feel the desperation coming off him in waves, like an animal on the hunt, about to attack.

'Could you answer, rather than nod your head!' A breath. 'You killed those girls didn't you? Astrid. Patricia. Jacqui. You killed them all, didn't you?'

Now Penhaligon was as hooked as Bilborough was. And there was something about him, she had to admit that, some inner strength, something. Kelly was crumbling before his mesmeric gaze. Was he going to say it? She held her breath, aware Bilborough was doing the same, half poised across the table.

And then Kelly spoke. 'It appears so.'

Bilborough grinned, sat back in his chair with a sigh. He shot Beck a triumphant glance.

Beck got up from his chair at the table, walked around behind Kelly. 'So. You kill her. She's reported missing. Nobody knows she's dead, except you. You get a buzz out of that. But that buzz wears off. You want her found. You want it all over the papers. Next time you kill you leave her where she drops. Third time an even bigger buzz. You do it on a train, a moving train, with people all around. What next?' He bent low, breathing smoke from his roll-up onto Kelly's face. Kelly coughed, tried to look away. His gaze landed on Bilborough, was deflected right back to Beck, who held him with his words. 'How do you top that? Do it on stage? Sell tickets?'

Kelly closed his eyes. Penhaligon sat quite still. Watching. Thinking. What had Beck said? *The buzz wears off. You want her found.*

Beck took Kelly's chin in his hand, pulled the man round to look at him. 'You did it, didn't you? Didn't you?'

And Kelly finally fell apart. 'I want to confess.'

The tension in the room pressed against Penhaligon in waves.

Bilborough and Beck exchanged glances. Beck stubbed out his roll-up. Then Bilborough said: 'We're listening.'

'I want to confess . . .' said Kelly. '. . . to a priest.'

Bilborough uttered a short laugh. 'No.'

And Penhaligon looked back at Kelly. He looked like he was about to cry. 'I wanted you to find another body. I wanted to prove to myself – oh, to you as well, but mainly to myself – that I couldn't have done these things, killed those girls.' He licked his lips. 'Can I have some water?'

Bilborough shook his head. 'When you've finished.'

Was that a flash of anger in Kelly's eyes? Penhaligon looked more closely but the expression had faded.

'So . . . if another girl died and you were watching me, then you'd know I couldn't possibly have done these things. And that would be it. The proof I needed.' And now he did start crying. A single tear sliding along one cheek. 'And then I realised what I was praying for. For another human being to die so I could be at peace . . . and now . . . and now it's happened . . . and another family . . . and it proves nothing. Nothing!'

When Kelly finally calmed down, Beck took him away. Penhaligon waited behind, caught Bilborough's eye as he was about to leave the interview room.

'Yes, Penhaligon. What is it?'

Penhaligon licked her lips. Bilborough wasn't going to like this. 'Well, sir. It's like Beck said. The buzz wears off. You want the body found.'

'Yeah. So?'

'Well don't you see? That works for Kelly but it also works for the man who phoned as well.'

Bilborough remained calm, almost magnanimous. 'We've got a confession. The rest is just details.'

Penhaligon frowned impatiently.

Bilborough added, 'Do *you* think a Catholic priest would lie?'

'Sir ... I have no proof the man on the phone was a Catholic priest.'

Bilborough sighed. 'Penhaligon, you're a good copper, I know that. Why would Kelly confess if he didn't do it?'

Penhaligon shrugged. 'I don't know.'

'There you are then.' He smiled, and the smile transformed his face. Suddenly Penhaligon had an inkling of how young he really was. 'Come on. Drinks're on me tonight.'

He left the room, leaving Penhaligon to stare moodily at the tape recorders on the interview room table.

21:30–23:00

Mark was on the phone when Fitz got home. 'Are we paying for that?' The comment earned him a black look from Mark. 'Cos if we are I don't want you on there an hour and a half like you were the other day.'

Mark sighed. To the phone, he said, 'Hang on.' He cupped his hand over the mouthpiece and said, 'They're paying. And Mum's been.'

Fitz leaned against the wall, looked hard at Mark, imagined the words he didn't speak, *And you've been too, haven't you Dad? Down the pub getting rat arsed.*

'I can smell the sulphur.'

Mark shrugged. 'She said she'd be back later. Something she wants to tell you, or something.'

'I'll look forward to that then. Did she say when?'

'No. And there's a copper here to see you. Told her I didn't know when you'd be back, but she insisted on waiting anyway. She's in there,' Mark gestured towards the sitting

209

room before returning to his phone conversation.

Fitz moved unsteadily towards the sitting room. 'Did you offer her a cup of tea?'

'Do what?'

'I said, did you – never mind.'

Fitz entered the sitting room. Penhaligon was perched uneasily on the sofa. As he entered she rose. Fitz gazed at her narrowly. Took in the slight flush, the narrowed lips where normally there would be a carefully neutral expression. 'You've had a drink or two, haven't you, Panhandle?'

'Penhaligon.' Cold. But patient. 'And yes, I have had a drink.'

'With the lads?'

'Yes, with the lads.'

'Got a confession from Kelly then?'

'Bilborough thinks so.'

'But you don't?'

'Fitz . . . do you ever stop asking questions?'

'Why do you want to know?'

Penhaligon sighed. 'You've had a drink too, haven't you?'

'Indeed I have. As I said, I like it.' He studied Penhaligon narrowly. 'It is OK to do things that you want to once in a while, Panhandle.'

Penhaligon stared at Fitz. 'You've got me for one week.'

Fitz smiled. 'I had pleurisy once. For two.'

Penhaligon laughed. Her face changed completely when she laughed, Fitz realised. He couldn't quite work out how, exactly, but the change was definitely appealing. 'Drink?'

'Think I've had enough, really.'

Fitz shrugged. Emptied some vodka into a glass. 'So what made you change your mind?'

'Women's privilege.'

'Aha.' Fitz sat down, set his drink on the floor beside the chair and eased off his shoes. 'Women's privilege.'

'Yes.' Penhaligon sat down too. 'You know. Maybe I will have that drink.'

Fitz got back to his feet, poured Penhaligon a vodka. 'Tonic?'

'No.'

'Ice?'

'No thanks.'

'Lemon?'

'That's what causes the brain damage.'

'I'm not sure I follow.'

'As in, the lemon causes it, not the alcohol.'

'I see.'

'It's just a stupid joke. Something my dad used to – something my dad says.'

Interesting slip. Was it just the booze, or was there something more there waiting to be uncovered? Fitz smiled ingenuously. 'Right,' he said in a businesslike voice. 'No sex.'

Penhaligon made an admirable job of remaining expressionless.

'Our relationship will be strictly platonic.' Fitz gulped at his vodka. 'Keep your hands to yourself. I know it's going to be hard; there's nothing I can do about that. OK? It's just hands off.'

Penhaligon looked at him as if he were quite mad. 'I'll try,' she said, deadpan.

Fitz tried to divine what thoughts were running through her head.

Penhaligon downed her drink in one. 'I have to go.'

'Meeting someone?'

'No.'

'Going somewhere?'

'Just home.'

'Something in the oven?'

'No.'

'Another drink then, before you go?'

Penhaligon rose. 'I really don't think so, Fitz.'

'You're not driving, I hope?'

Penhaligon hesitated. 'I'll call a cab.'

Fitz took a breath. 'Tell me about your father.'

'What?' The reaction was out of all proportion to the question. Penhaligon flushed, blinked several times, seemed suddenly to become highly agitated. 'What? Tell you about my father? Why would you want to know about my father?'

211

Fitz shrugged. 'Just making conversation, Panhandle.'

She sighed angrily. 'Fitz, I'll see you tomorrow morning. If you want to see Kelly you'll have to get there early to beat the crowd.'

Fitz shook his head. He began to speak, but the sound of the front door opening cut him off. He looked around. The door hadn't banged so it hadn't been Mark going out. With an apologetic look to Penhaligon, he sloped out into the hall.

Judith was just closing the door. She turned and saw him.

Fitz stood quite still. 'Judith. This is unexpected.'

'I've come to sort things out. Last night didn't really go very well did it?'

I'm a bit pissed now, Judith, darling. Do us a favour and come back another day will you? When I can handle it. Or perhaps another life. When I'm a more mature person.

'I suppose not.'

Judith took off her coat. 'Well then, perhaps we ought to sit down and discuss things.' She glanced at the glass in Fitz's hand. 'Rationally.'

'Um,' said Fitz. 'Judith. I have to go out again. It's the case. I'm close to cracking it.'

Judith stopped, took a breath. He could see her containing the anger. She looked at him. Sighed. 'You're not playing games are you?' She looked him up and down, took in the glass for a second time. 'No. That's not it.' She bit her lip, considering. 'Alright, Fitz, I'll tell you what I'm going to do. I'm going to wait for you while you go out. And then when you come back we're going to talk. Alright?'

Even as she spoke Judith was heading for the sitting room. Suddenly an awful premonition ran through Fitz. The sitting room: where Penhaligon was sitting. Drinking. In civvies.

Shit.

Fitz leaned his head against the wall. Then he followed Judith into the room, found her staring at Penhaligon. She didn't say anything.

Fitz introduced them. 'Judith, this is Detective Sergeant Panhand – sorry. Penhaligon. Detective Sergeant Jane Penhaligon. Penhaligon: this is Judith. My wife.'

Judith nodded cordially by way of greeting. But her voice

was cold. 'Correct me if I'm wrong, but I thought police officers weren't supposed to drink on duty.'

Penhaligon got up from the sofa and smiled. 'I'm not on duty.'

'I see.' Judith did an abrupt about face, walked back past Fitz without saying a word, put her coat on. Fitz watched her silently, head rotating like a great fat owl.

With her hand on the front door, she turned to face him. 'I wanted to talk tonight, Fitz, I really did. I spent all day working out what I was going to say, thinking about what you might say in response. I was going to tell you that I wasn't taking the train to Leeds tomorrow, wasn't taking Katie to Mum's. I wanted to get things clear between us.' She swallowed hard, appeared to be having difficulty getting her breath. 'It appears sorting out our marriage isn't as important to you as it is to me.' She opened the door. 'You know what Mum's number is.'

Oh no, Judith, wait! Can't you see it's all been a misunderstanding? What do you think? That I'm having an affair, now? Christ Judith. I love you!

'You're still going then?'

Judith seemed on the point of speaking further, then shook her head. Her voice was weary as she said, 'Goodbye, Fitz.'

Judith walked out of the house and closed the door behind her before Fitz had a chance to reply. He leaned his head against the wall. Banged it a few times. If he did it hard enough it might knock some sense into himself. If he was lucky. He laughed. Fat chance of that these days.

Penhaligon came into the hallway. 'I have to go. Tomorrow, right? Early. I'll pick you up.'

And Fitz leaned back from the wall, suddenly stone cold sober, his encounter with Judith like a bucket of ice water in the face.

'No.' Fitz shook his head, ignored the pain in his forehead from banging it against the wall. 'Tomorrow's no good. It has to be tonight. It has to be now. Do you understand?'

Penhaligon sighed. 'Fitz. You're well over the limit. If they catch us there, it's curtains for you and a charge of professional misconduct for me.'

'Then they'll bury us together in unmarked graves.'

'It's not a joke.'

'Neither is condemning an innocent man to life imprisonment. So let's get on with it, shall we?'

The Custody Sergeant offered a token resistance when Penhaligon took Fitz into the holding area. 'I thought Fitz was off the case?'

This was all she needed. 'Well you thought wrong.'

The Custody Sergeant was obviously unconvinced. 'Look, if the boss finds out –'

Penhaligon sighed impatiently. '– I'll carry the can, OK?'

She stared at the Sergeant until he let them into the cells.

Kelly was awake. He looked like he hadn't slept in weeks. He was sitting on the edge of his bunk. Penhaligon stood aside to allow Fitz entry into the cell. Fitz didn't say anything. He didn't need to. Kelly was on his feet in a moment, compliant, trusting, almost desperate.

Fitz looked at the Custody Sergeant. 'We'll need to take him to the interview room.'

The Sergeant looked at Penhaligon.

'In for a penny, in for a pound.' That was Fitz. There was no trace of levity in his voice.

When Kelly was seated once more and the Custody Sergeant had left the interview room, Fitz gestured to Kelly to sit.

When Kelly had done so Fitz turned to face one wall, as if thinking out a strategy. When he turned back again his face was set in a determined expression. Kelly recoiled from that look. Even Penhaligon felt the pressure of it, felt glad it wasn't aimed at her. When he spoke, the words broke the silence like the first crack of thunder in a storm.

'You did it.' He stared at Kelly. 'I won't bore you with the details, but suffice to say the killer is Catholic, late thirties, single, clean shaven.'

Kelly wasn't offering even token resistance. He sat in the chair, broken, dejected, face crumpling, as his mind may well have been crumbling, before Fitz's onslaught.

'How do I know he's clean shaven?' Fitz reached into his

pocket, produced a cut throat razor, dropped it on the table in front of Kelly. 'Because he shaves himself with the razor he's just used on his victim.'

Kelly's eyes dropped to the razor. He reached out a trembling hand to touch it.

'Go on. Touch it. Feel it in your hand. Feel the strength it gives you. Pick it up!'

As Penhaligon watched Kelly recoiled from the last instruction, which Fitz barked in a harsh voice. But the razor was in his hand. What the hell did Fitz think he was playing at?

'Feel that, do you? Feel how smooth it is? How sharp? You could split a hair with that blade. Open it. Go on. Open it up. Feel the blade, let it out into the air, into the light.'

And Kelly was opening the razor, clumsily, two handed, awkward even when you took into consideration the more flexible cast on his arm. He held the razor in front of him, blank faced, his arm apparently supported by nothing more than Fitz's words. And Fitz was moving closer. His voice becoming more intimate, worming its way into Kelly's head, into her own as well.

As Penhaligon watched, Kelly lifted his eyes from the razor to Fitz, who abruptly pointed at her.

'Look at her!' His voice cracked in the silence, thunder in the night, not breaking the tension, adding to it, layer on layer.

'*Look at her!*'

And Kelly was looking. At her. Holding the razor. Blade out towards her. And she saw herself reflected in his eyes. Saw herself as he might have seen her.

Fitz's voice continued to build. 'What do you see? A victim?'

Kelly began to shake. He glanced at the razor, then back to her.

'There are some women out there who are just asking for it and she's one of them. A victim. Am I right?'

'Please.' Kelly's hand was trembling now, little glints of light gleaming off the blade, reflecting into her eyes, like sunlight through a dirty carriage window. 'Please stop this.'

But Fitz wouldn't stop. Couldn't stop. And now his words were attacking her as well, every image another turn of the screw. 'You can read her like a book, can't you? The childhood. The petit bourgeois parents who lived in an area they couldn't afford to live in. Not many friends – except the other girls who couldn't make friends, of course. They huddled together for comfort, bitchy, bitter . . .'

Penhaligon felt herself begin to tremble. How could he be so accurate? What was going on here? Christ! He'd given Kelly a razor and now he was deconstructing her! She looked at Kelly. His mouth was working: *Please. Please stop this*, but no sound was coming out.

'. . . sitting in her little group of rejects, watching the other girls. They always seemed to have more fun. They didn't seem to feel the cold. They got offered parts in the school play; she didn't. They got the boys; she didn't.'

And now Fitz was looking at her, not Kelly, the both of them a wall of eyes, tunnelling into her, taking her back in time, back into her childhood, and why was he doing this, oh, why, why –

'Except for that one night, that first time. What was his name? Thomas? Frank? It doesn't matter. The girl he really fancied wasn't there but he thought he'd make do. Tried to slope off quickly, didn't want to be seen. Where was it? Behind the bike sheds? A quick knee trembler up some alley perhaps? Over in seconds, cold, unsatisfying. Straight home into a hot bath but, oh, the next day. The looks, the sniggers, the remarks. Everybody knew. The whole school knew.' And Fitz was looking back to Kelly, moving closer still, his face within easy reach, just inches from the razor. 'But that's what life's like if you're a victim, if you're a bloody victim. Isn't it?'

Penhaligon stood, her mind a storm, clogged with doubts, uncertainty, clogged with herself, with memories, with hatred. Hatred for her parents, her childhood, life, Fitz. Especially Fitz.

And he wasn't even looking at her. He was looking at Kelly. It was all for Kelly's benefit. And he'd known what she'd done without even having seen her do it.

'Ah. Big mistake. Never look away. Never stand and look away.' A glance at her to confirm his observation, then back to Kelly. 'It's just what you were looking for, isn't it? That first sign of weakness, vulnerability. You'll strike now. You'll kill now.'

And Kelly was moving, standing, face wretched, hand outstretched towards Fitz, razor clutched in white knuckled fingers, blade shimmering with light.

'It's your mission in life. Women like that, isn't it? Acting tough, in control, showing a bit of thigh, treating you like dirt when you look. Well you'll show her exactly what's what, won't you? You'll put her in her place. You can read her like a book. She's not tough. You'll put her in her place for keeps, won't you?' By now Fitz's voice had lost control, was rising in pitch, in anger, rising to a shout. How long could he keep this up? And Kelly was crumbling before him, visibly. There were tears on his cheeks. The fist was wrapped hard around the handle of the razor, just inches from Fitz. 'You're a killer. Your picture's been in the newspapers, on the television. Nobody's come forward to identify you. You're nearly forty years old and nobody knows you. Is that credible? I think not. There's only one possible explanation why people haven't come forward. Because you're a killer and they know it. They're terrified to come forward. Victims, the lot of them. Like her!' And his finger like an arrow, searching her out, and still Fitz wouldn't stop. 'You kill but you don't rape. You can't rape so you kill. That's penetration. For you that's penetration. Sex is disgusting. Women are disgusting. Better to kill than to penetrate. More moral to kill than to penetrate. You want to kill now don't you?' He moved closer, reached out to tap Kelly on the temple with one finger. 'I know it. I know what's going on in there.' And suddenly Penhaligon knew that much at least was so true it was terrifying. 'You want to kill, kill, kill, kill —'

And Kelly was moving, lunging with the knife, whipping around in a circular movement as Fitz's words took the rhythm of a train.

'Kill, kill, kill, kill, kill, kill, kill —'

Arm moving, blade flashing in the neon light —

'– kill, kill, kill, kill –'

– flashing like sunlight through trees, through a carriage window –

And then Fitz was finished. Gone. Done. Empty of words. But the tension in the room built as Kelly whirled into the silence, stumbled, put out a hand to protect himself, palm flat against an invisible wall, eyes completely gone, no trace of the present there at all.

And that was when Penhaligon realised what Fitz had done. He'd confronted him with the void, pushed him back into it just as he'd pushed her back into her childhood, back to the time of the murder.

She began to say something, but Fitz raised a hand instantly cutting her off. *No noise. Let this run its course.*

And Kelly was moving again, a brief look down at his feet, as if to avoid stepping on something, before

the light

before moving on up an invisible

the light glinted

corridor, smiling as if to greet

the light glinted through the corridor window as Kelly moved along, swaying to the rhythm of the train. It was so unusual to be back in the outside world after so long. Approaching the city where his parents had died so long ago.

Kelly stepped carefully over a crumpled beer tin, placed a hand flat against the wall to steady himself. He felt the vibration of the train travel through his palm, all the way up his arm to his brain.

It was so strange to be wearing normal clothes again. A shirt. A suit. Proper shoes. He wondered what the others at St Peter's had thought when he left. He knew what they said, but sometimes words concealed the truth. He'd learnt that much, at least, in a decade. That was why he'd left.

Another step forward and someone was coming out of the

carriage in front of him. A man. Middle aged, unassuming, balding, inoffensive looking. The man staggered against the outer wall of the train, defeated by the rhythmic movement. Kelly moved towards him, pulled down the nearest window. A blast of cold air partially dispelled the stranger's nauseous expression.

Kelly smiled, 'Travel sickness?'

The man attempted a grin.

Kelly attempted a joke, something light. Just to see if he could still do it. 'Have faith in God. He can cure anything.'

The man's smile faded. 'Are you a priest?'

Kelly shrugged. 'Right at this point I'm not sure. I suppose you could say I'm trying to rediscover myself. My faith.'

The man's reply puzzled Kelly. 'I've only ever loved two women you know. My mother and the Virgin Mary.' He hesitated. 'If you'll excuse me. I think I need some fresh air.'

Kelly nodded. 'I understand. Can I get you a cup of tea?'

'Thank you.'

Kelly pulled open the carriage door. A young woman was inside. Young. Beautiful. She was reading a book. She looked up sharply at the sound of the door. 'I'm getting your friend a drink. Would you like one?'

'He's not my friend. He's a bit –' She shook her head again. 'Never mind. Thanks anyway.' She went back to her book.

When Kelly returned from the buffet carriage, the window was still open but the stranger was gone. Puzzled, Kelly pulled open the door of the carriage he'd seen the man come out from earlier.

Sunlight flashed through the carriage window, onto the back of the man as he crouched over the girl, onto the cut throat razor he was holding in one hand.

The girl was thrashing feebly. A kind of gurgling noise came from her throat, pumping out with the blood.

Kelly put his hands out as if to push away the carnage. His hands were empty. That was odd. Hadn't he been carrying some tea? Two cups. One for himself, one for the

killer, the murderer

the stranger bending over the naked girl, the razor flashing *in an arc of sunlight, the carriage swaying as the train rocked, and his foot slipped in the fallen tea*

or was it blood

and Kelly lost his balance, tumbled in a flood of images to the floor, on to the girl's body, as the stranger jerked back in alarm before leaping forward to attack.

And then Kelly was fighting for his life, his hands and face and clothes covered in the dying girl's blood, the razor spinning towards him time and again, opening his clothes, his skin, while the man was breathing 'yesyesyesyesyesyesyesyes –' over and over again to the rhythm of the train.

And then somehow he was in the corridor, on his knees, then his feet, the stranger following, his voice lost in the noise of the train, a screaming whistle, the hysterical clatter of a door banging as he

fell

screaming from the train

across a chair and onto the

tracks, screaming onto the

floor, the razor flying from his grasp to fall unregarded into a corner as Kelly curled into a foetal shape, injured arm ignored in his attempt to escape from reality, from life, from the truth.

But Fitz was there, holding him tightly, whispering into his ear, bringing him back, back from the brink, and Penhaligon watched as Fitz picked him up with his words, with the sound of his voice, picked him up, stood him up, gazed at him with what she could have sworn was a mixture of admiration and love.

'That's it,' he said, his voice quiet, awed. 'That's it, you can come back now. Come back now. Come back now . . .'

And Kelly did. Slowly. And when he sat at the table the tears streaming down his face were tears of joy.

'I didn't do it.'

Fitz was beaming almost as broadly as Kelly. 'I know.'

'But now *I* know.' And his head was down on the table, the words almost obscured by a flood of new tears. 'I know I didn't do it . . .'

After that it was a matter of tying up a few loose ends. At Fitz's prompting Kelly remembered a figure leaning over him, removing his wallet from his jacket. He managed to give a reasonable description of Jacqui, although he remembered her clothes in more detail. When Penhaligon checked the coroner's report, she found his description matched the details of the report almost to the letter.

Then Fitz asked Kelly to describe the killer.

'He was . . . middle aged . . . balding . . . unassuming-looking.'

'Were there any clues to his profession in his clothes? Was he in uniform, did he wear any badges, anything? Think hard.'

Kelly closed his eyes. The tortured look was gone from his face, which now almost glowed with relief. 'He wore . . . a suit . . . smart casual . . . and glasses. He had glasses. And he wore an anorak, I think. Something waterproof. I thought it was odd at the time.'

At Fitz's curious glance, Penhaligon interjected, 'Summer, right? It was a hot day.'

And Fitz glanced at her. 'Of course. You were on the train, weren't you, Panhandle? You found the body.'

She nodded. *Don't ask me about the dreams. The nightmares. You do and I swear to God I'll –*

'I found the guard.'

Fitz frowned thoughtfully. Looked back at Kelly.

'Anything else?'

Kelly shook his head.

'Colour of eyes? Type of voice? Mannerisms?'

'Well . . . his voice was mild. Very calm. Calmer than his face, actually, I think.'

'What do you mean by that?'

Kelly shrugged. 'I'm not sure – it's difficult remembering

221

anything clearly from before the . . . anyway, what I meant was . . . though his voice was calm when he spoke . . . there seemed to be something . . . he was flushed. He looked embarrassed. And he was panting.'

'As if he'd been running, doing exercise of some kind?' *Wanking off in some toilet?*

Kelly frowned. 'No. More like . . . he was psyching himself up for something.' Kelly looked directly at Fitz. 'Will you be able to let me go now?'

Fitz bit his lip.

Kelly divined his thoughts effortlessly. 'I understand.'

Penhaligon came across the table, sat down opposite him. 'You have to understand. Bilborough has a confession from you. Or the start of one, anyway. We now have a confession of the exact opposite set of circumstances. In addition, everything you describe, everything you remembered . . . could still be interpreted in such a way as to indicate that you were the killer yourself.'

Fitz nodded. 'All we've done is responded to Bilborough's move. Now we're on an even footing again. In the eyes of the law you're neither guilty nor innocent. What we have to do now is prove what you say is true by finding the killer. And that way prove your innocence.'

'I understand.'

'In the meantime, I suggest you don't say anything else to Bilborough without my being there first, alright?'

Kelly nodded.

'We're going to take you back to your cell now. You'll be alright.'

Kelly stood. 'It's OK. Tonight I could sleep soundly on a bed of nails.' He smiled.

23:30–Midnight

After they'd taken Kelly back to the cells and handed him over to the Custody Sergeant, Penhaligon offered Fitz a lift home. The drive took place in silence. But as she braked to a halt outside Fitz's house, he looked at her and smiled.

'You know, I could get used to having my own private chauffeur. Drink?'

Penhaligon shook her head.

'Things on your mind, Panhandle?'

'Penhaligon. Or Jane if you must. Anything but bloody Panhandle. OK?'

Fitz lifted his hands in mock surrender. 'So. Drink?'

Penhaligon sighed. 'No.' She stared at Fitz. What was he thinking? What was going through his head? Elation? Pride? Between them they'd managed to even the balance a little. In the morning Bilborough was going to be as pissed as hell, but she didn't care. If he couldn't take the truth that was his problem. 'We were bloody lucky tonight.'

'I know.' He studied her narrowly. She could feel the push. 'Come on. One drink. For old times' sake.'

She smiled tiredly. 'Fitz. There haven't been any old times.'

'Oho. So you are awake. Just testing.'

Penhaligon shook her head, pulled on the handbrake. 'I'm going to regret this.' Fitz got out of the car. She followed him into the house.

Fitz cruised into the living room, dug through a stack of records hidden behind the sofa, switched on the record player.

'You'll wake up Mark.'

Fitz shrugged. 'He's probably stoned out of his tree at some techno party.' Fitz put the record on, dumped the needle onto it. At once Penhaligon smiled. 'Goldsmith. You like movies?'

Fitz went to the drinks cabinet. 'I like movie soundtracks. They're clever. Good ones hold up as musical compositions in their own right, while still fitting the images of the film.' His face crumpled into a quirky grin. 'Most of which are narrow minded, over romanticised, condescending, and commercially oriented crap.'

'But of course, it would be unlike you to generalise.'

'Of course.'

Penhaligon took the glass Fitz offered her. 'There are good films.'

Fitz took his own glass, turned from the cabinet, had second thoughts, grabbed the bottle too before sinking into the sofa with a sigh. 'Not many.'

'Oh come on. There are loads of good films.'

'Oh yeah? Name one.'

'No. That's what you want me to do.'

'See. You can't.'

'I won't be drawn, Fitz.'

'You won't name one because you're afraid I'll decon-struct it for you. Show it up with all its faults.'

'Spoil it for me, you mean.'

'Show you the truth, you mean.'

Penhaligon leaned forward in her seat. 'Why are you so obsessed with the truth, Fitz?'

'I'm not obsessed.'

'Is it because Judith's left you and you can't work out why?'

Fitz said nothing, sipped his drink.

'I could help you there. I'm a woman. I've got an insight into her mind. The way she thinks. I've got a head start on you, Fitz. All you have to do is ask me nicely.'

Still Fitz said nothing.

Penhaligon grinned and leaned back in her chair, relaxing for the first time in days. 'Everything's a game to you isn't it? But the game's not so appealing when someone else is writing the rules.' She imitated Fitz's deep voice. 'Am I right, Doctor Fitzgerald? I do believe I am.'

Fitz studied her narrowly. 'You're feeling good, right now, aren't you Panhandle?'

She smiled.

'I can tell because you didn't correct me when I used your nickname.'

Penhaligon felt her smile slip a notch.

'And you're knocking back that drink as though it were lemon squash.'

Penhaligon worked hard to suppress a flush of heat through her cheeks.

'So. You feel good. Relaxed. It's the first time in days, probably. The case is breaking. Fitz isn't such an old bastard, well, maybe he is, but at least he's interesting, right? Or you wouldn't be here, am I right?' There was something predatory about his grin. 'I am, aren't I?' The smile widened. Penhaligon felt it sucking her in. Vacuuming her up. 'Right, I mean.'

Penhaligon felt a rush of irrational anger flow through her. 'Fitz stop it. It's not funny any more.'

'Stop what, Panhandle? I'm just making –'

'– conversation? Bollocks. You're pissed. You're a fat, misogynistic bastard with an ego as big as your bloody stomach. You like baiting people. It turns you on. Why do you do it, Fitz? You don't know, do you? That's why Judith left you, you know. Why she walked out. She loves you but she hates the bullshit you're so full of. You can't stop it, half the time you don't even know you're doing it. So she left you. It was the only way she could deal with it. The only way she could deal with you.'

Fitz sniffed. Groped in his pocket for a packet of cigarettes. It was empty. 'Got a cigarette?'

'No I bloody haven't. If you took as much notice of me as you'd like to think you do, you'd know I don't smoke!'

The record finished playing. The needle lifted off with a gentle click. There was a long silence. Fitz put down the empty cigarette packet.

Looked at her.

'Do you want to tell me about your father yet?'

Penhaligon felt herself flush with anger so strong it bordered on fury.

'I can help you know.'

'You condescending bastard. You don't know anything about my parents! You don't know anything about me!'

Fitz looked closely at her.

And Penhaligon was on her feet, drink forgotten in her anger. 'You're so self important you make me sick. Look at you. I can see your mind working. I can feel that mighty intellect of yours hammering away at the problems it perceives, never once realising that the problems it perceives may not be problems at all to anyone else.' She glared at Fitz. 'Tell you about my father? Alright. I'll tell you about my father. He's a dead man. A dead man who's still breathing. My mother's put him in a coffin already. My brothers have helped. They want me to as well, but I won't. I can't.'

'Because you love him too much.' Smug. Self assured. The right answer.

Wrong. 'Because I hate him you bastard. I hate him for giving up. For letting them do that to him.'

Fitz's voice softened. 'A terminal illness is a difficult thing to cope with. Especially in close family. But you can get help. Hating your father just because he's ill won't solve anything.'

'Help? You really don't understand anything do you? I'm not angry with him because he's ill. I'm angry with him because he's committed suicide. He took paracetamol, you stupid bastard. He swallowed a whole bottle full when he couldn't stand the pressure from Mum any more. She bloody drove him to it and he never stood up to her. Christ. He could've stayed alive for years. Years. Huntington's is a slow killer. But no. He had to give in. They let him come home from the hospital. They pumped him out but it was too late. He'll be dead in a fortnight, probably less. And then Mum'll have won. And I'll have to watch him die. That's why I hate him. That's why I hate him so bloody much.'

Fitz was silent. He blinked. Penhaligon took no pleasure from the uncertainty she saw on his face, the realisation of just how wrong it was possible to be when given all the correct information.

He took a step closer, his face crumpling in sympathy.

'Don't you even think about it!' She turned and left the room, walked out of the house. Came back when she realised she'd left her car keys in her bag and that in Fitz's sitting room.

And he was waiting for her. With the truth.

'I prepared for the death of my father for years. I wanted to be centre stage. I wanted to be in charge. Well I got my wish, eventually.' He wasn't looking at her, hadn't touched his drink. 'Don't make the same mistake I made. It's his moment and his decision. Support him. Don't squander the love in here.' He thumped his chest just above his heart. 'And above all, don't be so bloody selfish.'

Penhaligon groped beside the chair where she'd been sitting to try to find her bag. Fitz held it up, dangled the car keys from one finger.

'I wouldn't be a very good friend if I let you drive home tonight, would I?'

Penhaligon felt close to tears. 'Fine. I'll call a cab.'

'I did it while you were outside.'

SIX

Saturday

Fitz was barely awake when Penhaligon banged on the front door the next morning. When he opened the door and saw who it was he ventured a smile. The smile was not returned.

'They're going to charge Kelly. This afternoon.'

Fitz blinked, wiped sleep from his eyes. 'What the hell does Bilborough think he's playing at?'

'Apart from giving me a severe bollocking, you mean?'

Fitz shook his head, trying to clear it of the after effects of the previous night's alcohol and stress. 'I don't understand.'

Penhaligon shook her head. 'You stupid bastard, Fitz. Think about it. We didn't tape the interview. There's no evidence. It's our word against the tape Bilborough made.'

'Oh for . . . we'll do another interview. Tape that.'

'Bilborough and Beck are already doing that. He thinks Kelly's twisting the truth. Thinks he did it and is now trying to cover it up. Kelly's going to crack any time soon. What with the stress of the amnesia, Bilborough's accusations and your bullying, I'm surprised he hasn't been sectioned already. He probably would have been except that Bilborough still thinks he can get Kelly to admit to killing Jacqui. And God only knows what Kelly will say now they've got him back in that interview room.'

'Christ.' Fitz opened the door fully and gestured for Penhaligon to come in.

'Cute pyjamas, Fitz. Who bought them? Your daughter?'

Fitz expelled an impatient breath. 'I have to get there.

228

Someone has to represent him. Bilborough and Beck will tear him apart.'

'It's no good.' Penhaligon closed the front door behind her. 'By the time they've finished with him he'll say anything they want. We have to get Sweeney ourselves. Otherwise the case is open and shut, Kelly's away for life and Sweeney's still at large.'

'An admirable thought but just how are we supposed to catch Sweeney?'

'I've already thought of that. I had Giggsy run our description of Sweeney through the computer. Single. Late thirties. Catholic. Balding, neat dresser, glasses. I got Giggsy to correlate this with the statements that were taken from the people on the train. We got two matches, both travelling on business. Michael Hennessy and Peter Frederickson.'

'You told Bilborough?'

'Do you honestly think there would have been any point?' Fitz shook his head. 'Who are we taking first?'

'Hennessy. His address is the nearest.'

'I'll get dressed.'

'What a good idea.'

Fitz glanced at Penhaligon. If he was expecting a smile he was disappointed.

Ten minutes later they were in Penhaligon's car heading along the high street towards the ring road. Fitz glanced at Penhaligon. No chat. No warmth. Still no smiles. 'Panhandle. Are you mad at me?'

Penhaligon changed down, jammed her foot on the accelerator and overtook a slower vehicle. 'No, Fitz, I'm not mad at you. That wouldn't be professional.'

Fitz winced as a set of traffic lights turned red just as they passed through them. He glanced at the speedo.

'Don't you think forty-five is a little fast for a built-up area?'

Penhaligon shot him a sideways glance, pressed the pedal further towards the floor. 'Do you?'

'As a matter of fact, I do.'

'You don't want to participate. And I'm ignoring all the warning signs.'

'Yes.'

'Just like you did last night.'

'Panhandle, this isn't funny —'

'And before that, in the interview. You did it then, as well.'

Fitz pulled the seat belt tighter. 'Alright, I'm sorry . . . I made you mad. I had to do that. You know I had to. How else could I get Kelly to crack? How else could I get at the truth?'

Penhaligon looked back at the road, overtook another vehicle, turned left onto the approach to the ring road without slowing.

Fitz couldn't take his eyes from the vehicles in front. 'It wasn't a priest, you know. On the phone. It couldn't have been. He broke the seal of the confession. That's number one in the top twenty of sins. That's above buggering the Pope. He's no priest. He's our killer. The reason he knew Astrid Reynolds was at the bottom of the canal was because he put her there.'

Penhaligon charged onto the ring road. The speedo needle crept up to fifty-five. Fitz jammed his feet against the floor, gripped the door with his left hand.

Penhaligon wrenched at the wheel, swung the Volvo into the outside lane. 'Then why the phone call?'

'Because he thought Kelly was dead. Shoved from a train doing sixty. And then suddenly he was alive. Bang — his picture was all over the paper. Kelly could identify him. He had to stick a spanner in the works. Fudge the issue somehow. Would you mind slowing down please?'

'Frightened?' Was that a perverse satisfaction in her voice?

'Yes.'

'Big mistake.' Penhaligon crossed to the inside lane, overtook again. 'Never admit you're frightened; it just encourages them. Tell me more.'

'We know he's not married. This is no Yorkshire Ripper that goes chasing prostitutes. In fact this guy idolises women; statues, sculptures, the Venus de Milo, the Virgin Mary, that sort of —' He recoiled as Penhaligon braked to avoid a slower

vehicle, then leapt into the outside lane and accelerated again.
'– thing.' He rocked with the motion of the car. 'White, hairless and smooth. Hairless being the most important. Pubic hair of course shatters all this, which is why he has to shave them. Look, if you don't slow down, I'm going to have to grab the wheel –'

Penhaligon glanced at him then and Fitz had some inkling of what might happen to him if he tried to act out his threat.

'There are men who are victims, Fitz, and you're one of them. A born victim. Right? Why the hair?'

Fitz found himself babbling. 'Well, in school he was probably the first or last to grow it himself. I would guess the first. This is where his neurosis comes from. He probably saw it growing on himself and not on others, and thought it was some sort of punishment from God.'

Penhaligon swung over to take an off ramp, and tapped the brakes as she headed down towards the residential streets, before immediately accelerating again.

'If I'm right, then he was born in August or September, which makes him one of the oldest in his –'

Penhaligon took the car round a corner, round a milk float chugging along in front of them and directly into the path of an oncoming heavy goods vehicle.

'– Jesus Christ! We're in the wrong lane!'

Tyres squealed as Penhaligon swung the Volvo back in front of the milk float. The lorry's horn blared as they shot past, dopplering back into the roar of the engine.

'– oldest in his class. Jesus Christ, Panhandle, can we slow down now? Please?'

'It's Penhaligon.'

'Alright. Penhaligon. Penhaligon! The Mona Lisa, anything, just slow down!'

The engine note descended to a smooth purr as Penhaligon brought the car to a stop in a residential street. She looked at Fitz and smiled triumphantly as she pulled on the handbrake.

Fitz didn't look back at her. He was too busy unbelting and getting out of the car.

By the time Penhaligon had also got out of the car, Fitz had regained some of his composure. He gestured for her to lead the way up the garden path of the mid-terraced house occupied by Michael Hennessy.

When she reached the door Penhaligon knocked firmly. There came the sound of someone moving around indoors. After a moment Penhaligon knocked again.

This time her effort was rewarded. The door opened and a man peered out.

He was in his late sixties or early seventies, though to Fitz he seemed much older. His hair was thinning, bleached white with age. His face held a deep, unhealthy flush. The smell of alcohol on his breath was apparent even from the doorstep. The man took a set of yellow headphones from his ears, switched off the Walkman attached to his belt. 'Sorry. Didn't hear you knocking. Had me music on.'

'Mister Hennessy?' Penhaligon opened the conversation on a standard note. Well, good for her. He'd be the last one to suggest they fly in the face of convention.

The old man nodded.

'Mister Michael Hennessy?'

Hennessy shook his head slowly, a curious expression playing about his lips. 'John. Michael's my son.' He smiled. The rather pathetic smile of the terminal alcoholic.

'Could we speak to him please?'

The smile faded. 'He's out.'

Penhaligon showed him her I.D., allowed the faintest hint of impatience to enter her voice. 'I'm a police officer. May we come in?'

'No.' Hennessy put his headphones back on and made as if to shut the door.

Penhaligon reached out, held the door open against the old man's full strength. 'We're investigating a murder. Now may we come in please?'

Hennessy sighed. Not impatience, or anger at the inconvenience. Indifference. Penhaligon might have been the pools coupon woman rather than a police officer investigating a murder.

'Alright. If you must.' He pulled the door open wider and gestured for them to come in.

The first thing that Fitz noticed as they followed Hennessy

along the hall was the crucifix hanging on the wall formed by the staircase. He pointed it out silently to Penhaligon. The crucifix was large, ornate, not a casual decoration. Photographs in frames were mounted either side of the crucifix. They showed a man recognisable as a twenty-something year old John Hennessy with a woman and a small child. Wife and son?

Hennessy took off his headphones again as they moved along the hall and into the living room. 'About that girl on the train, is it?'

'Yes.' Penhaligon. Keeping the firm note in her voice. Keeping control of the situation.

'Michael made a statement.' Hennessy stood aside to allow them to enter the living room.

Fitz blew out his cheeks. The place was a mess. Plates caked with old food. Magazines and newspapers spread all over furniture that had definitely seen better days. Cups on the table filled with the dregs of tea, their colour matching the old paper on the walls, the paint above the picture rail and on the ceiling.

Penhaligon looked around, taking it all in. Another crucifix and more framed photographs on the mantlepiece, coal in the scuttle. The television had a vase of flowers on it; bloody dangerous that. Cheap prints hung on two walls. The view from the window was of a narrow brick passage between the Hennessys' and the neighbours' house.

'This is just routine,' she said. Her voice held none of the disgust Fitz could see in her at the filthy state of the house.

Hennessy looked around at the mess, as if seeing it from his unexpected guests' point of view. The smile was back. 'Had a bit of a late night.' He shrugged. 'You know how it is.'

Fitz nodded. *The cheap booze, the loneliness, the self loathing, yeah, I know how it is alright.*

Hennessy began to collect together the dirty plates and cups. Stacking them precariously he took them through to the kitchen. Fitz followed him as Penhaligon began to make a more detailed examination of the living room.

'Where is Michael?' he asked.

Hennessy dumped the crockery amid a pile already in the sink. 'He's at work.'

'Oh yes?' Fitz sifted through a stack of papers on the kitchen table, pursed his lips and nodded when he found that day's edition. It was unfolded to the crossword. 'What does your son do?'

Hennessy drained the dirty water from the sink, put the plug back in, looked around for some washing up liquid as he ran more hot water. 'He's a health inspector. He goes round to hotels and he rates them: good, bad, indifferent.'

'Yeah?' Fitz made an effort to sound interested. 'Travels around a lot does he?'

'Oh yeah.' Hennessy extracted a teapot from the jumble of crockery in the sink, gave it a wipe and placed it on the draining board. 'Do you want a cup of tea?'

'No thanks.'

'Alright.' Hennessy plunged his hands into the hot water, winced, pulled them out, shook the water from them. He looked at the sink, then back to Fitz.

Fitz decided it was time for a push. 'Promiscuous.'

'Eh what?' Hennessy's head was up, the sink full of crockery forgotten.

Interesting. Fitz waved the newspaper and grinned. 'Five across.'

Hennessy grinned. Relief? 'I don't do 'em.'

'It's Michael's, is it?'

'Yeah.' Hennessy stared at the sink again, shook his head. 'D'you want a drink?'

It's obvious you do mate.

'Don't mind if I do.'

Hennessy rummaged in a cupboard for some glasses and a bottle. He nodded towards the living room, where Penhaligon was still sifting quietly through the detritus of an old man's life.

Fitz shook his head. 'Doubt it.'

Hennessy raised his voice. 'Here. Er ... d'you want a drink?'

Penhaligon put her head around the kitchen door. 'No thanks. Your wife's not in?'

Hennessy put one glass back in the cupboard. 'My wife died a year ago.'

'I'm sorry.'

Hennessy shrugged, affecting nonchalance. 'Yeah, well, you know how it is.' He poured two glasses of whisky, handed one to Fitz.

Fitz nodded his thanks and sipped from the glass.

Penhaligon aimed a savage glance at Fitz. To Hennessy she said, 'Do you know where Michael was on Monday, April third?'

Hennessy laughed, a wheezy, old man's laugh. Something unhealthy going on in the lungs there by the sound of it. 'I don't know where *I* was on April the third.' He chuckled again, glanced conspiratorially at Fitz. 'I don't know where I was last night.'

Fitz didn't react to Hennessy's glance. 'It was the night Patricia Garth was murdered at Oxenholme Railway Station. Do you remember that?'

Hennessy looked from Fitz to Penhaligon and back to Fitz. His manner changed subtly. The chuckles, the nonchalance were gone, replaced by animal caution.

'No.'

And Fitz gave a great big grin. *It's OK mate. I understand. The old memory can be a bit of a pain, can't it?* 'They thought they'd have to pull the match because of the coverage. United against Spurs.' Another push. 'Do you remember? It was live on the telly.'

Hennessy relaxed. 'Right. Yeah.'

'Did you watch it?'

'Oh yeah. Michael and me, you know, we like the football.'

'So you watched it together?'

'Yeah.'

Fitz shrugged. Interesting. 'Well, that's all we need to know.' He moved across to the mantlepiece. Picked up a photograph. A middle-aged man, balding, glasses, standing beside a handsome elderly woman. 'Is this Michael and his mother?'

'Yeah.'

235

Fitz nodded, put the photograph back. 'You don't go out much since . . .?'

'No.'

'I wonder if I could use your bathroom?'

'It's upstairs, yeah.'

'Right, fine.'

In the bathroom, Fitz flushed the toilet without using it, opened the cabinet and began to rummage inside. The first thing he found was a wad of cotton wool. Then some Germaline. Aftershave. A new packet of soap. Toothpaste. Three toothbrushes.

And three or four cut throat razors.

Fitz shut the cabinet.

The truth was close now.

Downstairs, Penhaligon was staring at the photograph Fitz had placed back on the mantlepiece. She turned as he re-entered the room. Her face was pale, shaken. Something had happened. He narrowed his eyes. *Alright?*

She gave a tiny shake of the head. *Later.*

'I think we've just about finished here, Fitz.'

He nodded. 'Fine. Thanks for your time, Mister Hennessy.'

Hennessy smiled and saw them to the door.

At the car, Fitz stopped Penhaligon with a look.

'Alright. What's up, Panhandle. You looked like you saw a ghost in there.'

Penhaligon swallowed hard. Was that fear in her eyes, or anger? It was difficult to tell.

'Michael bloody Hennessy was in my carriage. He was in my *carriage* Fitz. On the train. Christ. I thought he was going to attack me. He was sitting opposite me when the guard screamed. When he found Jacqui. Just a few feet away. Christ.'

Fitz pursed his lips sympathetically. 'There were cut throat razors in the bathroom. And Hennessy had a phony alibi.'

Penhaligon glanced at him. She was shaken, but not bowed.

'Don't you watch any sports, Panhandle? Hennessy claims to have watched the game with Michael live. They couldn't possibly have done.'

Penhaligon frowned. 'They had a telly.'

He pointed up at the outside of the Hennessys' house. 'But no satellite dish.' Fitz grinned when Penhaligon had no reply, opened the door and got into the car.

'That's it then.' Penhaligon joined Fitz in the car, pulled the driver's side door shut with a click. 'Michael Hennessy's Sweeney.'

Fitz nodded. 'And he's at work today. Did his father say where or when?'

'Leeds. Catching the 12:30.'

Fitz blinked. Leeds. Now why did that ring a bell –?

The radio bleeped, interrupting the embryonic thought. Penhaligon picked up the handset.

'Control to Oscar Three.' Bilborough. Anger and frustration apparent in his voice. 'Penhaligon. Are you there?'

A sideways glance at Fitz showed him Penhaligon was as frustrated at Bilborough's interference as he was. 'Oscar Three receiving, over.'

'What the bloody hell do you think you're playing at, Penhaligon? Fitz is off the case. A member of the public. You've let a member of the public interview a prime suspect in a murder case. And now this. Off on a wild goose chase to bloody hell knows where –'

Fitz snatched the handset. 'You've already heard the murderer, you officious prick! The guy Penhaligon spoke to on the phone was the killer. Michael Hennessy is Sweeney. Think about it and –'

But Bilborough wasn't interested. His voice cut across Fitz's, an angry squeak. 'Fitz, bugger off! Put Penhaligon back on. Penhaligon? I want you back here right now. Is that clear?'

Penhaligon took the radio. She glanced at Fitz. Was that a twinkle in her eye?

'This is Penhaligon here, sir. You're fading. Can hardly hear a word, sir. Must be some kind of fault on the radio.'

'Bollocks! You know and I know there's nothing wrong with the bloody radio, now –'

Fitz grinned as Penhaligon winked at him.

'Am on my way to intercept the 12:30 Manchester–Leeds intercity. Request assistance. Over and out.'

She put the handset down. Switched off the radio. Started the engine.

And then Fitz felt something go through him like a knife. A memory. His smile slipped; he felt the world lurch sideways.

Penhaligon noticed his expression. 'What is it?'

And there was another little glimpse of the truth. 'It's Judith. Her mother lives in Leeds, she's taking Katie there today, on the 12:30. She'll be on the train. Christ, Panhandle. *She'll be on the train!*'

12:35–13:05

Michael Hennessy felt the train move against his feet. Felt himself carried along as the machinery beneath him accelerated along the track. His mind accelerated with the machinery. He liked trains. They kept you moving. Kept you moving fast. When he was on a train he was moving fast, he was speeding, flying. It was better than the slow drudge he'd left behind in Manchester Victoria and the slower drudge that awaited him at Leeds Central. Fast was the thing. No; even fast wasn't really the thing. Fast was coasting, involved no energy; well, in a perfect, frictionless universe, would involve no energy. Newton had said that. Newton was a genius. Acceleration. That was the thing. The rush of air. The desperate gulp as the wind snatched the breath out of your mouth. The dizziness in your head as you fought the wind for your breath back. And then the moment. The moment when it all faded, the drudgery, the mundanity, the hopeless, inevitable ordinariness as it faded, and he was moving, faster and faster, at one with the speed, he *was* the speed. He *was* acceleration. He was a law of physics, an equation; no body, no physical being, just a set of intrinsically meaningless mathematical symbols. Meaningless because the only sense came from the relationship between the symbols, the shape they made when mapped onto the four dimensional universe. And because he was also a human being with free will, he knew that he could change the shape of the equation, the

238

relationship between the symbols, and hence the result of the equation.

Nearer to my God than thee.

That was what the equations were all about. Change. Control.

Outside the train the world rushed by. Embankments, tunnels, signals, rails. And beyond them, roads, houses, chimneys, people, sky. Was it Einstein who'd once asked, 'When does Oxford station arrive at this train?' Though he understood precisely the irony of the great man's observation, Michael didn't smile. He never smiled, although he did feel something stir inside him. Some emotion. It fuelled the change in himself. Fuelled his control over the change. Over the equation he was. And that was ironic as well because it implied the Chaos theorists had all got it wrong. It wasn't the equation that described you, it was you that defined the equation.

At that thought Michael felt an immense satisfaction.

The train moved faster, propelling Michael across his interior landscape at exhiliarating speed.

Nearly there. Nearly there. Nearly there. Nearly there.

Faster and faster. Faster and faster. Faster and faster.

Michael pressed his face up against the glass of the corridor window. He pulled down the window. The air that blasted in was tainted with dirt and smoke, the smell of oil, of thrashing machinery. It was like nectar. It *was* nectar. Manna for the age of technology, falling from the skies all over the country.

Michael slid the window up as the train's klaxon blew a long blast. He remained quite still as the sound faded away, red shifted into memory.

Time to find a carriage. A seat. Leeds was a couple of hours away. He looked at his watch. Not long now. Not long now.

The change was coming. Coming. Coming.

The change was coming. It was coming.

With the rhythm of the train.

And then something made Michael stop. The train was slowing. Glossop. Of course. First stop. Just local. Only

239

twenty minutes from Manchester. After Glossop the next
station was an hour away. The other side of the mountains.
Michael felt his breath quicken in his throat at the thought of
all that open space, all that time. Time. Time to do ...
whatever he wanted. To be liberated. To change. To be

nearer my God than thee

fulfilled.

The train slowed even more. Beyond the window the view
of the world was curtailed by stockyards and red brick
buildings. A platform. People.

Michael drew air into his lungs, filled his blood and his
mind with a fresh rush of oxygen. He leaned against the wall
as the train pulled into the station and drew to a halt. He was
tired. So tired. So tired.

Doors clashed in the distance, the metallic din overlaid by
a babble of sound; chatter, laughter. People on the train.
Pushing past him. Brushing against his clothes. Next to him.
Touching him. Oh. Touching him. Touching him.

He closed his eyes. That was good. Get some distance.
Some

touching him why did they keep

perspective, some

touching him with their hair, the tips of their fingers, their
luggage, their hair, their hair

privacy.

And then the bustle was past. People on. People off. A
whoop from the engine, the wheeze of pistons, the clank and
scrabble of machinery, and the train was pressing against him
again. Cool, solid, clean, sharp lines. Moving him. Accelerating him.

He opened the window even further, leaned into the wind,
opened his mouth. The wind moved into him, through him,
bled the breath from him, built a void in his mind. A dizzying
void into which he poured himself.

And the air was full of smoke. Just for a moment, as the
wind whirled it back at him, slapped his face with the smoke,
the smell, the sound of thrashing machinery. He sucked it in,
found pleasure in the dirt, used the pleasure to fuel the
change. The change in him. The change.

And once again he was *nearly there. Nearly there. Nearly there.*

Once again he was going *faster and faster. Faster and faster. Faster and faster and faster and* it was time.

Time to find a carriage. The carriage.

Time to find her.

Penhaligon brought the Volvo to halt directly outside the main entrance to Glossop station. Fitz was out of the car and running for the barrier even as she was locking the doors. She flashed her I.D. at the guard who was arguing with Fitz. Ten yards beyond him the train was beginning to pull away from the platform. Fitz was heading for the nearest carriage. Penhaligon grabbed hold of the guard and yelled. 'Get them to keep the train here. Do you understand? Stop the bloody train!'

The guard blinked, began to speak, but Penhaligon was away after Fitz. Feet pounding on the platform, grab the door handle, no, missed it, another then, quick as she could –

– and the train moving faster, picking up speed. And Fitz had yanked open his door, was climbing aboard –

'Fitz, wait for me, we have to stay together! It's procedure!'

'Fuck procedure! Judith's on there!' And Fitz was away as the end of the train flew towards her, and then she was running, running with the last carriage, opening a door and swinging herself aboard even as the end of the platform rushed towards her with Fitz's voice.

'And don't pull the emergency cord! He'll get away if the train stops!'

Christ this was a shambles. The train was moving, no stop for an hour. Fitz was insane. Fucking insane. Don't stop the train? Christ, what was he on?

The whistle blew then, pounding into her head, and Penhaligon jerked herself into the last carriage of the train as the door slammed shut with a sound she remembered all too vividly from her dreams.

Michael found her in a carriage just beyond the buffet car. In a compartment of her own. Young. Beautiful. Vulnerable. Alone.

He entered the carriage with a self-effacing grin. *Sorry. I'm in your space, I know, but not for long. I'll be away soon and you won't even know I've been here.*

She looked up. A smile of her own. Legs crossed. Then eyes down, back into her book.

Dismissive.

Michael hesitated. Leaned across her to put his case on the rack. That earned him another look. 'Excuse me.' Was that his voice? So slow, so unaffected by the speed, the acceleration he was feeling as the train propelled him

nearer my God than thee

from the past into the future.

He sat, weaved in time with the train, watched her do the same. Watched as the light through the window caught in her eyes, glittered from the pendant at her throat. Watched as the breeze from the half-open window moved her hair. Her hair. Her hair. Nearly there. Nearly there. Faster and faster. Faster and faster. Faster and faster.

Suddenly. He spoke suddenly. 'British Rail.'

She looked up then, a little glance, a nervous glance. 'Pardon?'

'Ten minutes late.'

'Oh. Right.' A thin smile, then back to her book.

'My name's Michael.'

'Helen.' Not even a look this time. Not even a glance up from her book.

Dismissive. *Dismissive.*

But nervous too, growing restless, agitated. One sign. One tiny sign. That's all he wanted. The permission. One sign. And he was nearly there. Oh. So nearly there. Nearly there. Nearly –

The compartment door opened and a woman came in accompanied by a child. The little girl was about ten. Not so little when it came right down to it. Both mother and daughter were beautiful. The girl ran to the window and stared out, the wind ruffling her hair. Her hair. Her hair.

The relief in Helen's face was evident as the woman put her bags in the overhead rack and sat.

• • •

Fitz barrelled through the first carriage, flinging open the compartment doors one by one, ignoring the looks, the accusations. Nothing. No Hennessy. No Judith. No Katie.

Christ. I'll do anything. I'll come back into the fold. I'll change. Just don't let them be hurt.

Fitz wrenched open the door between carriages, moved through into the next. Outside the world whirled past. Inside his head the past was unfolding with inevitable consequences into the present. Guilt. Terror. Anger.

And he was whispering a chant, a litany, a spell against the darkness. *Not them, not them, not them, not them.*

Helen turned the page of her book. Turned it back again when she realised she hadn't read a word for the last ten minutes. Opposite her the man who'd introduced himself as Michael kept staring at her. Oh he was pretending not to, she knew that, but she could see his eyes flicker every so often. Flicker around the carriage to take in the woman, seated by the door, the little girl standing at the window.

And he was watching her, of course. Watching her turn the pages. Over, over, over again. You heard stories. Men on trains. But that was fiction, wasn't it? Films? But what about the news the other night? What about that girl, what was her name, Jacqui? Was that it? She was killed on a train. The report hadn't been specific. Just that she'd been murdered. And the killer was still at large. Or, no. That was her over active imagination. The killer was in police custody. They'd been asking for friends or relatives to come forward. That was it. The killer was in custody. So this man in front of her, staring at her, wasn't the killer. Couldn't be the killer, wasn't planning to do to her what he'd done to Jacqui.

And anyway. There was someone else in the carriage. A woman, her daughter. She was safe. Safe while they were here.

The book slipped from Helen's fingers then. Clattered to the floor. She bent to retrieve it but the man was there first, handing it back to her with a strange look, a look as if he was trying to smile but didn't really know how.

The little girl turned from the window, interposed herself

between Helen and the man, broke the spell his eyes were weaving over her.

'Mum. I'm going to the loo, OK?'

The woman sighed. 'I'll come with you.'

The kid rolled her eyes at Helen. 'I don't need you to stand guard, Mum.'

'I'll come anyway.'

They left. Helen glanced up at her bag on the luggage rack, thought about following them as quickly as she could.

'Would you like a sherbert lemon?'

Helen blinked. The man was holding out a paper bag to her. And she was still seated, her bag still on the rack. She was still in here with him. Alone in here with him, now the woman had taken the little girl away.

'Should I take that as a yes or a no?'

Penhaligon had worked her way through three carriages now. Nothing. She wondered how Fitz was getting on. If he'd found anything. Anyone. She wondered how she'd deal with it if he had. She wondered how she'd deal with it if she found anything herself.

When Helen refused the sherbert lemon Michael folded the top of the paper bag neatly and slipped it back into the inside pocket of his anorak. Another object rested there, a comforting weight against his pulsing heart. He allowed his fingers to trace the shape of the object. Felt the ivory smoothness of the handle, the groove from which the blade would emerge.

He became aware Helen was looking at him. She was looking at him. Looking at him. No longer dismissive. Blank. A blank slate on which to chalk his own emotions.

The razor was in his hand now. Tucked comfortingly into his hand. And the train was pumping him into the future, pistoning him into the future, faster and faster, faster and faster. Nearly there. Nearly there. Nearly there. Nearly there. Yes. Oh yes. Oh yes. Oh yes. Oh yes, yes, yes, yes, yes, yes, yes, yes –

And she was up, moving, the first flicker of nervousness in her face turning to fear as he stood as well.

'Get out of my way!'

He took his hand out of his pocket.

She saw the razor. Saw the blade. Tried to run, to get past him.

It was the simplest task to push the blade into her.

The scream was distant. A hollow murmur of fear, like the wind through bare branches. It was enough for Fitz. He was away, charging through the carriage, past compartment after compartment, the scream building inside his head, the voice changing, deepening, becoming familiar.

Not them, not them not them –

Helen put out her hands to defend herself from the man. The blade took her in the shoulder. He was moving so fast. She turned, flung out a fist in a punch, but he was already somewhere else. She missed, lost her balance, turned again, falling onto the opposite seat, her legs buckling as if from an incredible weight. And then she realised there *was* an incredible weight on her, and it was him, it was Michael, and there was pain, bright, sharp little spurts of pain as the blade flickered through the air, through her clothes and skin, again and again, and the trickles of pain ran together, merged to form a river of agony that swept her away –

Penhaligon sidestepped the first person who got in her way. They were all reacting to the screams. She increased her speed to a run. Someone else got in front of her.

'What –?'

She shoved the man out of the way. Ignored his indignant cry as he toppled over a middle-aged couple, as more people rose from their seats, rose to fill the aisle with a moving wall of bodies –

The blade moved, faster and faster, sometimes missing, sometimes snagging in clothes. But sometimes what it snagged on was the girl. Was Helen. Screaming, squirming, but so slow, so slow, and the train was pushing him forward, accelerating him, every particle of him, until the knife was a relativistic blur moving backwards and forwards in time with the screams; backwards to Patricia, to Astrid, forwards to Jacqui, to Helen; backwards and forwards, scream after scream after scream after scream.

The first runnels of blood emerged from the cuff of Helen's cardigan, ran from the wounds on her arms, hands, face.

Merged with the blood jetting from Astrid's belly, Patricia's cheek, Jacqui's throat.

The blood spanned time. Took him

nearer my God than thee

back. Forward. Rocked him in the arms of time, the arms of his mother, the Virgin Mary.

And the change was coming. Oh. It was coming. Coming, it was coming it was nearly there. Nearly there. Nearly there. Nearly –

When Penhaligon burst into the compartment the girl was on her knees, screaming, begging, her arms thrashing, hands fluttering before her face, one flinging droplets of blood onto the floor, the seat, the towering form of Michael Hennessy.

Hennessy was whispering something. He didn't see her. Something snapped in Penhaligon. She smashed her fists down hard on the back of his head.

'You *fuck!*'

A rain of blows that caught him unawares, drove him forwards, to smash his head into the window frame before bouncing backwards towards her, turning as he stumbled towards her, hand outstretched with the knife glittering with sunlight, running with blood –

'Christ!' Penhaligon flung herself to the floor as he barged past into the corridor. She stuck out a foot and managed to trip him. He fell again, head crunching into the wall. He screamed with pain. The scream was that of a child who doesn't understand why his toy has been taken away from him; who doesn't understand the bad thing he has done, let alone the punishment.

And then he was gone, and she was scrambling to her feet, helping the girl up as well, assessing her wounds.

'You'll be alright. He's gone. You'll be alright now.'

246

But she kept on screaming.

Eventually Penhaligon left her there.

Where the hell was Fitz?

Fitz barrelled past a woman and child emerging from the toilet at the end of the carriage. As he drew level with them, Hennessy, charging along the passage in the opposite direction, ran straight into him. Fitz felt something tug at his chest. Bright metal. Sparks of fire beneath his suit. The warmth of blood.

Hennessy stared at him. For a moment they were locked, motionless.

Then something in Fitz gave way. Some fundamental part of his psyche just folded under the pressure. He grabbed Hennessy, swung him awkwardly around in the confined space of the passage. He was screaming at him. The words didn't make any sense. 'All bets are off! All bets are off now you bastard! I am Lobby Lud and I claim the fucking reward!'

Hennessy swung his arms, the blade tugged at Fitz's clothing, his hands. Pain flooded through his nervous system. He screamed at the pain, pushed it away, grabbed at Hennessy, missed his footing. And Hennessy was away, turning towards the stupefied woman, her screaming child.

'Judith! Get back! Get away!'

She grabbed the child, moved back, reached upwards for the emergency cord –

– and Hennessy was there too, grabbing for her, moving fast, the knife a blur as Fitz lurched towards him, knocking him clear of the woman towards the carriage door, and then the kid was running forward, 'Let her go, you leave my mother alone!' and she was kicking, she was kicking at *Fitz*, and Hennessy was at the door, was opening the door even as the train shuddered, began to slow.

The door swung back, out. Hennessy went with it. Slow motion, out into the daylight.

And Fitz was screaming something he would never remember, his mind gone somewhere far away, and he was after Hennessy, out of the door and into the cascade of noise and light and spinning ground and sky and pain exploded all along his left side as he hit the ground rolling, loose chippings and bits of wood smashing into him, biting into him, blinding him.

When he opened his eyes Hennessy was crawling away from him between the rails of the down line. Fitz got to his feet, fell, crawled after Hennessy. The down line stretched out ahead of them, turned a gradual corner and vanished from sight behind a copse of trees. Beside them on the up line the train, an enormous tonnage of metal, screeched to a halt, wheels locked, spilling runnels of water and oil onto the track; all this ignored as Fitz scrambled after Hennessy. The truth was there, right there, in front of him. He had it now, out in the open. It was trying to get away but he wouldn't let it.

He flung himself at Hennessy, grabbed him. They fell together between the rails.

Hennessy screamed as Fitz grabbed him. Terror. His face turned up as Fitz flung him to the ground. Blood. Scratches. Terror. Like Jacqui. But no second mouth like Jacqui. Not dead like Jacqui.

Not yet.

Fitz felt a warmth spread through his limbs. The warmth of realisation. That he could kill. He could kill Hennessy. He could kill the truth. And it would never make him afraid again. He could kill. It was easy. He could do it now.

He could kill now!

Hennessy screamed.

'What?' Fitz spat the word out.

'We're on the line. There's a train coming!'

Fitz glanced over his shoulder. Beyond the distant copse of trees a klaxon moaned. Even as Fitz watched the train rounded the copse. The klaxon screamed again, louder now, and Fitz imagined the look on the driver's face when he saw what awaited him on the rails. As if to confirm his thought, there came the hissing of brakes and a wild metallic screech sounded as the wheels locked.

Hennessy screamed again.

Fitz stared wildly back at him. 'I can't hear you!'

'There's a train coming!'

'I can't hear you, there's a train coming!'

'It's on this line! Let go of me you bloody maniac!'

Fitz didn't need to look to know that Hennessy was right. The train hurtling towards them was never going to stop before it reached them. 'I am a maniac,' he screamed. 'It's true! I am a maniac! I keep it all inside. Under control. You can't imagine. You can't imagine what I see sometimes. What I think of doing. How I stop myself doing those things I see.'

Hennessy was still screaming. The Lord's Prayer. Fitz shook him by the throat to get his attention back. Dimly he was aware of Penhaligon yelling something at him. He couldn't hear the words above the howl of the train, didn't care anyway.

'You don't know what you've done for me, do you? You've caged me. But you've liberated me as well.'

The train roared.

Hennessy babbled, all sense gone, sure he was going to die, Fitz could see it in his eyes, carried on screaming at him anyway.

'We're the bloody same, you and me. The bloody same. I could have killed her. I could have done that. You've showed me what I could have done. What I could still do to you. You've liberated me!'

Fitz looked up. The train was everywhere –

'You want to know what scares me the most?'

– coming closer –

'Do you?'

– filling his entire field of vision, blotting out the ground, the sky –

'I'll bloody tell you shall I?'

– the noise, the animal howl of it cutting across Penhaligon's yells, Hennessy's screams, his own voice, everything –

'The thing that scares me the most is that I don't know what the difference between us is!'

And he picked Hennessy up, threw him clear of the track, stumbled across the rails to fall beside him as the train thundered past, a wall of thrashing metal, wheels locked and screeching amid the stink of oil and smoke –

And Fitz, exhausted, propped himself up on one elbow to stare for a long moment into Hennessy's eyes.

'Isn't that funny?'

And he began quietly, determinedly, to laugh.

13:30–13:45

By the time the paramedics arrived Penhaligon had managed to staunch the worst of Helen's bleeding. She looked a mess, face, hands and arms covered with tiny, shallow defence wounds. There was a deep cut in her left shoulder which had bled heavily, but she'd been lucky. The wound stopped an inch from the major artery in her arm. As Penhaligon watched the paras tuck a thermal blanket around her still form as it lay strapped to a stretcher, Penhaligon wondered at the various forms of luck. Helen was lucky to be alive.

Perhaps for someone else, someone like her, luck was being able to say goodbye before it was too late.

Perhaps Fitz was right.

She glanced over to where another paramedic was treating the cuts in Fitz's hands and the shallower one across his chest. They'd spent fifteen minutes picking bits of gravel, dirt and splinters of wood out of his hands, legs and left arm. He didn't want to go to hospital. The paras weren't inclined to argue but the Doctor proved as stubborn as Fitz. In the end she shoved a needle in his arm.

'Antibiotics,' Penhaligon heard her say.

'Bullshit,' Fitz had replied, a moment before he went under.

It was almost funny. They loaded Fitz into the ambulance with Helen. Hennessy was to travel, sedated, in a separate vehicle.

Penhaligon turned to Bilborough. He stood with Beck as she walked towards him. Caught her eye as she approached. 'Good work.' His voice was warm, but his eyes, they told a different story.

Beck jammed his roll-up in his mouth, said nothing.

'Give you a lift back?' Bilborough again.

'No thanks, sir. I'm going with Fitz.'

And she walked towards the waiting ambulance, leaving Bilborough and Beck to survey the litter of gawkers, left over emotions.

Later she called at the Applebys', one last visit to tell them the news. She explained why Fitz couldn't be there, watched Ann's face run a gamut of emotions which ended in a flood of tears.

Sweeney was going down. He was going down and the grieving could begin, and after that, the healing.

As she left the Applebys' house Fitz's words of the night before thundered through her mind. Love. Guilt. Honesty. Selfishness.

Ann Appleby's healing had begun.

Her own would take considerably longer.

SEVEN

Sunday

15:30–16:00

The English countryside sped past outside the windows of the Volvo. In the front passenger seat Fitz thought the grim, drizzly weather was doing a pretty good job of reflecting his mood. He ought to feel fine. He felt like shit. Several kinds of shit in fact.

From the driving seat Penhaligon glanced at him. 'So Judith wasn't even on the train then?'

'Katie made her late. They got the 13:30.' Fitz shook his head. 'That woman I pushed out of the way wondered what the hell I was going on about. Her kid kicked me you know. Kicked *me*. There's no justice.'

Penhalgion shrugged. 'Kids. They never understand do they?'

Fitz glanced sideways at the detective. Her words had a double meaning and he knew it. He also caught the little glance that allowed her to make sure he knew. Interesting.

From the back seat, Kelly said, 'I think you turn right at the next junction.'

Fitz looked at Kelly over the top of his glasses, said indignantly, 'I can read a map, you know.'

Kelly nodded, unsmiling.

Fitz consulted the map, said to Penhaligon, 'Officer Pan-handle, I'd like you take a right at the next junction, please.'

'Penhaligon.' She worked hard to suppress a grin. 'And are you sure you know your right from your left, Fitz?'

'Only when I'm drunk.' Fitz crumpled his face into that

grin, angled a look back at Kelly. 'So. You didn't even know your parents were dead?'

'No.'

'The Falklands, the Gulf, the Berlin Wall, Gazza's belly – all that really meant nothing to you?'

Kelly shook his head. 'Nothing. But it's coming back. Slowly. I have you to thank for that.'

Fitz chewed on his lower lip. 'Perhaps you should have stayed in your ivory tower.'

Kelly looked out of the car window, out at the streaming rain falling across countryside painted grey by the lack of sunlight. 'If I'd acted differently, she'd be alive. That's what you're thinking.'

Fitz was about to reply when Penhaligon stopped the Volvo by a massive set of gates set into a stone wall. Beyond the gates a long driveway meandered through well kept gardens until it reached a towering, slate grey building. The Monastery of St. Peters.

Kelly opened the door and got out. After a moment Fitz joined him, turning his collar up against the rain. 'Why are you going back?'

Kelly looked up at the dull sky. Rubbed one finger beneath his eye. 'I had doubts about my vocation. I left the monastery because I wanted to see the world outside. I've seen it now. And you can keep it.'

Fitz frowned. 'If you'd wanted to get yourself banged up for life you should've done a bank job, something to deserve it.'

Kelly looked at Fitz; there was something scary about that gaze. A hollowness, an emptiness that Fitz, in all honesty, could not decide if he was partially responsible for.

'I belong in there,' Kelly gestured beyond the gates, turned the movement into a goodbye wave to Penhaligon.

She smiled out from the driver's window. Nodded a goodbye.

Fitz held out his hand. Kelly took it for a moment. Firm grip. A grip that could shake the world. Or the grip of a man whose world had been shaken, right to the core, right to the very foundation. A man desperate for that last hope to clutch on to. The hope represented by God and not the world outside the monastery walls.

'I'll pray for you Fitz.' Kelly let go of Fitz's hand, turned and opened the gates, began to walk up the drive.

Fitz closed the gates behind Kelly, remained watching until he was a tiny figure lost amongst the bulk of the monastery. At one point he turned, waved. Fitz strained his ears but anything else he might have said was lost in the distance, and the rain.

Penhaligon turned the car around. Fitz climbed back in. 'Do you fancy a quick one?'

Penhaligon laughed out loud. 'No.'

'I'm talking alcohol, not sex.'

'No to the former, you must be bloody joking to the latter.'

Fitz rubbed his chin as Penhaligon stamped on the accelerator. 'Do you get much, then, Panhandle?'

'Tell me about your wife. Surprise me with the reason she left you.'

'Do you ever cop off in uniform? Do men go for that the same as women?'

'What made her leave you?'

'You know why a uniform turns a woman on? It reeks of death. Death, Panhandle, the finest aphrodisiac in the world.'

'Come on, Fitz. Out with it. What made her leave you? The gambling? The drinking? The fact that you're an arrogant, self-loathing, misogynistic slob?'

'Flatterer.'

'Which was it? Why did she leave?'

'You tell me. You said you knew last night.'

'Last night I was drunk.'

'There's a pub over there,' Fitz pointed. 'Take a right.'

'No.'

'Yes.'

Penhaligon indicated left, turned onto the main road, changed from second directly into fourth, stamped on the accelerator.

And as the car belted along the A-road, Fitz wound down the window. 'Do you know, Panhandle, for the first time in days, the prospect of your self destructive driving doesn't scare me.'

'Shame.'

'You want to know why?'

'Don't tell me, you've got a brain tumour.'

Fitz rolled his eyes. *Because even though Kelly's banged up for life inside his own head, even though the girl on the train was injured, perhaps badly, even though Judith's walked out on me and split the family in half, none of that matters. None of that matters because the game's still on. It's still on, Panhandle, and the only thing that's changed is the rules.*

'Never mind,' he said. He looked at Penhaligon, allowed his face to crumple into that grin. She caught the glance, for the first time smiled back.

And there was that moment, the ripe, shining, glittering moment when it happened, and you had the whole of your future in the palm of your hand.

And inside you were spinning, a whirlpool of emotions, visions, controls, and all of it meshing perfectly, encapsulated in the brief moment of her smile.

It was the off.

ACKNOWLEDGEMENTS

The Do-It-Yourself TV
Novelisation Kit

Ingredients:

1. 20,000 words. High quality script by Jimmy McGovern.
2. 80,000 words. Inventive improvisations around the central theme (You may do this yourself if nobody else is willing to do it in the required time or for the money offered.)
3. 1 filing cabinet's worth. Excellent editorial comments and suggestions, medical research, pathological thoughts and psychological traumas by Paul Hinder, Andy Lane, Molly Brown, Liz Holliday, Lee Brimmicombe-Wood, Jon Cooper, Michelle Drayton and Martin Wesley.
4. ½ tblspn of research (Bodies and Crimes) supplied unbeknownst to his good self by Doctor Denis Hocking.
5. 1 teaspn. Detailed copy-editing by Peter Darvill-Evans, Rebecca Levene.
6. .00001 teaspn. Humorous comments by Andy Bodle and Kerri Sharp.

Method:

1. Sift script until all the chunky bits of emotional drama are separated. Place in covered jar to foment.
2. Lightly baste the improvisations, then stir in emotional drama. Whisk until mixture thickens into deeply rooted, character-driven psychodrama.
3. Add editorial comments from Paul, Andy, Molly, Liz, Lee and Jon, then beat with a firm motion until the clichés,

256

clunky writing, anthropomorphising, and other non-consumable items separate out. Place these in a plastic bin liner and discard. (Or give them to the cat; it's not masochistic – cats *will* eat anything; especially if you put a lid on it first.)

4. Sprinkle on medical research by Michelle, extra forensics by Martin, copy-editing by Peter, Rebecca *et al*.

5. Spice with humorous comments from Andy and Kerri and the odd line from a number one hit single.

6. Cover with reasonable grade (preferably recycled) one-side-gloss artpaper and allow to stand in book press for two to three hours.

7. Carve off excess glue from spine (another cat meal if you like) and allow to stand on bookstore, airport, garage, hairdressers and all other good retail outlet shelves for one day before serving to public with a liberal dose of back cover copy.

Note:
Avoid reviewers' comments by telling them it all came out of a box anyway. (Don't tell them which box – or they'll all be doing it.)

In addition to the above, serious thanks are due to the following people: Mum and Dad (you know why), Joanne and Jonathan (you don't – keep guessing), Peter (for taking yet another editorial risk), Rebecca (for picking up the pieces afterwards), Andy Dymond (for lending me the mixer and other stuff, time without end), Rachel (who for her sins laughs at my jokes and has excellent taste in romantic poetry) and Albert Elkins and the builders working for the Easton Renewal Scheme who waited six weeks to rebuild my house (cheers guys – couldn't have done it with you, couldn't have done it without you!)

And:
Martin, Martin, Nacula, Esther, Ollie, Huw, Mel and Elliot, Jo and Nick, Lynne and John, Lizzie and Co., Harvey, Graham, Adam and crew, Sam and Barney, Raoul and Sam,

Andy and Ilona, Sara, Emma, Annie, Nige and Debs, Alan and Alys, Owen and Jackie, Maureen, Phil, Angie, Sheila, Bill, Lisa, Wayne, Sam, Dave, Patricia, Rodders and the bods at BSFR.

Soundtrack by mammal. *'Pay To Play? No Way!'*

This novel was first serialised on the labels of 80,000 SOOCHI T-shirts.

Be excellent to each other, dudes. Outtahere –

The Cracker Writers

Jimmy McGovern

Jimmy McGovern's scriptwriting career began in the early 1980s with plays for Liverpool's Everyman and Playhouse theatres. His Merseyside association continued with scripts for over eighty episodes of Channel 4's soap opera *Brookside* between 1983 and 1989. During the 1990s he has written for over a dozen films and television series, including *EL CID*, *Backbeat* and, of course, *Cracker*.

Jim Mortimore

Jim Mortimore was born in London in 1962. At various times he has enjoyed employment as a rubbish shoveller, library assistant, social services clerk, printer, commercial musician, and graphic designer. His interests include: origami, cycling, reading, writing, painting, music, and video/computer art/animation.

Jim lives in Bristol, and has reluctantly agreed to the removal of all jokes from this biog.

The Cracker Stories

The first three Cracker stories, first broadcast on British
television in 1993, were all written by Jimmy McGovern.
Based on the original scripts, Virgin's Cracker novels add
depth and detail to the televised stories.

The Mad Woman In The Attic
Adapted by Jim Mortimore

Dr Edward Fitzgerald, who insists that everyone call him
Fitz, is a psychologist with an apparently conventional life.
He teaches and practises psychology; he has an attractive
wife, two children, and a big house in a pleasant suburb of
Manchester. But he's also addicted to gambling, booze,
cigarettes, and pushing his considerable bulk into any situation he finds intriguing. His wife Judith has had enough. She
leaves him. Fitz's life is beginning to fall apart.

When one of his students is murdered, Fitz can't resist
becoming involved. The police have a suspect; they are sure
he's the serial killer, but he's claiming complete amnesia. The
police reluctantly hire Fitz to get a confession.

As Fitz investigates, he finds that the police theory doesn't
fit the facts. He discovers, in solving murder cases, a new
focus for his life. And he meets Detective Sergeant Jane
Penhaligon.

To Say I Love You
Adapted by Molly Brown

People do strange things for love.

Tina's parents had nothing but loving intentions when they turned her into a talking guide dog for her blind sister. Sean, full of bitterness and fury, is prepared to kill for the love of Tina. And Fitz, psychologist and occasional catcher of murderers, would do anything to win back the love of his wife Judith – if only he didn't find himself working so closely with DS Jane Penhaligon.

In this, the second Cracker thriller, Fitz can find a murderer, prevent a catastrophe, and still find time to flirt with a pretty policewoman. But he also knows only too well the motivations that drive Judith into another man's bed and that push him to the edge of self-destruction.

Compared to the complications of Fitz's own life, tracking down a team of cop-killers is simple.

One Day A Lemming Will Fly
Adapted by Liz Holliday

Everything's going to be all right. Judith is back home, Penhaligon's falling in love, and Fitz has a new problem to solve from the police.

It's an open and shut case. A schoolboy – a young, effeminate, scholarly and often bullied schoolboy – is found murdered. His English teacher – male, single, lives alone – tries to commit suicide. It's obvious: the teacher killed his pupil. The police think so. The boy's parents think so. Everyone in the family's neighbourhood thinks so. And Fitz thinks so. It's just a matter of obtaining a confession.

But the truth is as elusive as trust and honesty, and the case goes badly wrong.

In this, the third Cracker story, Fitz reaches the crisis in his personal drama. He has to choose between Judith and Jane. And that's the least of his problems.

Three new Cracker stories are appearing on television in the autumn of 1994. These will be adapted into novels which will be published in the spring of 1995.

700145

0800

04